P9-DUD-566

The Pillars of Ponderay

NO LONGER PROPERTY OF
SEATTLE PUBLIC LIBRARY

The Pillars of Ponderay

Lindsay Cummings

KATHERINE TEGEN BOOKS
An Imprint of HarperCollins Publishers

Katherine Tegen Books is an imprint of HarperCollins Publishers.

Balance Keepers, Book 2: The Pillars of Ponderay
Copyright © 2015 by PC Studio, Inc.

PC STUDIO

All rights reserved. Printed in the United States of America.
No part of this book may be used or reproduced in any manner whatsoever
without written permission except in the case of brief quotations embodied in
critical articles and reviews. For information address HarperCollins Children's
Books, a division of HarperCollins Publishers, 195 Broadway, New York, NY 10007.
www.harpercollinschildrens.com

Library of Congress Cataloging-in-Publication Data
Cummings, Lindsay.
    The pillars of Ponderay / Lindsay Cummings. — First edition.
        pages   cm — (Balance keepers ; #2)
    Summary: "Eleven-year-old Albert Flynn and his teammates must restore
balance to a hidden underground realm before the Imbalance causes the western
coast of the United States to be consumed by earthquakes, hurricanes, and other
disasters"— Provided by publisher.
    ISBN 978-0-06-227521-9 (hardback)
    [1.   Adventure   and   adventurers—Fiction.   2.   Magic—Fiction.
3. Friendship—Fiction.   4. Imaginary creatures—Fiction.   5. Animals,
Mythical—Fiction.   6. Natural disasters—Fiction.]   I. Title.
PZ7.C91466Pil   2015   2014047918
[Fic]—dc23   CIP
                                                                    AC

15 16 17 18 19   CG/RRDH   10 9 8 7 6 5 4 3 2 1

First Edition

As always, to my dad, who writes like a boss and is also a good boss, too. And to Patrick Carman, who knows why.

Table of Contents

The Core

The Tower

Observatorium

Belltroll

Lake Hall

Professor Asante's Quarters

Professor Bigglesby's Quarters

Main Chamber

Treefare

The Pit

Library

Cedarfell

Waterfall of Fate

Canteen

Heart of the Core

Watchers' Cavern

Ponderay

Professor Flynn's Quarters

Calderon

Cave of Whispers

The Path Hider

The Way Inside

The Realm of
Ponderay

Ten Pillars of Ponderay

Canyon Cross

The Realm always provides the Means

Tunnel to the Core

Silver Sea

Path of Pillars

Ring of Entry

CHAPTER 1

New York, New York

Albert Flynn stood inside Calderon Peak.

Below him was the Sea Inspire, and outside, the Realm of Calderon, alive with angry flames that threatened to swallow the world whole.

He could hear his friends Birdie and Leroy calling for him to save them. They were trapped far below, held tightly in the claws of a great black beast—one that, in a few moments' time, would drop them into the flames. They would be gone forever, and it would be Albert's fault.

"I'm coming!" Albert screamed. He'd never let anything happen to them, not if he could help it. Albert concentrated, focusing on the magic of the Master Tile that hung from his neck.

It was the only one of its kind in the Core, and if Albert focused hard enough—squeezed his eyes shut and really, really *tried—he could get the Tile to do anything.*

Even make him fly.

He concentrated, fists clenched, sweat dripping down his back.

I want to soar like Superman.

He pictured the symbol in his mind, one that he'd recently mastered, which looked like the outspread wings of a bird.

But nothing happened.

Albert reached for the cord at his neck, fingers itching to grasp the Tile.

But he felt nothing at all.

"No," Albert gasped.

Beneath him, the monster roared. Albert heard the cries of his friends as the beast released its talons, dropping them into the flames of the Sea Inspire.

It was too late to help them.

Albert's Master Tile was gone.

Albert awoke with a start. Two bright blue beams of light shone into his eyes, and he had to clap a hand over his face before he was blinded.

"Farnsworth," he groaned, reaching out to touch his dog's head. How Farnsworth's fur could be both soft and rough at the same time, Albert wasn't sure. But he did know one thing. "You aren't supposed to use your flashlight eyes outside of the Core. Come on, buddy. Shut them off, before someone sees!"

Farnsworth whimpered, and the light faded from his eyes. Albert dropped his hand and stared at the dog. Or, rather, he stared at the Canis Luminatis.

It still blew Albert's mind that the dog was his. Farnsworth wasn't from the surface of the earth. He came from *inside* of it, deep in the center of the earth. Most people, like scientists and Albert's bald, sandal-wearing schoolteacher, insisted that the Core was full of molten metal.

But a select few knew better. They were called Balance Keepers, and Albert was one of them. Their mission? To go to the Core when they were called, and access hidden Realms through a set of sealed gateways. When the Realms were out of Balance . . . well, the world on the surface was, too. Things went bad, and *fast*. And until the Balance Keepers could go into the Imbalanced Realm, find the Means to solve the problem, and fix it in a flash, things on the surface only got worse.

Albert was only eleven, a newbie in the Core.

Not anymore, he thought, smiling to himself as he lay in bed beside Farnsworth. Just a few months ago, Albert and his two teammates (and new best friends) on team Hydra, Birdie and Leroy, had saved the world by setting the Balance right in the Realm of Calderon.

The place Albert had just dreamed about.

Albert reached up, almost instinctively, to touch his neck.

The Tile was there, just as it always had been. Albert could never lose it.

It was too powerful.

Too important.

And in six months' time (which was way too long, as far as Albert was concerned), he'd be going back to the Core. Back to his favorite place in the world, where his teammates would greet him. And *oh yeah*, there was also his dad, a Professor in the Core, who was totally awesome in Albert's eyes. Professor Flynn was the one who'd given Albert the Balance Keeper gene, after all.

"ALBERT! Breakfast is ready!" Albert's mom called.

Her voice drew Albert from his thoughts. He looked at the clock on his bedside table. 7:34 a.m. *So much for sleeping in on a Saturday.* He rolled out of bed and threw on a fresh pair of jeans and a T-shirt that said *Seismologize THIS!* It was Albert's favorite new seismology blog— something he'd recently become fascinated with, when school and homework and his obnoxious little half siblings didn't get in the way. After all, anything that had to do with the earth's natural activities . . . well, it sort of reminded Albert of home. The Core.

"Let's go, Farnsworth," Albert said, tightening the laces on his Converse. "I smell waffles!"

Farnsworth didn't have to be told twice. Waffles were his favorite treat, just like they were Albert's friend Leroy's. The second Albert opened the door of his bedroom, the little dog sprinted away and scurried down the stairs.

Most of the year, Albert lived in New York City with his mom and stepdad and three half siblings. Their apartment wasn't large, by any means, and often the mornings were so chaotic that Albert *almost* felt like he was back in the Main Chamber of the Core.

There were way too many pairs of tiny tennis shoes on the stairs, a line of dolls with horrible haircuts, and a rubber duck that squeaked like a mouse when Albert kicked it out of the way. He crawled onto the railing and slid face-first down the stairs. When he got to the bottom, he did a sort of awkward flip-roll onto the floor and rose to his feet.

Hey, it wasn't as cool as things he could do in the Core. But he had to try. Life could get pretty boring in the real world.

The smell of his mom's cooking was a constant in the apartment, and Albert's stomach rumbled as he made his way down the hall to the kitchen. His half sister, Susan, sprinted past him.

"KITTY!" she screamed, her blond hair whipping Albert in the face as she chased the family tabby cat.

"Susan, leave the cat alone," Albert groaned. The poor thing's striped tail was puffed up like a duster. It was constantly being chased. And not just by the kids. Farnsworth was also one of the culprits, and he'd gotten in great shape since moving with Albert to the city.

Another sibling ran past. Sam, Albert's redheaded younger half brother, was always shooting rubber darts at Albert's face. Sure enough, he had the dart gun.

"Hands up!" Sam said, stopping in the middle of the hall. He aimed right at Albert.

"Whoa! Not today, little man!" Albert said. But Sam launched a dart toward him anyway. Albert ducked just in time, and the dart lodged itself into the cuckoo clock on the wall behind him.

CUCKOO! CUCKOO!

It chirped nonstop, and soon Albert's stepdad, Rick, emerged from the downstairs bedroom, rubbing sleep from his eyes, complaining about how badly he wanted to tear the clock apart.

"I'll help you. Heck, I'll tear it apart myself!" Albert said, laughing as he scooted past Rick. Albert enjoyed the chaos. It was familiar to him, comforting in a way, however odd it might seem to outsiders.

In the kitchen, Albert's mom stood with her back to him, filling the waffle maker with a fresh batch of batter. Her hair was up in a ponytail, brown curls spilling down her back. Farnsworth sat at her feet, devouring any crumbs the moment they hit the floor.

Albert swept a row of army men off his usual chair and sat down across from his other half brother, Peter. He looked similar to Albert, but he was only three, and was really scrawny for his age.

"I loooove waff-ulls," Peter said. His face was covered in sticky syrup.

"Yeah, looks like it," Albert laughed. "Mom, can I have a couple?"

His mom turned to look at him, a grin lighting up her face. She shared Albert's green eyes and kind smile. "Your appetite has exploded since you got back from Herman," she said. "What on earth did your father have you doing over the summer?"

Oh, right. That was another thing. Albert's mom, no matter how trustworthy she was, could never know about the world of the Core. She was still convinced, and would be for the rest of her life, that Albert spent his summer vacations in Herman, Wyoming, with his dad and Pap, doing all sorts of small-town things.

"Oh, you know, just boring things," Albert said, thinking quick on his feet, "like sorting through dead letters in the town post office. And playing Tiles with Pap."

Not out saving the world. He hated not telling his mom the truth. But regular humans just wouldn't be able to handle the truth about the Core. If the secret got out, it would be dangerous.

"I'm just growing up, Mom," Albert continued. "No big deal."

It was the wrong thing to say, apparently, because Albert's mom was suddenly at his side, squeezing him in a hug that could have rivaled a wrestler's choke hold. "My little boy." She sniffed, and Albert was *pretty* sure she was tearing up. Moms did that kind of thing, some-times. "Don't grow up too fast, okay?"

He patted her arm gently. "Don't worry, Mom, I'm still only in the sixth grade."

She nodded and let Albert go, her usual smile hav-ing returned. "Well, in that case, you'd better eat three waffles." She handed him a heaping plate, dumped a big gooey mess of syrup on top, and placed a fork in Albert's hand.

After breakfast, Albert went to Rick's office to check out *SeismologizeTHIS!* He sat down in the plush leather chair and clicked the mouse. The screen came to life, showing Albert three smiling faces of his half brothers and sister, melted ice-cream cones held in their little fists.

Albert wasn't in the picture.

"It must have been taken last summer," he said to himself. It didn't completely upset him. He was more annoyed about being left out than any other feeling—it was the same annoyance he felt toward those gnats that liked to hang around the hot-dog stand on Fifty-Fourth Street. "Whatever."

Albert typed in the familiar website address, and the home page popped up. There were all sorts of links to articles about the earth's tremors and waves, includ-ing historical graphs that showed their patterns over centuries. There were lots of pictures of places around the world where earthquakes had happened, showing buildings toppled over and streets cracked in half.

Albert hadn't checked in since Thursday, and today, there was a new story. The headline, in bold black letters, read:

Abnormal Seismic Activity off the Coast of Southern California.

"Abnormal?" Albert said out loud. "There was nothing like that two days ago. . . ."

"Abnormal" sort of sounded like *Imbalance*. And that sounded like Core business. Which couldn't be good, because Albert's family was leaving for San Diego in a few days to visit their crazy great-aunt Suze for Christmas. The last thing Albert needed was his family in danger again, just like last summer, when the Realm of Calderon was out of whack.

"Here goes nothing," Albert said. Heart racing, he clicked the article link, then scanned the paragraphs, looking for anything important.

The article interviewed a college professor named Sally Robertson, whose hair looked an awful lot like someone had dumped a bowl of overcooked noodles on her head. Albert smiled and read on.

"We've been tracking the underwater activity one hundred miles off the coast of San Diego," Robertson said, from her office at the University of Southern California. "There's been an unprecedented number of tremors in

*the Pacific, and so far we haven't been able to trace the
exact cause. There's no logical explanation, but citizens
need not worry. We're measuring things around the
clock. . . ."*

"That's abnormal, all right," Albert said. He scanned a
little farther down.

There was a map of the Pacific, with lines showing the
paths the tremors followed. It sort of looked like a spider
web, spreading out from a few miles offshore. Usually,
something *caused* them, from way out in the sea.

But these were simply there.

Farnsworth leaped into Albert's lap and licked his
chin.

"This isn't looking good, buddy," Albert said.

Just then, a chat application on the screen popped up,
showing a video call was coming in.

It was from Leroy!

Albert clicked Accept, and his best friend's face
appeared.

Leroy Jones was tall for his age, with messy black hair
always hidden beneath a baseball cap. He wore thick
black-rimmed glasses. In the surface world, Leroy wasn't
really a big reader. But in the Core, his Tile gave him
wicked-smart mental skills, so Albert had *always* thought
of Leroy as one of the mega-intelligent guys who would
someday make millions. The glasses helped.

"Dude! What's up?" Leroy was chewing on a strawberry Pop-Tart, and there were crumbs all over his T-Rex shirt.

"Isn't it, like, five a.m. or something where you are?" Albert asked.

Leroy lived in Texas. He wasn't a cowboy, but he'd shown some pretty cool horseback riding skills back in the training Pit in the Core. "Yeah, but I needed a snack so I got up," Leroy said. "This is dessert. And so was the bowl of ice cream I had before this."

Just then, Birdie's call button showed up. It was practically the middle of the night where she was, but Albert couldn't blame her for not being able to sleep. He clicked her into the conversation. Birdie had crazy curly blond hair, mixed in with pink streaks, all pulled together into a ponytail that hung over her shoulder. She had an attitude that often reminded Albert of an angry cat's.

"Have you guys seen the news?" Birdie asked. Albert was pretty sure that if Birdie were standing right in front of him, she'd have her hands on her hips.

"Hello to you, too," Leroy said, shoving another bite of Pop-Tart into his mouth. Farnsworth barked and wagged his tail at the screen. He loved Albert's friends.

"There's food on your face," Birdie said, frowning at Leroy.

Albert laughed, but quickly composed himself—he wanted to get back to the tremors. Birdie took her cue.

"Well," Birdie said, chewing on her bottom lip. "Albert—I know you've been obsessed with this earthquake data for a while, so I've been keeping track, taking a few notes." She lifted up a notebook full of scribbled pages. "And I think you're right."

"A few notes?" Leroy laughed. "That's practically a novel!"

"It's not *that* much." Birdie waved him off. "Anyway. Albert, have you heard from your dad? Maybe he could let us know if something's going on?"

Albert shook his head. "He texts me every now and then. But not lately." It had kind of hurt Albert's feelings, but he understood. Professors were always kept busy in the Core, and they didn't exactly have stellar service down there.

Leroy smiled. "I'm sure he'll get in touch soon."

"Yeah," Birdie said, catching on. "No worries."

Albert wanted to change the subject, and fast. "What are you guys doing for Christmas break?"

"I'm going snowboarding," Birdie said, grinning like the Cheshire cat. "I can't wait to try out the new half-pipe they just installed!"

"My mom signed me up for a cooking class," Leroy groaned. "She said if I'm going to eat all of her food, I might as well learn how to help make it."

Albert wasn't too excited about visiting Aunt Suze, but at least San Diego had a ton of beaches. Last time they'd visited, Albert's half siblings had made him pretend to be a dolphin, and cart them across the waves on his back. Maybe Farnsworth could take over that role this year. . . .

Albert's phone chirped from his pocket. While Birdie and Leroy chatted, he checked the screen. "Hey, I have a text from my dad!"

"Open it!" Birdie and Leroy said at once.

Albert's heart skipped half a beat. He opened the text. And what he saw made him yelp in a very Farnsworth-like way.

> **Hey, kiddo. I know you're probably all packed and ready for your trip to California, but how do you feel about spending Christmas break in the Core instead? We need you.**

CHAPTER 2

The Return to Herman

I t took some tough convincing and about ten phone calls from Albert's dad, but Albert's mom finally agreed to let Albert leave for Christmas break. After a few hours of begging *almost* as skillfully as Farnsworth, Albert was on his way to the airport with his family. Albert would head to Herman, and his family would head to California as planned.

Rick was catching a flight later in the week, so Albert even got to sit in the front seat of his mom's minivan, which was great, considering that Sam and Peter were playing a game of "who can scream the loudest" in the backseat.

"They're having a rough winter in Herman," Albert's mom said as she drove the car through the winding streets of New York City. It was snowing big fat flakes of white, dusting the sidewalks just in time for the Christmas season to roll around.

"I know!" Albert said. "Dad said I could start snowboarding!" He hoped the made-up activity seemed genuine.

His mom nearly veered off the road and hit a biker.

"With a helmet, of course," Albert added, but what he was really thinking was, *Mom, if you only knew the dangerous stuff I was doing in the Core you'd never let me out of New York.*

They stopped at a red light, then passed by Albert's favorite place in the city, Central Park. It was the one place in New York that Albert had memories of going to with his dad when he was just a little boy. They'd gone hiking all through the winding trails, and when Albert was too tired to walk, sometimes his dad actually paid for them to ride in one of the pedicabs.

"You'll call me, right?" Albert's mom asked. She gunned the engine, and soon Central Park was just a speck of snow-covered trees in the rearview mirror.

"Yeah, of course I will," Albert said. "Don't worry, Mom."

"You're growing up, I understand," his mom said. A taxicab cut them off, and she laid on the horn, then smiled sweetly as soon as the driver sped away. "But you're my firstborn, and this will be my first Christmas without you."

"I'll send you lots of pictures," Albert said. "And I'll be

back before you know it."

His mom sighed. "Just promise me you'll be careful?"

Albert reached across the center console and touched her arm. "Always."

It was a sweet moment, and Albert's face got red. Just then, a sticky wad of gum flew from the backseat, landing itself right into Albert's mom's coffee. It splashed everywhere, and Farnsworth howled.

His mom gave Albert's half brothers her best evil eyes in the rearview.

The drive to the airport was going to take a while at the rate things were going. The snow was really picking up, too.

Albert leaned back in his seat and closed his eyes, dreaming of the second he would set foot in Herman.

This was going to be the *best* Christmas ever.

The plane ride wasn't bad, and taking off in the snow was exciting. It was one of those really cool two-story planes, the *huge* ones that had a staircase in the middle. Albert loved hearing the engine roar. His heart raced faster than a flying Guildacker the second the wheels left the runway.

Because he was an unaccompanied minor, the flight attendant, Annie, kept sneaking him free cookies every time she passed by. She even gave Farnsworth a handful of pretzels. When they landed, and all the passengers were clear, Annie drove Albert through the airport on one of those indoor baggage trucks, whizzing through the halls to deliver him right to his dad.

Except Bob Flynn wasn't waiting at baggage claim.

It was an old man, one with white hair and wrinkles on his face, and what looked like a permanent *I know all of your secrets* type of smile.

It was Albert's grandfather, Pap.

Albert knew from experience that sometimes the elderly weren't the best of drivers. On that score, Pap had long been in a league of his own. Herman, Wyoming, was covered in five feet of snow. Most people would drive with caution, slow as a turtle. But Pap drove his old, rusted pickup truck like a race car, whizzing through the snowy streets as if he were behind the wheel of a brand-new Ferrari.

"So," Pap said, watching the road with squinted eyes, "I hear you've become interested in seismology. Been keeping up with the news in Southern California?"

Albert clutched Farnsworth as the car soared down a big hill, tall snow-covered firs racing past them in a blur. "Yep, and I think that's why my dad asked me to come. It's probably an Imbalanced Realm. My mom and siblings are going to California. Do you think they'll be okay?"

"That's what Balance Keepers are for." Pap winked,

then swerved around a corner. A rabbit dove out of the way just in time.

To anyone else, Pap looked like a normal old man, but Albert could see the difference. There was something quite otherworldly in Pap's blue eyes. As a retired Balance Keeper, he knew lots of secrets about the Core, secrets that Albert had yet to discover. Maybe he even knew why things were going so strangely in the Core these days.

"Why are the Realms so messed up lately?" Albert asked. "It seems sort of soon for another Imbalance, doesn't it?"

Pap clicked his teeth, then swerved around another corner. The back tires of the truck hit the curb, and Farnsworth's eyes flashed a brilliant, electric blue.

"Only the Core knows the truth," Pap said. He reached over and patted Albert on the shoulder. "But the Flynns are curious, and smart, and if you search hard enough, the secrets might unravel."

Albert was about to ask what in the heck Pap was talking about, when a lonely street sign came into view.

ENTERING HERMAN. POPULATION, 512.

"Almost there," Pap said. "You've never seen Herman in the winter, have you?"

"Nope, I haven't." Albert pressed his face to the window

as Pap pulled off the interstate. His breath fogged up the glass, and when he wiped it away, he gasped.

Herman was *way* cooler this time of the year.

Pap gunned the engine, and they turned right into the familiar ring of evergreen trees, then down the bumpy little road that spat them out onto the edge of town. Night was falling, and all the multicolored houses in Herman were covered in twinkling lights.

There was a man in a Santa suit passing out candy canes on the main road, where shoppers were all bundled up, towers of gifts in their arms.

A little girl with her dog ran past. Farnsworth whimpered like he felt sorry for the other animal—it was wearing reindeer antlers on its head.

"The tree lighting was last night," Pap said, and as they cleared Main Street, Albert saw a glimpse of a tall fir tree, lit up as bright as the Chrysler Building, ornaments and tinsel on its snowy branches.

They stopped at the one traffic light in Herman to let a few kids run past. Then they were on their way to Albert's dad's house. It was the only one on the street that didn't have lights on the roof, and Albert knew it was because even though the townspeople *thought* he was their mailman, Bob Flynn really spent most of his days in the Core, overseeing the Calderon Realm. It was more than a full-time job. It was a way of life.

"Hey, at least there's a wreath on the front door,"

Albert said as he and Farnsworth jumped down from the truck.

Inside, Bob Flynn's house was warm and cozy, a fire crackling in the corner of the living room. There was Pap's favorite recliner, a permanent indentation on its cushions.

"Dad! I'm here!" Albert set his bag down and raced to the kitchen, expecting to see Bob Flynn with his *Kiss the Cook* apron on, stirring up his favorite deer stew.

Instead, the kitchen was empty. An untouched fruit-cake was sitting on the wooden table, along with a single white envelope.

Albert slumped into his usual chair, the one with the uneven legs that always sat crooked. "He's not here? I thought we'd have dinner and watch TV. You know, the usual."

Pap hobbled into the room, Farnsworth on his heels. "He wanted to be here. But he has duties." He crossed to the table and scooped up the envelope. "He *did* leave you this. An early Christmas present."

Albert looked at the envelope. Sure enough, Bob Flynn's horrible handwriting was on the front, in bright red ink.

Albert ripped open the envelope, and something fell into his lap. It was a silver key.

"What's this?" Albert asked Pap.

Pap winked. "Read the letter."

So Albert did.

Hey, Kiddo,

Sorry I couldn't be there to greet you. Things are a little demanding right now in the Core, and you'll understand soon enough. Take tonight and get some rest—you leave first thing in the morning. The rest of Hydra will meet you in the Core.

Because there's so much snow, you and Farnsworth will have a little trouble finding the Troll Tree. Which is why I picked up a little surprise for you. Pap will show you in the morning.

See you soon!

Love, Dad.

P.S. Wear a helmet.

Albert didn't know what it meant.

But if helmets were involved, tomorrow was going to be one of the best days of his life.

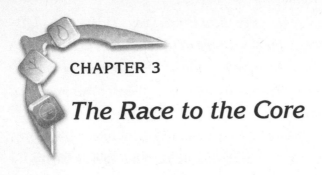

CHAPTER 3

The Race to the Core

Albert couldn't sleep.

He tossed and turned all night, holding the silver key. He imagined all sorts of things where a helmet would be required.

Most of them, like skydiving, or bull riding, or snowboarding, wouldn't be very helpful in getting Albert to the Troll Tree.

But hey, a boy could dream, right?

When morning came, Albert and Farnsworth wolfed down their eggs and toast. Pap stood there the whole time, patiently waiting.

Finally, he spoke.

"Let's go to the garage, shall we?"

Albert swallowed his last sip of milk, then threw on

his gloves, boots, and coat, and followed Pap out the back door.

He almost tripped over his own feet.

Sitting right across from him, parked next to his dad's mail truck, was one of Albert's dreams come true.

A *snowmobile*.

And not just any snowmobile. It was an IceBlitzer 3000, jet black and sleek as a stallion, just waiting for Albert to hop on and speed away.

"That's for me?" Albert's voice squeaked.

Pap laughed. "If the key fits."

Albert crossed the garage in two steps, hopped up onto the seat of the IceBlitzer, and put the key in the ignition.

It roared to life, louder than a lion.

"Can I drive it?" Albert shouted to Pap over the sound of the rumbling engine.

"It's yours for the day!" Pap nodded, then scooped a helmet off of the tool shelf up against the wall. It was black to match the snowmobile.

"Don't go too crazy, all right?" Pap put the helmet on Albert's head and fastened it tight.

He showed Albert how to work the controls, then guided him as he backed out of the garage.

"How about a hug for your old Pap before you go?" Pap asked.

Albert put the IceBlitzer in neutral, then gave Pap the best hug he could. "You can't come with me, can you?"

Pap laughed and shook his head. "The Core doesn't need me any longer. But you, Albert . . ." The wind blew, and snow started to fall. Pap shivered and pulled his robe tighter around his body. There was a strange look in his eyes, something Albert hadn't seen before. "Something tells me you're going to be needed more than ever. And soon."

His voice was strangled, and it gave Albert a chill that didn't come from the snow. Pap shook his head and smiled. "When you get there tell the Path Hider that old Pap wants a rematch in Tiles. He's the only one to ever beat me."

"You should play Leroy," Albert said. "And Birdie."

At the thought of his friends, warmth spread over Albert. He'd see them in just a few hours!

"Ride fast," Pap said, and with a mischievous smile, he waved Albert away. "See you soon! And use the shovel in the compartment under the seat when you get to where you're going!"

"Bye!" Albert clicked the snowmobile into gear. Farnsworth leaped into Albert's lap, and together they sped away.

Albert had to drive slowly across town, winding around an old woman who walked with a stack of books balanced in her arms.

"Cold days ahead, my dear Francis," she said to Albert as he passed.

"This place gets weirder and weirder." Albert laughed.

Soon enough, the edge of the woods came into view. The trees blew in the wind, and they seemed to whisper secrets to Albert, beckoning him to come closer, to have more adventures. He stopped just before the tree line. There in the snow, somehow surviving through the cold, was a cluster of tulips. Springtime flowers, and these had purple tiger stripes on them.

It was the magic of the Core, seeping through the cracks of the earth into Herman.

"You ready for this, Farnsworth?" Albert asked.

The little dog yipped.

"Hold on tight!" Albert called out. He gunned the engine, angled the IceBlitzer into the trees, then sped off.

It was amazing. The wind whipped Albert in the face, and he felt like a pro, one of those guys who could do backflips and crazy spins all over the mountain. He could probably even outrun an avalanche on this thing!

Farnsworth put his paws on top of Albert's hands as if he wanted to help steer. Then Albert really laid on the speed. The IceBlitzer purred beneath him, running like a champion. It carried them up the hill, and they got big air on the way down. Almost ten feet, at *least*, launching Albert right over a frozen stream.

The snowmobile hit the ground on the other side and kept going. "Yeehaw!" Albert screamed, channeling a little bit of Leroy's Texas flair. "I'm in the lead!"

They went left between two fat trees, dodged right, nearly missing a thornbush, and then zoomed up one hill and down another.

Up ahead, there was the familiar slingshot tree that had once been a path marker on Albert's first journey through these woods.

"We're halfway there!" Albert yelled.

He squeezed the gears as hard as he could. Farnsworth barked. His ears flapped like a bird's wings in the wind.

Sometimes, the path ahead seemed to blur. Trees appeared in places that they hadn't been, only seconds before.

"This is getting tricky," Albert groaned.

He knew the Path Hider was at work here, hiding the paths to the Core. Farnsworth, being the clever Core dog that he was, knew how to read those hidden paths. Every few seconds, Farnsworth barked, alerting Albert of the changes.

A few times, Albert thought he saw the shadowed figures of his friends, walking through the woods, but he couldn't be sure. The Path Hider was also concealing Birdie's and Leroy's paths as they moved, but only for a second or two.

Finally, Albert saw a clearing up ahead.

"I think that's it," he said, and angled the IceBlitzer toward it.

Sure enough, as they got closer, Albert felt that strange lightness in his body, sort of like he was sitting on a cloud. The Troll Tree loomed in front of him, a ghostly being with its branches all dressed in white. The trunk of the tree was three times as large as it was tall, and with the snow so deep, the secret door that led to its hollow center was probably out of sight.

"We made it," Albert breathed.

He turned off the engine, removed his helmet, and slid off the seat. When he lifted it, inside, just like Pap said, sat a portable snow shovel.

"I don't think I've ever had to shovel snow," Albert laughed. Farnsworth barked in agreement, and together they approached the Troll Tree.

In the summer, Albert had had to circle the trunk several times before the door appeared. He did just that, walking as best he could in the deep snow. When he was sure he'd circled at least three times, he saw it.

The top half of the door.

"Oh, man, this is gonna take all day," Albert groaned. He looked down at Farnsworth, who was wagging his tail. "Help me dig, will you?"

They began, Albert with the shovel, Farnsworth with his paws. It was exhausting, and before too long, Albert's shirt had grown damp with sweat.

If only Tiles worked outside of the Core, Albert thought. *I'd use that Fire symbol I saw in the Black Book and melt this snow to smithereens!*

Over an hour later, when Albert was sure his hands were going to fall off, the digging was done. The door stood before him, its old brass handle just begging for Albert to turn it and go inside.

"Farnsworth?" Albert looked down at his dog. "Lights on, please."

The dog barked joyfully, and as Albert turned the handle and swung open the door to the Troll Tree, Farnsworth's laser eyes were burning a bright blue.

"After you." Albert smiled.

Farnsworth scurried inside, and Albert followed.

CHAPTER 4

Trouble Is Brewing

The last time Albert had been here, he'd been ter-rified out of his eleven-year-old mind. He'd even gone so far as to think that, somewhere in the darkness, a cyclops was waiting to devour him whole.

This time Albert was *in the know*. And rather than feeling fear, Albert's entire body hummed with excite-ment. He followed Farnsworth through the darkness of the tree, falling onto hands and knees when the space became too small for standing. They entered the tunnel-like maze of roots that led deeper into the Troll Tree, and in turn, deeper into the earth.

Down and down they went, squeezing their way through roots tangled so tightly they could have been fishermen's knots. Faster and faster, Albert's heart raced.

I'm almost home. I'm almost back in the Core.

Soon, but not soon enough, the dim orange light of the Path Hider's door came into view. Albert squeezed through a last knot of old, gnarled roots, and found that he could stand again.

"Here we go!" Albert smiled down at Farnsworth.

A pair of blinding blue eyes answered him.

Just like last summer, Albert had to press his hand up against a gooey glowing substance in the door. It oozed over his skin, covering it up so whatever magic the lock held could read Albert's Balance Keeper genes.

In seconds, the goo released him.

The door clicked open, revealing a familiar orange platform just beyond.

The ride down into the Path Hider's domain was just as thrilling as the last time. Only now, Albert could really enjoy it, without fear or doubt.

He knew exactly where he was going, and he knew that he belonged.

The faster the platform sank, the more excited Albert grew. Even Farnsworth was yipping away, almost as if to say, *Our friends are down there!*

The platform slowed, and as the familiar hissing pipes and steam vents came into view, Albert leaped.

He landed on the hard flooring of the Path Hider's domain.

"We're home!" Albert screamed.

He was just about to make his way through the maze of pipes, when he saw two shadows running toward him. One was tall and thin. The other was shorter with a mess of curls.

"ALBERT!" he heard his friends scream in unison.

He didn't have time to react. In seconds, Albert was enveloped in what had to be the most backbreaking hug of his life.

It was worse than his mom's, which was really saying something.

"Okay, okay! Let me breathe!" Albert laughed.

When the hug broke, he was staring at his two best friends' faces. He couldn't believe how much he missed them! Birdie's hair was up in its usual ponytail, her pink and blond curls hanging across her shoulder. Leroy had on a new baseball cap, one that read *Papa's Pancake House*. Albert laughed, and before he could stop himself, he hugged them both again.

"I got here first," Birdie explained, bobbing up and down on her toes. "I got the message right before an exam. Close call on that one. I was so wrapped up in the reports about California, I hardly had time to study! Of course, I still would've gotten . . ." She froze midsentence, because both Albert and Leroy were stifling laughs.

"*What?*" Birdie demanded.

Albert smiled. "I'd forgotten how much Birdie talks."

"Birdie is nothing," Leroy said. "Mom managed to

squeeze me into *one* cooking class before I left. You don't want to *know* what all those girls were talking about. I have nightmares about them giggling."

The three friends exploded into laughter, but it stopped when someone behind the trio cleared his throat.

Albert turned, and through the steam, a man emerged. The Path Hider.

He was tall, *very* tall, with long spidery fingers. His rust-colored hair was topped with an old miner's helmet, and the man blinked at the trio with eyes in two different shades, one copper and one blue.

"Welcome home." The Path Hider bowed low to the ground. "My dear young Balance Keepers."

"Hello again," Albert said.

"'Sup?" Leroy waved and accidentally smacked the side of a pipe. It hissed out steam that spit right in Birdie's face.

For a second, Albert thought Birdie might punch Leroy (she liked punching boys far bigger than she was). But instead, she was busy staring at the Path Hider, a strange look in her eyes.

The Path Hider had always been, well, strange. Albert guessed it was because the Path Hider had been down in this steamy room for centuries, all by himself, hiding the paths to the Core.

He was good at keeping people away.

Farnsworth nearly leaped into the Path Hider's arms.

His eyes blazed a brilliant sapphire blue, and the Path Hider stooped to scratch him behind his ears.

"All right, Farnsworth, that's enough for today." The Path Hider stood up and gave the trio a half smile. "I thought we might enjoy a sip of coffee before I pass you along."

He turned and made his way back through the pipes, ducking and dodging the steam like a champ. The pipes were like a tangle of snakes, some as thick as giants' legs, others as thin as kindling sticks.

On the far side of the room, an old oil-stained couch sat beneath a jumble of copper wires. Beside it was a water cooler filled with steaming hot coffee.

Albert, Birdie, and Leroy took their places on the couch. The Path Hider sat across from them, lounging in a recliner that Albert guessed was only held together by magic.

It was quiet for a moment. The Path Hider studied them all with his strange eyes, and Albert felt like he was underneath a microscope.

"So. How's it been, you know, down here?" Albert asked. "Same old, same old?"

The Path Hider nodded. "Hiding the Core's location is of the utmost importance. A little modification here, another alteration there." He waved his spidery fingers in the air. "The secret is forever safe."

A crackling noise drew Albert's eyes from the Path

Hider. It was Leroy, unwrapping a piece of red candy.

"Really?" Birdie laughed. "You've been here five minutes, and already you're eating?"

Leroy shrugged. He looked at the Path Hider. "What do you eat down here? Besides coffee, I mean."

The Path Hider leaned farther back in his recliner and propped up his feet. He wore old leather boots, the same kind Albert and Birdie and Leroy had, as well as everyone else in the Core. But his were worn and tattered. It was time for a new pair.

"I eat what they send me," the Path Hider said. "But enough about me. I want to hear about the great Calderon First Unit." His blue eyes fell onto Albert. "Is it true?"

"Is what true?" Albert asked. "If you're talking about what happened in Calderon last summer . . ."

"No, not that." The Path Hider leaned forward, hands on his knees. His eyes flitted to the cord around Albert's neck, where his Tile was concealed beneath his shirt. "The rumor that *you* hold the Master Tile."

"Totally!" It was Leroy who piped up to answer. "Albert's a pro now! He can do anything. Show him the Tile, Albert!"

Albert's face grew as hot and as red as a bowl of tomato soup. "It's just a Tile, guys."

But his friends were excited to show him off, pride on both of their faces. Albert lifted the cord from his neck, revealing the Master Tile. It was different from all the others in the Core, a shiny black color with a white symbol on it. The symbol was shaped sort of like an old scale, the kind with two arms that levered up and down, depending on the weight placed on each side.

"Magnificent," the Path Hider breathed. He reached out, eyes wide, almost as if he wanted to touch it. But at the last second, he drew his hand back and gave Albert a glittering smile. "I'm proud, Albert Flynn. I've watched you for years, as I do all the Balance Keepers. I knew you'd be a special one, considering your family's blood-lines. But I never suspected the Master Tile."

He was looking at Albert like he was royalty.

"Um, thanks," Albert said. "That means a lot, I think."

The Path Hider nodded, then went on to ask Birdie and Leroy about their Tiles, too. Birdie's was a Water Tile, while Leroy's was a Synapse Tile. The Path Hider looked impressed with theirs, too. "I've seen lots of Tiles come through here over the years. The ones you three hold are rare. Quite rare, indeed."

"You should see Leroy in the Tiles tournaments," Birdie said, folding her hands in her lap. "He's a whiz! No one can beat him!"

"Or so you think." The Path Hider nodded. "Someday, Leroy Jones, I will challenge you to a game of Tiles." He winked and stood up, seemingly done with his ques-tions. "I guess I should send you on your way. The path tells me stories, and secrets. But I wonder"—the Path

Hider rubbed his chin—"if you could ask that shopkeeper Lucinda to come and visit me soon?"

Birdie smiled knowingly. Lucinda had a major crush on the Path Hider. "She talks about you sometimes. I'm sure she'd love to come visit!"

"Very well, then," the Path Hider said. "Farnsworth?"

The little dog came tearing across the room with a chunk of copper wires in his mouth. The Path Hider yanked the wires out and shook off the slobber. "This will take days to repair. Ah, well. Lead the way, old friend."

Farnsworth barked, then set off down the dark tunnel that led to the gondola. Albert, Birdie, and Leroy followed, but just before they were out of earshot, the Path Hider whispered a warning.

"Watch your backs, young Balance Keepers. I sense trouble brewing in the Core."

Albert looked back. He saw not even a shadow.

But the Path Hider's voice followed them into the darkness.

"You never know who you can trust."

CHAPTER 5

Darkness Is Coming

The gondola whizzed along its track, tossing Albert, Birdie, Leroy, and Farnsworth back and forth. The cave around them was as large as the night sky, and just as dark. As they got closer to the end of the ride, something black and fuzzy flitted into the open window.

"Oh, come *on*! Not again!" Leroy yipped like a dog.

"The Memory Wipers!" Birdie laughed and held out her arm. One of the bats landed on her wrist. It was almost as big as Farnsworth. "I love these little guys!"

"Little?!" Leroy squawked.

"I'd forgotten about them," Albert said, reaching out to touch the furry black bat. It was soft like a newborn kitten, and it started to purr.

"I guess that means their songs really do work," Birdie said, stroking the bat.

At first, Albert wasn't sure what she was talking about. But as he stared at the bats, a memory reformed in the back of his mind. It was from last summer, when Albert and his friends had left the Core to return to their normal lives. The Memory Wipers had swooped in and out of the open windows of the gondola, singing their strange songs. It had forced the trio's memories of the Core to fade like near-forgotten dreams. The Memory Wipers were a vital part of protecting the Core's secrets, keeping it safe from the outside world, and Albert smiled as he realized they'd done their job.

"Did it work on you, Leroy?" Albert asked. "Even with your Synapse Tile?"

Leroy groaned. "Yes. And I'd be happy to forget them all over again."

The Memory Wiper flew out the window, singing its song. Hundreds of others joined in, their voices strangely human. But before they could lull the trio to sleep, Farnsworth barked twice, and the gondola sped back up, carrying them away from the cave.

After a few more drops of the gondola, and several screams (some happy and some not) from Albert, Leroy, and Birdie, Albert finally saw the blue flames of Lucinda's shop come into view.

"You're late!" Lucinda shouted. As they got closer,

Albert saw a familiar black shape coiled around Lucinda's neck and shoulders. It was her pet snake, Kimber. Farnsworth growled and barked at the sight of it, probably remembering the giant Hissengores in the Calderon Realm that had attacked the poor dog last term.

Lucinda's shop was basically a booth made of metal scraps fused together. It sat on a floating platform, and beside it, there were barrels tucked into the cave walls, overflowing with shadowed things.

The gondola came to a stop just in front of Lucinda.

"We came as quickly as we could," Birdie insisted. She leaned forward and whispered, "The Path Hider has a message for you."

Kimber hissed and curled tighter around Lucinda's shoulders as Birdie whispered in Lucinda's ear.

When Birdie was done, Lucinda smiled and fanned her face. The trio laughed, and then Albert remembered something. "Last time, you gave us a bag of Core stuff. What do we get this time around? Colored Tiles? New boots?"

Lucinda's smile fell. She leaned forward on the booth, and the old metal creaked and groaned. "I have nothing for you this year but a warning."

Albert, Birdie, and Leroy leaned forward, too. Even Farnsworth stood on his back paws to get closer to Lucinda.

"The Core hasn't been the same since a few weeks

after the Balance in Calderon was restored last summer,"
Lucinda sighed. "There's a change in the air around us.
It feels colder, somehow. Even the flames in the tunnels
don't burn as bright. The other Balance Keepers who
were able to make it here on such short notice have been
training around the clock. The Professors are pushing
them hard, due to the emergency."

"Emergency?" Birdie asked.

Lucinda shook her head. "I can't say for sure what's
going on. But I know that the Core is changing, and not
for the better."

"The Path Hider gave us a warning, too," Leroy said,
sitting back on the gondola bench. "So what's *really* the
problem?"

"There's an Imbalance, isn't there?" Albert asked.

"You can tell us," Birdie chided.

Lucinda's voice lowered to a whisper, and her eyes
grew as large as two moons. What she said next chilled
Albert all the way down to his toes.

"It would be in your best interest to stick together.
Train hard, and be prepared for the worst. Darkness is
coming, children. And I fear that the Core may not be
ready to face it."

She stared into the distance, a faraway look in her
eyes. Kimber coiled tighter around her neck. Before
Albert could say another word, Lucinda waved her arm.
"Be safe," she said. "And be careful who you turn to

when times get hard. Now move along, you three. The Core needs all the help it can get."

The gondola carted them away.

The three friends sat back in their seats, and not another word was spoken until they reached the final platform, where massive double doors stood before them—the entrance to the Main Chamber of the Core.

"That's two sets of warnings in one day," Leroy's voice cracked.

Birdie looked back and forth at the two boys, then pointed at the doors to their right. "What do you think we're going to find when we get inside?"

It was Albert who stood up first. "I don't know," he said. He straightened his shirt, tightened the laces on his boots, and smiled back at his friends. "But there's only one way to find out."

He leaped from the gondola, and the others followed behind.

The doors to the Core seemed to notice their presence, because as soon as Albert's hand touched the old, ancient wood, there was a creak and a groan as they unlocked.

"Here we go," Albert said.

Birdie cracked her knuckles. Leroy swallowed, hard. Farnsworth pawed at the ground like a racehorse ready to run.

Together, the three friends pressed hard, putting all their strength into it, and the doors to Albert's favorite place in the entire world (really, *inside* the world) opened wide. Farnsworth raced between Albert's legs, disappearing into the chaos of the Core.

Albert was home.

Even though Albert had been here before, the Main Chamber still felt like walking into a dream.

Three glittering streams flowed across the floor, leading to ancient doors that were the gateways to the three Realms. Overhead, a wolf with eagle's wings perched on the giant copper chandelier that lit the cave. The room was warm and open, and as Albert took a step farther inside, he felt lightness in his heart that could only come from a place as magical and wonderful as this.

"We made it," Albert breathed.

An older girl ran past, with a flaming orange and red bird perched atop her head. Its feathers left a trail of sparks in their wake.

"Hey, that's a phoenix!" Leroy said. "She didn't have that last time!"

"I *love* your bird!" Birdie yelled after the girl. Her voice echoed in the cavernous space.

Throngs of people were scurrying past, both young Balance Keepers and adults alike. The last time Albert had set foot in here, there was laughter. People playing games, boys and girls diving into the rivers and riding on the CoreFish.

All of that was missing now.

"Something's different," Birdie said. "Lucinda was right."

"It's so quiet," Leroy added. "Remember how it felt last time?"

Birdie nodded. "It was like walking into a storybook. Where are all of our friends? Why does everyone look so serious?"

Albert looked at the faces of everyone passing by. None of them were smiling. Everyone was in a rush to get to where they were going, none of them stopping for conversations along the way, and there weren't as many people as usual. It felt strangely empty.

Albert closed his eyes for a moment and remembered the very first time he'd walked into this room. There had been so much life then, a sense that adventure was hiding around every corner. That first time, it had almost felt like the Core was so full of magic that the walls could hardly hold it all in. Today, it was as if someone had stolen the very heart away. Now all that was left were fragments, and Albert was determined to discover *why*.

"What's going on?" he asked a Cleaner, a woman wheeling a big copper bin stuffed to the brim with trash. His voice almost seemed too loud for the silence around them.

The woman stopped to sweep dust from the floor, her dark curls falling into her face. "Trouble," she said. "Toil and trouble, my boy."

She moved along, leaving Albert, Leroy, and Birdie to

stare at one another.

"Okay—that was straight out of some creepy Hallow-een movie," Leroy said. "What is going *on* around here?"

Birdie rubbed her hands together. "It's, like, freaking me out, you guys."

They stood and stared for a while, not sure where to go, what to do. Last time, Trey had been here to guide them. Today it seemed that there wasn't any time to waste on Hydra's return.

Just then, a ground-trembling roar came from one of the tunnels. People screamed and dove for cover. Leroy ducked behind Albert. A pink cat screeched and leaped onto Farnsworth's back, claws out. A big, muscular Core worker tripped and toppled into one of the streams.

But Birdie stood tall and calm, a smile spreading across her face.

Seconds later, a winged beast emerged from the far tunnel, the one that led to the girls' dorm. It had large, leathery wings, sharp talons, and an even sharper beak.

"JADAR!" Birdie screamed.

The Guildacker howled, a sound that was quite doglike, and took flight, its wings barely missing the chandelier overhead. It swooped down and landed soft as a feather in front of Birdie.

She fell against him at once, wrapping her arms around his big neck. "I've missed you!"

Jadar whimpered and stooped lower. Birdie kissed him on the beak, and he ruffled his wings. The crowd relaxed; people came out of their hiding spots. Jadar was the most fearsome beast in the Core, straight from the Calderon Realm.

He was also one of the reasons Albert, Birdie, and Leroy were able to save the world last summer.

"Hey, Jadar," Albert said, waving at the Guildacker. He nudged Leroy in the stomach.

"Oh yeah! Hey, there, um, dude. What's up?" Leroy wouldn't look the beast in the eye. He was probably still a little afraid of him from last term. Albert held back a laugh.

Birdie turned back to her friends, and Albert thought he saw a few tears sparkling in her eyes. "Do you guys mind if Jadar and I go for a little flight? It's been way too long!"

Albert smiled. "Go ahead."

Birdie hopped on, sitting like a queen atop a throne. But before Jadar could soar to the sky, a voice called out.

"Hydra!"

All three of them turned.

Across the Main Chamber, standing on one of the arched bridges, was a small boy with dark hair and glittering eyes.

Petra.

CHAPTER 6

Trouble from Within

Petra wasn't a Balance Keeper, but as far as Albert was concerned, he was every bit as brave. As Albert, Birdie, and Leroy approached Petra on the bridge, Albert recalled how when they'd first met Petra last term, he was an awkward boy with a voice that rivaled a field mouse's squeak.

"Hydra!" Petra yelped again.

I guess that hasn't changed much.

Petra knew secrets about the Core that not even the oldest students did, so it hadn't been surprising to Albert when Petra ended up discovering what the Master Tile *really* did. Last term, Petra had been a die-hard supporter of team Hydra during the Pit competitions. Eventually, Albert had come to think of Petra as a part of the Hydra team.

And by the looks of it, the Core had recognized Petra's value, too.

"I'm a Messenger now," Petra said as Albert, Leroy, and Birdie followed him across the Main Chamber and into one of the tunnels. "Basically, I do runs for every Professor. Not just Bigglesby. And that's good, because that man enjoys handing out detentions, even if I'm just a *second* late!"

Albert loved listening to Petra talk. Sure, he usually said too much, but the guy had a certain awkward charm. He was a Pure, someone born and raised here. And he was a great friend.

"So where are we going?" Albert asked, sidestepping a giant black cat the size of a horse, with three eyes and six legs.

Petra smiled. "To see your dad, of course!"

Albert's heart felt instantly lighter. He was so happy to be back in the Core, but with all the weird warnings they'd gotten so far, he just felt a little *off*. Professor Flynn almost always had the answers Albert needed.

The four of them entered the familiar tunnel that led to Professor Flynn's office. Blue flames lit the way, flickering on the rounded walls. When they were almost to the end, Farnsworth took off, sprinting as fast as his paws could carry him.

"Is there something going on lately? I mean, besides the tremors off the California coast?" Albert asked.

Petra nodded as they came to a stop at Professor

Flynn's door. "Unprecedented things. I'm sure your dad will explain it all. This is one of the first emergency sessions we've had in a long time."

He lifted his hand to knock, but suddenly the door swung open.

It was Trey, Professor Flynn's Apprentice. He was tall and thin, with an English accent that most girls in the Core adored.

"I see you've made it back," Trey said, looking down his nose at the three of them. He nodded once at Petra.

"Yeah, right on time," Albert said, grinning. Trey was intimidating to most of the Balance Keepers, but not to Hydra. They'd learned that while he was mostly about business and rules, he also had a soft spot for those who loved the Core. After a while, he wasn't so bad.

"Did you miss us?" Birdie popped her hip.

Trey nodded. "The Core needs every Balance Keeper it can get right now." He had a file of notes in his arms, and he shifted the papers as if he was eager to move along. "I do have to get going, though."

Albert wasn't ready to let Trey go yet. He needed answers, and he needed them now. "Can you please just tell us what's happening around here?"

"I'm afraid my duties have called me elsewhere right now. No time to explain," Trey said. "I've got to be on my way. But good luck, and please, Hydra. If you've learned *anything* since I saw you last, remember to stay out of trouble."

"Aye, aye, Captain," Leroy called after Trey's retreating figure.

Albert turned to his friends as soon as Trey rounded the corner. "What was *that* about?"

Birdie's face was bright red. "Is he mad at us?"

Leroy just held his palms out as if to say, *I don't know.* Farnsworth simply scratched at his collar and let out a burp.

"He's been very busy lately," Petra explained. "Professor Flynn has had him doing work *all* over the Core, all hours. He's probably exhausted. I wouldn't worry."

But Albert was beyond worrying. He felt nervous from his head to his toes. There was definitely something off about the way everyone here was acting. Emergency or not, it was still the holidays. He'd expected bright lights and trees and presents all around, maybe even some fake falling snow.

"I'll wait for you guys out here," Petra said, waving Hydra through the open door. He looked into the room with longing, and Albert remembered how badly Petra wanted to be a Balance Keeper.

"It's great to see you, buddy," Albert said. Petra smiled as Hydra disappeared into the room.

The door shut behind them and memories flooded into Albert's mind at the sight of this place. As they rounded the corner into another towering cave, Albert saw the Waterfall of Fate.

It spilled from the ceiling, pouring glittering blue

water into a deep pool below. Beneath the surface, thousands of Tiles were waiting for new Balance Keepers to
come and claim them. Albert remembered the feeling
of swimming deep down, stretching his arms to try and
grab a Tile. He remembered the strange feeling he got
when his fingers closed around the Master Tile, and the
way his dad had looked at him when he'd emerged from
the water.

"Albert!"

His dad's voice drew him from his thoughts, and
Albert ran across the cave. He almost tackled his dad in
a giant hug, totally losing his cool. But hey, they hadn't
seen each other in *months*. Sometimes it was okay to act
like a little kid again, even for world-saving, Master Tile–
wielding Balance Keepers.

"I knew you'd make it safely here," Professor Flynn
said. He pulled away from the hug and smiled down at
his son. He had the same three freckles on his nose as
Albert, the same messy mouse-brown hair (only with
flecks of gray). Professor Flynn wore his usual glittering
green Professor's outfit, but Albert loved that in his eyes,
his dad still held the magic of youth.

"The IceBlitzer was awesome!" Albert said, grinning.
"You should have seen the air I was getting on that thing!
Best. Present. *Ever.*"

Professor Flynn laughed. "Well, it was the least I could
do. I hated to miss you at the airport, but"—he spread his

arms wide—"the Core needed me here."

"Yeah, I know," Albert said. "I've been monitoring the tremors. Which Realm is acting up?"

"It's Ponderay, isn't it?" Leroy asked.

Professor Flynn nodded. "Very good, Leroy. Ponderay hasn't acted up in hundreds of years. Not even a hint of an Imbalance. I'm afraid we here in the Core have taken its peaceful state for granted and have thus found ourselves quite unprepared to deal with this Imbalance."

"If there's an Imbalance for real," Albert said, realizing that his suspicions about the tremors had been correct all along, "then that means what's happening off the coast of California is because of Ponderay."

Professor Flynn nodded.

A lump formed in Albert's throat. "But Mom and the kids are in California! They're in danger. We should tell them, and get them out of there."

Professor Flynn put a hand on Albert's shoulder. "Everyone is in danger, Albert, just like last term. You know, as well as I do, that we can never share the news of the Core. This simply means that we must train harder than ever before. If we do our job right, your mom and everyone else in California will be okay."

Birdie stepped forward, her arms crossed over her chest. "You called us here, even though we're the First Unit for Calderon. So does this mean . . ."

"As one of the highest-ranking teams from last term,

you have been called here to do an emergency training session in case we need another team to enter the Realm behind the Ponderay First Unit," Professor Flynn said.

"YES!" Birdie fist-pumped the air. Leroy sighed and adjusted his glasses, but there was a ghost of a smile on his lips. Albert felt a flutter of excitement in his gut, but he couldn't celebrate like the others. That was twice in one year that his family was in danger on the surface of the earth. *What are the odds of that happening?*

"We'll do the job right," Albert said, putting on a brave face. "We'll fix the Imbalance."

"I'm glad to see you're excited," Professor Flynn said. "This doesn't usually happen, and as a result, while you're here, you won't be entering Calderon at all. Ponderay must take precedence. Next term, if everything returns to normal, you'll resume First Unit responsibilities for Calderon. You'll help train the next backup units in the Pit. But for now, with Ponderay, keep in mind, this is still a competition. You'll be starting over, in a sense, competing against another team to see who will go inside the Realm."

Albert's stomach twisted. "Just one other team? Who will we be competing against?" *Please don't be Hoyt's team. Please don't be Hoyt's team.*

But looking into his dad's eyes, Albert knew.

"Argon," Professor Flynn said. "So yes, you will be competing against Hoyt. I know you would rather compete against almost anyone else, but Argon was the only other high-ranked team who could assemble on such short notice."

Albert groaned, scuffing the ground with the toe of his boot.

Professor Flynn nodded. "We've spoken to Argon about this, and they've promised to be diplomatic about the entire competition."

"Sure they will," Leroy said, joining Albert's side.

"Oh, this is going to be good." Birdie rubbed her hands together.

Professor Flynn clicked his tongue. "News of the competition is not why I had Petra bring you here this morning."

He sat down at his old wooden desk, the chair creaking under his weight. The three of them took their seats across from him. From here, Albert could really see them now: the dark circles underneath his dad's eyes. Professor Flynn was *exhausted*. Both mentally and physically.

"What's wrong, Dad?" Albert asked. "Why's the Core so tense? I mean, besides the obvious Imbalance."

"You remember the events that unfolded last term," Professor Flynn explained. "Well, with a second Realm acting up, that's two in one year. Almost unprecedented."

"It hasn't happened since the eighteen hundreds," Leroy added. Albert guessed his Synapse Tile was kicking in, now that they were back in the Core. Its power gave Leroy the ability to notice *and* remember the details of anything he saw, from directions to pages in a history book.

"True indeed," Professor Flynn sighed, and continued. "What I'm about to tell you three is top secret. Not to be shared with *anyone*."

He looked pointedly at all three of them, and they each nodded.

"The problems in the Realms are being caused by one of our own."

Albert gasped. Birdie clapped a hand to her mouth, and Leroy nearly toppled out of his chair. Farnsworth growled.

"What?" Albert asked. His voice squeaked like Petra's. "How do you know? And who would do that?"

Professor Flynn shook his head. "I know it's hard to believe, but whoever is setting these Realms off Balance is entering them from *inside* the Core. The Imbalance in Calderon last term, and this one now in Ponderay, is too drastic to be caused by natural means."

"But why?" Birdie asked. "Why would someone want to do that?"

Farnsworth whimpered and leaped into Albert's lap.

"Sometimes Balance Keepers turn bad," Professor Flynn said, his voice sad. "Sometimes, when given great power, people lose control."

It felt like someone had just dumped a bunch of

fifty-pound weights inside Albert's stomach.

"That's horrible. We have to find them. We can find them, right, Dad?"

"That is the hope," Professor Flynn said.

But he didn't look very convinced. He stood up, motioning for Hydra to do so, too.

"For now, work your hardest in the training Pit. Become the best Balance Keepers you can be."

"We will," Albert, Birdie, and Leroy promised together.

They turned, ready to leave. But before they were out of earshot, Professor Flynn called out.

"Albert?"

Albert turned. "Yeah, Dad?"

"Don't worry about your mom and siblings. Your mom's a smart woman. She'll get them out of there safely."

"I hope so," Albert said.

His dad lowered his voice. "Watch your back, kiddo. If there's a traitor in our midst, a Tile like yours might be the very thing that person wants to seize for their own."

Albert nodded.

He turned and followed his friends out of the room, a chill running up and down his spine.

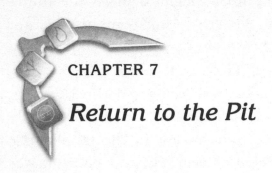

CHAPTER 7

Return to the Pit

When Petra saw the looks on his three friends' faces, he frowned.

"That bad, huh?"

"Worse," Albert sighed.

Leroy patted Albert on the back. Birdie's shoulders drooped, and Farnsworth sang out a mournful howl.

"Then I guess this is a bad time to tell you that you're due in the Pit, like, now?" Petra said. He was looking at Hydra like they'd be seriously disturbed.

But Albert's face broke into a smile.

"No, Petra," he said, walking a little bit faster. "That's the best news I've heard all day!"

"Let's go!" Birdie clapped her hands.

"I never thought I'd say this," Leroy sighed. "But let's do this, dudes."

Farnsworth yipped and sprinted down the tunnel with Albert, Birdie, and Leroy fresh on his heels.

They didn't see the worried look on Petra's face as they left him behind.

The pathway to the Pit was the most welcome sight Albert had seen since his return to the Core. Being a Balance Keeper made Albert *crave* danger, the same way Leroy craved cake.

"First one to the top wins!" Albert shouted as they burst through the old wooden door that led to the pathway to the Pit.

"Then that'll be me!" Birdie giggled, shoving past the boys.

Inside was a massive, towering cavern, and an uneven pathway that zigzagged left and right, higher and higher. Leroy groaned—no doubt at the lack of railings. Waterfalls fell at random over the path, creating a misty, dreamlike atmosphere.

Albert sprinted forward. Farnsworth wiggled past him and raced up the narrow pathway, barking and howling.

Birdie was fast and light on her feet.

But Albert had been secretly training while he was back in New York, running on his stepdad's treadmill every night. He pulled ahead, the soles of his boots just barely hanging over the edge of the path.

"Oh, no way!" Birdie yelled behind him.

Albert could hear her breathing, so he really laid on the speed.

Left, right.

Through a waterfall, then skidding to a near stop as the pathway went left again.

Albert reached the top and dove onto the orange platform where Farnsworth was already waiting. The little dog howled as if to announce Albert as the winner.

Birdie came up just a few seconds behind him.

"You were using your Master Tile!" she groaned, wiping sweat from her forehead.

Albert shook his head. "Nope. Just plain old Albert magic, nothing extra added on."

"Rematch next time, then," Birdie said, bending to stretch her legs. "Hey, where's Leroy?"

Together, Albert and Birdie looked down. Far below, Leroy was inching his way up the path, as slow as a worm in the mud.

"It'll probably take him a day or two to settle back into the way things are here," Albert said. He cupped his hands over his mouth and yelled down. "Come on, Leroy! Let's go!"

"We're gonna be late, Leroy!" Birdie shouted. "Pick up the pace!"

"Haven't you read any books, you guys?" Leroy's voice echoed up toward them. "Slow and steady wins the race!"

Birdie and Albert burst into laughter, then sat down to wait for their friend.

A few minutes later the platform rose high into the air with Albert and his friends on board, carting them away from the pathway below.

Cool air whooshed into Albert's face. He held his arms to the sides and let out a happy scream. He felt like himself again. This was where he was meant to be. Birdie and Leroy joined in, and even Farnsworth let loose a happy howl.

The platform stopped a few seconds later, and the door to the Pit swung inward.

"Ladies first," Albert said to Birdie.

She smirked, and held out her hand. "Then go ahead, you two."

Team Hydra entered the Pit with their heads held high.

"There you are! It's about time," a voice said, as they stepped through the doorway. Someone emerged from the shadows ahead. "I was beginning to think you'd chickened out on me."

Albert almost gasped when he saw who was talking.

It was a tall dark-haired girl with muscles so big that Albert figured she'd be able to punch him all the way back to the surface if she wanted to. There were scars covering her arms and neck, even a few on her face. Not to mention the dark, almost-black eyes. The girl was the description of intimidating.

"You're Tussy," Leroy said. "Professor Asante's Apprentice."

The girl nodded. "That's right."

She held up a copper clipboard. "I'll need you three to sign this form for me. Just a few formalities, now that we're in the middle of the worst Imbalance the Core has ever seen. Training will be far more dangerous than you've ever experienced. Sign on the dotted line, please."

Birdie took the clipboard and together the three of them read through the papers that were attached.

Leroy finished in about two seconds flat. "Chance of . . . hold on, does that say *dismemberment*?"

Tussy shrugged. "The training exercises for Ponderay are quite grueling. But I assure you, nothing like that has happened in at *least* ten years."

"I'm gonna be sick," Leroy whispered.

Albert patted him on the back and signed the documents. But even his hands trembled a little. Birdie signed next, and with lots of encouragement, Leroy finally signed, too.

Tussy grinned, but it sort of looked like the expression belonged on a hungry shark.

"Great," Tussy said. "Let's get started."

She turned on her heel and marched around the edge of the Pit to the bleachers where a few Core people were already sitting, ready to watch the action.

Right in the front row were three people who made Albert's hands curl into fists.

Hoyt, Slink, and Mo. Team Argon.

They were Hydra's archenemies, and total jerks. Hoyt smirked as soon as he saw Albert and his friends. He turned and started whispering to his team, and they all laughed louder than was necessary.

"Wow, really mature," Birdie growled. "Looks like they haven't changed a bit."

Tussy hardly seemed to take notice as she stopped at the edge of the bleachers.

"You'll be wearing these today."

She scooped up three bags and tossed them to Albert, Birdie, and Leroy.

"The climate in Ponderay will be completely different from what you're used to. This is no Calderon, if you get what I mean."

She laughed, but no one else did.

Albert opened up his bag and peered inside. It was a pair of thick blue pants, almost like a wetsuit, and a long-sleeved blue Hydra shirt to match. Knee-high boots were also included, and these had a similar waterproof feel to them, with Velcro and snaps. Birdie and Leroy had the same stuff in their bags.

Tussy pointed to a small, curtained-off area at the edge of the Pit cave.

"Change, please. And quickly. There's no time to spare."

Birdie went first, and a few minutes later, all of Hydra was decked out in their new gear.

The clothes stuck to Albert's skin like glue. It was weird, but he felt like he was about to be some kind of space hero or underwater traveler. He was sweating in minutes, and he hoped the temperature inside the Pit would be better suited for this kind of gear.

Tussy nodded in approval and motioned for Albert and his friends to enter the Pit. As usual, there were two orange platforms, one on either side of the Pit. This meant Hydra would already be *competing*. No warm-up, no practice, just full-on head-to-head from the start.

Albert looked across the Pit. Hoyt's team was piling onto their platform, wearing similar outfits in shades of orange.

"You know, I think I'd almost rather be back in that cooking class right now," Leroy said.

Albert sighed, but he felt the familiar weight of his Master Tile around his neck. He had to be a leader.

"We beat them last term," Albert said, facing his friends, "and we'll do it again now."

Birdie and Leroy nodded, then all three of them walked back to Tussy.

"This training will be quick and dangerous," Tussy said, filling them in on what she'd apparently already shared with Argon. "We've calculated that we have seven days—just one week—before the situation in Ponderay becomes so dire that we'll have to send in another team. At the end of those seven days, whoever has the highest score on the leaderboard will become the Ponderay First Unit, and along with Professor Asante, will enter the Realm to try and find the Means to Restore Balance."

"Wait," Leroy said. "Professor Flynn said we'd be competing to be a backup unit to the Ponderay First Unit. Now we're competing to *become* the Ponderay First Unit? What happened to the old First Unit since this morning?"

Tussy sighed. "They quit."

"They *quit*?" Albert, Birdie, and Leroy said in unison.

Tussy nodded. "Like I said, this is a terrible Imbalance we're facing, and we don't totally know what we're dealing with since no one's entered Ponderay in decades. Not everyone is brave enough to stick around and put their lives on the line. Anyway, now we're replacing them, and seeing as you three did so well last term, you're first on our list of prospects."

Tussy crossed to the bleachers and stood at the ready while Albert and his friends piled onto their platform.

"This is just great," Leroy said. "The First Unit actually chickened out!"

"Didn't we see them last term?" Birdie asked. "Wasn't their leader, like, totally fearless?"

"Apparently not." Albert shrugged.

Tussy clapped her hands to get everyone's attention. "All right, Balance Keepers, enough standing around. Let's begin!" She blew a whistle, and their platforms began to sink.

The last time they'd been in the Pit it was full of all sorts of Calderon things: tall twisting spires, hanging vines, and suspended barrels that spun like King Fireflies.

But today, as their platform reached the floor, Albert had no idea what he and his friends were in for. Right now, the Pit was empty. Just a big, deep hole in the ground. Albert hopped off of their platform, and Birdie and Leroy followed suit.

The ground was the same, at least. That strange, trampoline-like floor that acted like it wanted to suck Albert's feet under.

Overhead, Tussy blew her whistle, and suddenly the ground started to tremble.

"What's going on?" Leroy asked.

"Who knows." Birdie shrugged.

Albert was too busy watching to say anything at all.

Across from him and his friends, ten holes appeared in the floor, at least three feet wide each. There was a big *boom* that almost made Hydra topple over.

Faster than a bullet from a gun, ten rock pillars shot out of the holes, stretching so high that Albert had to squint to see their tops.

"Whoa," Albert said, his mouth hanging open.

"Sweet molasses," Leroy added.

From overhead, Tussy spoke into a MegaHorn.

"Today's task is straightforward. At the tops of these pillars—which I'm sure you know are stand-ins for the Ten Pillars of Ponderay—are ten large Tiles. You want your team to collect more Tiles than the other team, plain and simple."

"What are the rules?" Birdie called up.

Tussy smiled like a shark again. "There are none."

"Nice," Albert said, bouncing on his toes.

Across from him, he saw Hoyt sneering his face off.

"Balance Keepers, are you ready?" Tussy yelled into the MegaHorn.

Six voices answered. "Ready!"

The whistle blew and the madness began. "Let's split up!" Albert said to his friends. "Each of us take a different pillar, and try to work our way to the top."

"How?" Birdie asked. "We can't just *shimmy* up a pillar that size!"

Leroy, who had been busy staring at the pillars, shrugged like he'd figured out a plan ages ago. "There are holds in the pillars, every four feet or so. We can use those to scale the sides."

Albert turned to stare at the pillars. Sure enough, he saw the holds Leroy was talking about, little divots in the rock formations. Perfect for putting a hand or a foot inside. It was just like a rock-climbing wall.

"He's right." Albert grinned. "Let's go. Move fast. And watch out for Hoyt. I have a feeling he's not going to take this lightly."

"Got it, boss." Leroy nodded. He turned his hat backward.

"Let's cream them!" Birdie clapped her hands.

His friends both raced away. Albert sprinted across the Pit floor, losing sight of them as he zigzagged between pillars. Albert heard someone scream and looked up to see Slink falling through the air. He smacked the ground next to Albert, only to be sucked under and shot right back up again.

"Nice one, butterfingers!" Hoyt screamed.

Albert looked up. Hoyt was already halfway up a pillar, using his Speed Tile to scurry like a Hexabon. Across from him, Birdie was just starting the climb.

Leroy was nowhere to be seen.

Move fast, Albert.

He reached an empty pillar, and started the climb. It was tough work, especially after having been away from the Core for so many months. *It couldn't hurt to practice with my Tile.* Albert closed his eyes for a second. He pictured the symbol that he'd studied back in his room in New York. It sort of looked like a dumbbell. *Iron Grip.*

Still focusing on the symbol, Albert made his way

slowly up. Iron Grip was working, because even though Albert's arms and legs were tired, his fingertips never slipped from the pillar. He was climbing fast, and in seconds, he was halfway up.

"Just a little farther!" Albert told himself when he saw a handhold about a foot over his head.

He reached for it, was about to grab a hold, when it simply disappeared.

There was nothing Albert could do.

He fell, fast, toward the bottom of the Pit. When he hit the floor it sucked him under like a soft blanket, then shot him back up in the air.

Iron Grip! Albert thought, focusing on the dumbbell symbol again, and as he soared past a pillar, he reached out and grabbed hold.

"Hey!"

Albert looked down to see Birdie a few feet below him on the same pillar, clinging to its side like a spider.

"The handholds disappear, be careful!" Albert said.

Birdie nodded, a fat bruise on her forehead. "I learned that the hard way! Keep going, I'll move to another pillar!"

Someone screamed, and Albert saw Leroy and Hoyt fall off opposite pillars across the Pit.

"Move, Albert!" Birdie cried from below him. It spurred him back into action.

A few times, Albert's hand or footholds disappeared,

and he nearly fell off again. But with some major Tile concentration, and a determination burning like fire in the pit of his stomach, he climbed until he was perched just below the top.

A little bit more! Albert stretched, picturing his little half siblings reaching as hard as they could for the countertop where his mom hid the candy jar. Finally, Albert's hand closed over something smooth and hard, about the size of a salad plate. The Tile!

"Albert Flynn is the first to collect a Tile!" he heard Tussy say into her MegaHorn. Overhead, the crowd cheered, and Farnsworth howled. "One point for Hydra! They're in the lead!"

"Yay, Albert!" Leroy screamed from across the Pit. "You . . . did . . . it!"

From up this high, Albert watched as Hoyt summited a pillar across from him.

"One point for team Argon!" Tussy yelled, and Albert frowned. Hoyt had grabbed a Tile and was waving it in the air for the screaming crowd.

Uh-oh, Albert thought. *Time to step up my game.*

Hoyt dropped down to the floor, then raced to another pillar and started the climb. It was almost like instinct, what Albert did next. Tussy hadn't said you had to climb *all* the pillars. You just had to collect the Tiles on top of them. Albert was already high in the air. He tried to hoist himself up higher and get his whole body on top of the pillar. That way, he could simply stand and leap from one to the other. But Albert soon realized he wasn't strong enough. His muscles were screaming with exhaustion.

I need to use the Strength symbol, Albert thought, and he focused with all his might on an image of what looked like a mountain, tall and strong.

Albert felt his arms and legs start to tingle as the Master Tile worked its magic. He put all his effort into hoisting himself up, and sure enough, it worked. Albert was crouched on top of his pillar like a mountain lion on a boulder.

"Two points for Hydra!" Tussy screamed, and Albert saw Birdie with a Tile clutched in her hands.

"Yes! Nice job!" Albert screamed.

"Another point for Argon!" Tussy yelled, as Mo grabbed a Tile off the farthest pillar, then leaped down to the floor.

Albert stood up on top of his pillar. Even though there was no wind in the Pit, he thought he could feel his pillar swaying. A little to the left, a little to the right.

That was when it started to move.

And it wasn't just his pillar. It was *all* of them. They were spinning in a wide circle around the Pit.

They weren't moving fast, but the spinning disoriented Albert, nearly causing him to topple overboard.

It's just like being on a merry-go-round, Albert. No big deal.

But just as Albert got his balance, the pillar began to move faster.

Okay, like being on a slightly demented merry-go-round.

As they rotated faster, the force picked up and threatened to knock Albert to the Pit floor—along with the Tiles.

"The Ten Pillars have minds of their own!" Tussy said into the MegaHorn. "When the Realm of Ponderay is balanced, the Pillars stand strong and steady in the middle of the Silver Sea. But the Imbalance seems to have caused the Pillars in the Realm to begin rotating like this. Better think fast, and grab more Tiles, before the spinning knocks them off!"

Almost as if in response to Tussy's words, the pillars sped up even more. Now they were moving at a speed Albert was definitely not comfortable with—there was no way his mom would have let him ride a merry-go-round at this speed. Albert's mind buzzed, and his body felt wobbly and wrong. He just *knew* he was going to fall.

"Abandon ship!" Leroy screamed from somewhere below.

Albert didn't want to give up. He stooped to his knees and clutched the edges of his pillar as it zoomed around. He could see the next pillar in the circle just a few feet away and the Tile on top. If he could just jump far enough . . .

"Another two Tiles for Argon!" Tussy yelled into the

MegaHorn, and it was enough to distract Albert from picturing the symbol he needed to make the leap. He saw Slink and Mo both waving Tiles in the air, smiles on their faces.

"No!" Albert stood and tried to leap, but the momentum from the spinning pillar threw off his jump. He knew he wouldn't land on the next pillar, but he wouldn't go down that easy. As he began falling toward the Pit floor, Albert stretched with all he had left in him. His hand scraped the top of the next pillar, and his fingers closed over a Tile. He clutched it to his chest as he continued falling to the floor.

"Hydra barely snatches a Tile!" Tussy cheered. "Four total points!"

Seconds later, Hoyt grabbed a final Tile. "That makes six for Argon!" Tussy shouted, just as Albert landed hard on the Pit floor, his legs crumpling beneath him. Ten Tiles were claimed, four for Hydra, and six for Argon.

The pillars slowed to a stop, signaling that the competition was over. Argon had actually won.

"We were so close, bro," Leroy said, helping Albert up. Birdie stumbled over. Her ponytail looked like a giant cat had just used it as a toy. Across the Pit, team Argon was celebrating.

Tussy barked out a command. "What are you doing, teams? I didn't tell you to stop competing!"

Albert's jaw dropped. He wanted to say something,

but Hoyt was quicker to react.

"But all the Tiles are gone! We won!"

Tussy laughed, but it sounded more like a dog's deep bark. "Not so. You need to learn the meaning of exhaustion, Balance Keepers. I've given you one minute to take a break, while the Pit resets itself. When it's ready, you'll begin again. You'll go until I tell you to stop."

The pillars stood at the ready, and somehow they looked even bigger to Albert.

Tussy took a deep breath, and blew her whistle. As the Balance Keepers began again, Albert thought he saw her smile.

The competition went more slowly this time. Exhaustion began to settle in.

After another hour had passed, everyone was injured in some way. Leroy had lost a shoe and stubbed several toes. Birdie's nose was bleeding, and Albert had a big gash on his shoulder.

Still, they put everything they had into it.

It was Birdie who grabbed the ninth Tile, and Hoyt who grabbed the tenth.

Finally, Tussy blew her whistle.

The pillars sank to the bottom of the Pit and Albert's knees went out from under him. Everyone was lying, all broken and bent, on the trampoline floor.

Hoyt hardly had the energy to celebrate when Tussy

announced that Argon had won the second round 6–4, too.

Albert put his head in his hands, and Leroy muttered something about needing a strawberry milk shake.

"I can't believe it," Albert whispered, still gasping for a good breath.

Last term, they'd won so many competitions in the Pit that Hydra became a First Unit. They were pros now, a part of the big leagues in the Core. They'd saved the world.

But today was different.

Today Hydra lost.

CHAPTER 8

The Guildacker Float

Albert felt a strange sense of déjà vu as he and his friends left the Pit.

"I can't believe that just happened," Birdie said.

She clenched her jaw so tightly that Albert was afraid her hair was going to rip out. "They beat us. They actually *won*!"

"We're just a little rusty is all," Albert offered. But he felt downright defeated. "Hoyt's a Pure, remember? He's probably been sneaking into the Pit like we used to do, training up for this while we've all been on the surface. And it's not really fair. If we would've known Tussy was going to make us work so hard . . ."

"We can't use that as an excuse," Birdie countered.

"You're right," Albert said. "I guess we just have to

suck it up, guys. We lost, fair and square."

"It's never fair when you're up against Hoyt," Leroy added. He was wringing his hat in his hands. "But what if we've just lost our mojo?"

"You can't just *lose* mojo," Birdie said. "Especially because it's not a real thing."

"Oh, it's real," Leroy argued.

Albert laughed. "We're a team, guys. We were named the First Unit for Calderon only a few months ago. We're just getting back in the swing of things."

Farnsworth yipped in agreement. His flashlight eyes turned a cool ocean blue.

"See? Farnsworth agrees." Albert said.

The dog howled, and Albert, Leroy, and Birdie were in high spirits again, having decided that tomorrow things would be different. Tomorrow, they'd do everything they could to show Argon what Hydra was really made of. They rode the orange platform up and out of the Pit, then left the room and walked the jagged path back to the old wooden doorway.

Outside, Petra stood waiting for them, his back up against the cool stone walls of the tunnel.

"I'm sorry, guys," he said, shaking his head. "Hoyt's such a jerk. He already shouted Argon's victory to the whole Main Chamber the second he got out here. But no worries, right?"

Albert sighed. "Yeah. Sure."

"Aw, come on, you guys are Balance Keepers. You

can't get upset about one loss! And besides"—Petra bobbed up and down on his toes, reminding Albert of one of his half siblings when they begged for a cookie late at night—"I have a surprise for you."

"Unless it involves food, I'm going to Cedarfell and crashing," Leroy groaned.

Birdie elbowed him in the stomach, and they started to argue.

Albert shook his head. "At least some things never change. Lead the way, Petra. Farnsworth and I want to see what your surprise is. And I'm sure those guys will too, just as soon as they're done arguing like little kids."

Petra smiled wider than ever, then turned on his heel and walked briskly down the hall. While Birdie and Leroy talked about whether or not the blue flames were made of a natural or man-made substance, Petra filled Albert in on the latest Core gossip. Albert thought if Petra ever wanted to leave the Core, he would make an awesome reporter on the surface. Maybe even a detective.

He led them back into the Main Chamber, past a group of girls who giggled as they put pink bows all over Professor Asante's sleeping Guardian cat. Albert hoped the thing didn't wake up anytime soon, or those girls might be lunch. Or maybe just an appetizer.

Right as they were about to head into one of the tunnels, something caught Albert's eye. A large copper countdown clock had been hung on the wall beside the door to Ponderay. A big, glowing 7 sat on its face.

"I have a feeling that's, like, totally going to stress me out," Birdie hissed as she stared up at the clock.

Albert knew she was probably right.

"Come on, let's go!" Petra squeaked excitedly. He took a sharp left into a tunnel that Albert had yet to explore. It was lit by the same blue flames, but there were other doors here, locked doors, which Albert was just itching to get behind.

"What's in there?" Albert asked, pointing to a black door with an old, rusted handle.

"No one knows." Petra shrugged.

Albert's eyes widened, and again, he was filled with that same sense of adventure that struck him on his very first day in the Core. He loved this place, no matter the trouble, no matter the danger.

At the end of the tunnel, Petra stopped before a locked door. He turned to his three friends and gave them a sly grin. "What lies behind *this* door is only for us."

Farnsworth's eyes flashed a darker shade of blue.

"And Farnsworth," Petra corrected himself. Farnsworth's tail thumped on the dusty stone floor. "Here we go."

Petra pulled out an old rusty key from beneath his shirt, turned it in the lock, and swung the door open.

Albert peered inside, past Petra's shoulder.

It was not at all what he'd expected.

"This . . . is . . . ahhhhmazing!" Birdie shouted, holding her hands up in the air. "It couldn't be more beautiful, Petra!"

She walked over and then climbed up on a Guildacker-shaped float, the kind that Albert watched every year in the Macy's Thanksgiving Day Parade in New York.

This float was twice the size of Jadar and it took up most of the room. It looked so real that Albert was tempted to reach out to touch its chest and feel for a heartbeat.

"It's taken me months," Petra said. "And you guys get to help me finish it! I mean, there's no way I could do this all by myself."

"But you have!" Albert gasped. "You made this?"

"You have some serious skill, bro," Leroy said as he stared at the float.

It looked like some sort of famous sculpture artist had done it, not tiny little Petra. Albert didn't know the guy had it in him to be so creative.

The base of the float was made up of glittering gold coins—old ones that, apparently, Lucinda had given to Petra to use, as long as he promised to return them (with interest). The Guildacker's wings were covered in some sort of sparkling purple webbing. Albert reached up to touch it, but Leroy stopped him.

"That's that crazy moss stuff that made my fingers go all balloony on me last term."

"Oh, yikes." Albert pulled his hand away just in time.

"I had to wear special gloves for that part," Petra said. He stepped up beside Albert in the shadows cast by the Guildacker float's widespread wings.

"This is really awesome, Petra. But what's it for?" Albert asked.

Petra bobbed on his toes. "The Float Parade, of course!"

Albert just stared.

"Oh, riiiight," Petra squeaked. "You don't know about the parade. Technically, it's usually just for Pures, since we're the only ones here during the holidays."

Birdie hopped down from the Guildacker's back, careful not to mess it up with her boots. "I've never heard of it."

Even Leroy shook his head. "I'm coming up empty, dudes."

"It's only the biggest Pure event of the year," Petra explained, eyes as wide as the coins on the float. "First there's the Float Parade. Then there's a dance and a dinner, and whoever's float gets the most votes wins. It's a *huge* Core tradition for the Pures. And since you guys are here for the emergency session, the Professors have decided that everyone gets to join!"

"I can't wait!" Birdie giggled and clapped. "And you're so going to win the float competition. It looks just like Jadar!"

"I was hoping you'd say that," Petra's cheeks grew red

as cherries. "And I might have also been hoping that you three would, um, ride on the float. Please say yes! It'll be just like last year, when you guys saved Calderon! The entire Core will go nuts when they see it!"

Albert didn't really like being in the spotlight. He was good at saving the world from behind the scenes, then slipping quietly away with his best friends and dog.

But Petra looked so excited, and Albert couldn't even imagine how much time his friend had put into building this thing. It was cooler the longer he looked at it, with tons of detail. Even the Guildacker's claws looked razor-sharp, made of copper pipes that Petra had somehow chiseled into outspread talons.

"I'm game if you guys are," Albert said.

"It would be an honor, bro," Leroy said, patting Petra on the back.

"I'll do it on one condition," Birdie piped up. Her arms were crossed, and Albert knew she wouldn't back down. "I'll ride the Guildacker, even go to the dance . . . *if* I don't have to wear a dress."

All three of the boys laughed. Petra was at such a loss for words that Albert knew instantly he'd made the right choice.

The four of them piled their hands on top of one another's. Farnsworth laid a paw on top of the pile.

"Deal," Albert said. "We're definitely going to win."

CHAPTER 9

The Pillars of Ponderay

A s they climbed down the staircase and saw the glittering pool below them, the floating docks with old wooden tables and all of the Core people waiting below, Albert felt a thousand times lighter. They'd arrived at Lake Hall, where lunch was the biggest and best meal of the day.

This term, icicle lights hung from the cavernous ceiling like falling stars. The lights cast dancing shadows on the crowd below.

"You all right, Albert?" Birdie nudged him with her hip as they reached the bottom of the stairs.

"I'm good," Albert said. "I still can't believe we lost today."

"Things will get better," Birdie promised.

Albert wanted to believe she was right. This was the Core, after all. Things changed every single day, and tomorrow, he hoped they'd beat Argon.

"I'm so hungry I could eat an entire Guildacker!" Leroy yelled. His voice echoed across the Hall.

There was a deafening roar from the companions' table, which was closest to the bottom of the staircase where the trio stood. Jadar had heard Leroy's joke, and by the look of his coiled talons and snapping beak, he wasn't happy.

"My bad!" Leroy said, holding his hands up. "Totally my bad!"

Birdie smirked and waved Jadar away. "Serves you right, Leroy Jones."

"You guys are crazy," Albert said, holding back a laugh.

The three of them stood by the water's edge, waiting as the turtles swam to greet them.

"Oh, I've missed these little guys!" Birdie knelt down and patted her turtle on the head. It winked an ancient, knowing eye at her, then let her hop on. Albert and Leroy followed suit.

The turtles seemed to know exactly where Hydra belonged today. The turtles floated past Albert's old table, where he and his friends used to sit. Today it was empty, reminding Albert that even though he was back in the Core, it wasn't reason to celebrate. He was only here because of an emergency, and if Albert wanted to help set things right, and keep his family and everyone else in California safe, he needed to focus.

The turtles took a left, stopping at the edge of a black dock, where a few of the other students sat. Albert recognized some of them, especially Jack, an older Balance Keeper who had taken Albert and Leroy under his wing in Cedarfell. Albert didn't know Jack was a Pure. Some people, like Hoyt, flaunted it like a shiny new gadget, while others, like Petra, didn't think of it as something that needed to be said.

"'Sup, Hydra?" Jack waved from the dock.

"Hey, Jack! Nice to see you, man." Albert waved and hopped off his turtle. He knelt down and patted it on its glittering shell. "Thanks for the ride!"

The turtle blinked at him, then disappeared beneath the surface of the dark water.

There were three empty seats at the table. Albert, Leroy, and Birdie sat down. Leroy tucked a napkin into the collar of his shirt, then grabbed his fork and knife. "Let's do this."

"Albert Flynn," someone said.

Albert looked to his left, and was surprised to see Tussy there.

"Shouldn't you be sitting with the Professors?" he asked her.

Tussy had a fresh cut on her left eyebrow.

"Shouldn't you be a little more . . . disappointed right now?"

"I'm confused," Albert said.

"You lost today. The great Albert Flynn, the boy who wears the Master Tile around his neck. Part of the heroic team that saved Calderon. And today, you failed your first Pit exercise."

Albert felt like Tussy had just slapped him across the face.

"We haven't been here in months. It's natural to be a little out of touch."

Tussy clicked her teeth. "If you say so."

Albert could feel his face grow hot. "My team and I work really well together. You'll see."

"I'm expecting you to win in the Pit tomorrow," Tussy said with a pointed glare. She nodded her head across the lake, where Hoyt and his cronies were making gross faces. "I'd hate to see the fate of the world land in their hands."

"I can agree with you on that." Albert nodded.

"One week." Tussy took a gulp of her drink. "You'd better be ready."

Then she raised a scabbed eyebrow, stood up, and walked away.

Whimzies began to swoop down from overhead, carrying baskets full of steaming hot food. The smell alone made Albert's stomach rumble. As the rest of the table started loading their plates, thoughts of Albert's conversation with Tussy faded away.

He ate spaghetti and meatballs until he felt like he was going to explode.

Leroy, as usual, filled his plate three times, and left not a scrap of food to spare.

"You're *such* a glutton," Birdie said, shaking her head at Leroy. "It's really quite something."

Leroy shrugged. "Wha—oo—uh—mean?" A noodle hung from his chin.

"She means," Albert said, flicking the noodle away, "that you eat like a pig!"

Leroy swallowed, then laughed. "Pigs are usually fat and happy!"

As plates started to empty, Albert felt himself growing excited. Free time was next. And then, finally, a good night's sleep back in Cedarfell inside his warm tent.

But before anyone could stand up to leave, Tussy took the stage. A MegaHorn sat on a podium there, and she tapped it. A squeal reverberated throughout Lake Hall.

"As you may well know, we've brought several surface-dwelling Balance Keepers back to the Core, something we don't usually do on such short notice."

Heads nodded. Companion creatures hooted and roared and hissed.

Tussy went on. "I'll let Professor Asante relay the

news, as she has just recently returned from the Ponderay Realm. Everyone, give her a warm welcome."

Everyone clapped as Professor Asante took the stage. The sound was strangely weak compared to last summer, when Lake Hall was so packed with people that not a single dock or chair was left empty.

Professor Asante looked even larger today than she usually did. Albert had to crane his neck to look up at her.

"Sometimes I wonder if she's fully human," Birdie whispered to Albert and Leroy.

The boys both nodded. "Half giant, maybe," Albert said.

"Or half cyclops," Leroy mused, pushing his glasses farther up his nose.

Birdie sighed. "She has two eyes, Memory Boy. Cyclopses have only one."

Albert sighed and turned back to the stage. Professor Asante was covered in scars and cuts, just like Tussy. But she also had tattoos that wrapped around her neck and arms. There were *tons* of them, all a bunch of Core symbols. Albert knew some of the symbols; others he'd yet to study in the Black Book.

Professor Asante waved a large hand, and the room fell silent. "Welcome, Balance Keepers, especially those who were able to arrive so quickly. And greetings to everyone else in the Core, whose importance is not to be forgotten."

She gave the crowd another moment to cheer before silencing them again. Her eyes glittered as she surveyed the room. "These are dark times. I won't hide that from any of you. Rumors spread quickly in the Core, and I will shed light on the most recent one. The Realm of Ponderay, a place very dear to my heart, is indeed facing a terrible Imbalance."

The last time an Imbalance had been announced everyone gasped, but not today. Everyone had already sensed it. And with the reports coming in from California, Albert suspected he knew exactly how bad the Imbalance was. Soon, it would make things on the surface much worse. His stomach churned as he thought of his family.

"Let me assure you, this is something we Professors are taking very seriously. As you know, whenever a Realm has an Imbalance, *the Realm always provides the Means*. We are working around the clock both inside the Realm of Ponderay and through research efforts here in the Core to find the Means to Restore Balance."

Professor Asante went on. "The Balance in Ponderay has not been off in hundreds of years. There is a system set in place, one that has been there since the beginning of time, that has always ensured this. I regret that we don't know much about the system—we've never needed to—but we do know it involves the Ten Pillars of Ponderay that stand in a ring in the middle of the Silver Sea."

"I bet that's usually a gorgeous sight," Birdie whispered.

Professor Asante continued. "But now, as some of you know, in an event never before documented in Core History, the Pillars have begun to rotate in their ring, moving in a clockwise circle. They are not moving *too* fast, but we believe it is this movement that is causing the massive tremors off the coast of Southern California."

Several people did gasp this time, but Albert and his teammates just nodded solemnly; Professor Flynn had told them as much this morning. Albert suddenly wished he hadn't eaten so many meatballs. When he thought of his family in San Diego, his stomach started churning.

"I've been to the Realm myself," Professor Asante said. "Along with my Apprentice, Tussy, and we have yet to find the Means to Restore Balance. We don't yet know why the Pillars have begun to rotate. We will continue our search. What I ask now is that the Balance Keepers training for Ponderay step up their preparations."

She took a deep breath, and even from here, Albert could sense the tension in her shoulders, the exhaustion in her voice. Her eyes fell right on Albert, and as she spoke, a shiver tiptoed down Albert's spine. He felt like she was talking only to him, that they were the only two in the room.

"The time may come, very soon, when you will be asked to serve the Core."

Albert's heart skipped a beat. He thought of his family on the surface, and the desire to defeat the Imbalance burned like hot oil in his gut.

"Hydra and Argon should report to the Pit early tomorrow morning, for an emergency lesson on Ponderay before competition," Professor Asante added.

The speech ended.

Tussy took over and led the Core song. Everyone joined in, even Albert, and somehow, the familiarity of the moment seemed to take a bit of the chill away.

The song faded, and Albert, Leroy, and Birdie headed back toward the Main Chamber. When they got there, the clock with its glaring red number caught Albert's eye once again. *Seven days.*

"That was intense, dudes," Leroy said.

"Yeah, after that announcement, I think I need a good night's sleep." Birdie yawned and looked at Albert. "Do you guys mind if I head to Treefare early? I think I'll go hang out with Jadar and some of the girls for a while."

"Yeah," Albert said. "That sounds good. We'll need to be rested if we're going to beat Hoyt's team tomorrow."

"And with your Tile, you'll need to study up, bro," Leroy said, nudging Albert. "We can spend some time reading the Black Book."

They turned a corner, passing the tunnel that led to the girls' dorm. "I'll see you guys bright and early," Birdie said, waving. She patted Farnsworth on the head and disappeared down the dimly lit tunnel.

"She's crazy," Leroy said. "Spending time with a Guildacker!"

"Sometimes I think Birdie's braver than anyone I've ever met." Albert nodded.

They kept walking toward Cedarfell. There was a dip in the tunnel where a few of the blue torches had grown dim.

Albert felt a chill at the back of his neck as they walked. He thought he heard footsteps behind them, and when he turned, he was *sure* he saw someone quickly slink back into the shadows. But when he looked a little harder, there was no one there.

"Leroy," Albert whispered, "I feel like someone's watching us."

"Ohhhh, creepy," Leroy said, casting a glance behind them. "Naw. Nothing but darkness, bro."

"I'm just tired, I guess," Albert said. But he *felt* it. They kept walking, their footsteps echoing across the tunnel. Albert thought he heard a third pair of steps again, clacking along behind them.

At the last second, before they reached the door to Cedarfell, he whirled around.

Was that a person's shadow, hanging on the edges of the darkness?

No, I guess not. Man, I need some sleep.

He blinked and looked a little closer, and there was no one there, just a bunch of flickering blue flames and an empty tunnel. And the lingering scent of mint and cloves?

"Albert?" Leroy asked. "Are you all right?"

Albert blinked. "Yeah, yeah. I'm good."

Leroy turned the handle and kicked open the door. The familiar sounds of Cedarfell came pouring out, and Albert's body relaxed. He shook off the feeling, and followed Leroy and Farnsworth inside.

CHAPTER 10

The Apprentice's Secret

Cedarfell was all dressed up for the holiday season. There were bright, twinkling lights wrapped around the trunks of every tree, twisting up to the tops of the branches far overhead. A light dusting of snow danced down upon Albert's nose, but it wasn't cold. It was more for looks than anything, and it gave the entire forest a comforting feel.

"I missed these things," Leroy said, scooping up a giant acorn from the forest floor. He broke it open across his knee and slurped down the fizzy cream-soda drink that was inside.

"Man," Albert laughed, leaping over a fallen log. "You're a bottomless pit."

Leroy shrugged, and they sat down at a campfire where a few other guys were gathered.

Albert recognized two boys his age, both Pures who were training for Belltroll last term. One was redheaded with freckles all over his pale face. The other was tall and thin with a mop of dark brown hair. They kind of reminded Albert of himself and Leroy.

"I'm Pete." The redheaded boy smiled. There was a large gap in between his two front teeth.

"Does it always look this way when it isn't summer term?" Albert asked. He motioned to the lights in the trees.

Pete smiled. "Naw, this is just holiday stuff." He scooped up a handful of the strange, noncold snow and let it fall through his fingers. "It's cool, though, that you guys get to be here to see it."

The dark-haired boy nodded. "Even cooler that you guys could make it here on such short notice."

Albert shrugged. "Hey, that's just what had to be done. Let's hope my team can figure out the Pit. Ponderay's training is tough."

"I know you've heard this before," said Pete with an encouraging look, "but it'll get better."

"Thanks," Albert said.

A few more boys joined them, and someone pulled out a bag of marshmallows they'd purchased in Lucinda's Core Canteen in the Library.

"Now *that* is what I call a good surprise," Leroy said, stuffing his face.

They made s'mores, had a snowball fight, and when

the red birds overhead started to sing their evening song, Albert knew it was time to retire for the night.

At first, his sleep was peaceful. But it didn't last long. Soon, Albert was tossing and turning in his bed, not able to get comfortable, not able to shut down his mind. He wished it had an off switch like a video game console. Instead, he had more of his crazy dreams.

Albert and his team were failing in the Pit.

Birdie was on the floor, clutching a broken arm. Across from him, Leroy was busy battling a creature that looked like it was half shark, half monkey. The creature gnashed sharp, lethal jaws at Leroy's head. He was barely able to fight him off.

"Albert!" Birdie cried out. "Help me!"

"No, Albert!" Leroy shouted. "Help ME!"

Albert didn't know what to do.

Argon was crushing Hydra. Hoyt stood on top of a pillar, snickering as he held an armload of Tiles. And in the background, sitting on the stands, Professor Flynn shook his head in disapproval at Albert. "You're just not cut out for the Core this year, kiddo. Better luck next time."

"No!" Albert shouted. "Give me a chance!"

He could do this, he could fix things and help Hydra win. He reached down, ready to use his Master Tile.

But his fingers clutched at an empty cord.

*   *   *

In the morning, after a full meal in Cedarfell (two full meals for Leroy), Albert and Leroy met Birdie at the entrance to the Pit.

Her hair was up in a messy bun today, the streaks of pink showing through like yarn in a blond bird's nest. She had a huge grin on her face.

"We got new beds in Treefare," she said, holding open the door for the boys. Farnsworth scurried through and raced up the jagged path to the Pit. "I slept ah-mazingly. How 'bout you guys?"

"Like a newborn baby." Leroy yawned, stretching his long arms over his head.

Albert yawned, too, but it wasn't because he felt rested.

"We have to win today, guys," he said over his shoulder as he jogged up the path. "I was awake all night thinking about it."

"We'll win," Birdie said from behind him. "Right, Leroy?"

"The odds are actually pretty even, bros," Leroy shouted from the rear.

That made Albert feel a little bit better.

They rode the platform up, wind whipping them in the face. Birdie chatted on and on about the Pure girls in Treefare, how she felt like they were all incredibly talented.

When they reached the top, the doors swung open.

Professor Flynn stood on the other side.

"Dad?" Albert's voice squeaked like one of Farnsworth's chew toys. "What are you doing here?"

Professor Flynn waved them in, then escorted them to the edge of the Pit. "I'm here to give you a quick lesson on Ponderay, as a favor to Professor Asante. You'll get more info in a classroom session later, but for now, this will have to do. Professor Asante would do it herself, of course, but she's in the Realm searching for the Means to Restore Balance."

"Well, that's cool with me," Albert said.

Professor Flynn chuckled. "And afterward, can't a father watch his son kick some tail in the training Pit?"

Albert laughed. "I don't think people say *kick some tail* anymore, Dad."

Professor Flynn straightened his emerald jacket. "In that case, go team!"

Birdie muffled a laugh as Professor Flynn marched off and took his place in front of the stands. Trey was on the top row, scribbling furiously into a notebook, his hair messier than usual, his clothing a little rumpled. What was up with that guy lately? Team Argon marched in late, as always, and sat on the far left of the stands, while Albert, Birdie, and Leroy sat on the far right.

"Professor Asante wanted me to fill you in on how Ponderay would act during a typical day, without an Imbalance," Professor Flynn said.

He paced back and forth, totally in his element. Albert

smiled. How had he not known, all these years, that his dad was a part of something bigger and better than delivering mail in Herman, Wyoming?

Professor Flynn began his lesson. "In Balance, Ponderay is an incredible Realm. As you already know, the Ten Pillars stand in the middle of what we call the Silver Sea, a massive expanse of water in the center of the Realm. Usually, those Pillars stand steady and strong. From our Core records, we also know that each Pillar has a Tile on top. We're assuming those Tiles have something to do with maintaining Balance—hence all the climbing and grabbing of Tiles you've been doing. Last night, during a journey to the Silver Sea, Professor Asante also learned that there are slots on top of the Pillars that hold the Tiles. Today, you'll be collecting Tiles from slots as well as putting Tiles into slots."

Birdie raised her hand and spoke. "Professor, you've been to Ponderay?"

Professor Flynn laughed. "I have, a few times. Every Professor must enter and complete a small task in *all* of the Realms, before they are chosen to lead one. But that's another story for another time."

Albert wanted to know that story *now*. But he had to focus on learning about Ponderay, if he and his team were going to end up going into the Realm at the end of the six days they now had left.

Professor Flynn went on. "The Realm has its own

magnificent creatures, ones that you'll soon encounter in class under the supervision of Professor Asante. Those creatures work in perfect harmony with one another, each creature doing its own job to help keep the Realm in Balance. Typically, they're peaceful creatures. But when the Balance is off and they can't do their jobs, they might not be so peaceful," Professor Flynn said, with a serious tone sliding into his voice. "And I'm afraid that's where we're at now, because as of last night, the Imbalance has progressed to what we're calling Phase Two."

Albert put his head in his hands. Across the bleachers, Argon stopped their whispering.

Professor Flynn continued. "The Pillars have begun to rotate at breakneck speeds. The creatures have become predictably hostile."

Albert exchanged a look with Leroy—he didn't know what creatures lived in Ponderay, but he definitely didn't like the word *hostile*.

"Unfortunately," Professor Flynn went on, "if the Pillars continue spinning like this, the tremors off the coast of California will get worse." His eyes met Albert's, and he swallowed hard before continuing. "The Core Watchers—the people responsible for monitoring Imbalances—believe that this will soon lead to tidal waves on the surface. Hurricanes, strong winds, raging storms."

"That sounds terrible," Birdie whispered.

"But what about my family?" Albert asked. His voice cracked as he spoke the words, and he couldn't help but picture his mom and siblings, caught in the middle of an angry, roiling sea. What were they doing right now? Albert's great-aunt Suze lived about thirty minutes from the coast, but from what Albert knew about hurricanes, half an hour was nothing in terms of safety.

Professor Flynn seemed to notice the look on Albert's face. "We have to trust the process, Balance Keepers, and train hard. Professor Asante and the Core Watchers are working around the clock to discover the Means to Restore Balance. I have faith that we may still be able to solve this. But in case, we must be ready. Should we come upon a Phase Three, the Core will be facing one of the worst Imbalances in history."

Just then, the door to the Pit sprang open. Tussy marched inside with a look of pure determination on her face. As always, she had fresh cuts, and she looked like she'd just gotten done rolling in the dirt. Albert knew she'd been going into the Realm with Professor Asante. Apprentices were bound to the Core, which meant that if they did enter the Realms, it sapped their strength twice as fast as it would a normal Balance Keeper's. No wonder Tussy always looked so ragged.

"A quick word, Professor Flynn?" Tussy asked.

Professor Flynn nodded, and the two of them stepped to the side of the bleachers to speak in hushed voices.

Albert leaned in, wishing he knew of a symbol that could give him super hearing.

"You scared, Hydra?" Hoyt hissed from across the bleachers. "I can smell your fear from here!"

"Ignore him," Birdie said.

"He's just trying to rile us up before competition," Leroy added.

Albert sighed and focused on his dad and Tussy.

As Tussy spoke, Professor Flynn's smile slipped away. He nodded once, put a hand on Tussy's shoulder, and whispered something into her ear. She sighed and shook her head before she turned back to the stands to go sit with Trey.

"What are you six doing, just sitting there?" Tussy shouted suddenly. She motioned to a stack of fresh Pit clothing that was piled on the lowest bleacher. "Get dressed and ready! This isn't playtime, Balance Keepers!"

Albert wanted to ask his dad what was going on. Instead, he grabbed a stack of clothes and headed to the dressing area to prepare for competition.

"All right, teams!" Tussy called out. She was already standing on the edge of the Pit, MegaHorn in hand. She also had a camera set up on a tripod, ready to record the day's events. "Let's get moving! Today, we've got an exciting challenge set up for you. And Professor Asante will be watching the recording when she gets back from Ponderay tonight." She chewed on her bottom lip and glanced sideways at Professor Flynn in the stands.

"They know something we don't," Albert whispered to his friends. "What do you think is going on?"

"No idea," Leroy groaned. "But I'm not good with cameras. No pressure, right dudes?"

Birdie shouldered him. "Suck it up, Memory Boy. I *love* being on camera. Makes me feel like a movie star!"

"Yeah, it'll be good," Albert said. "Maybe we can watch it later and see what we can improve on."

Leroy nodded as Hydra and Argon lined up on their platforms. They sank to the bottom. Just like yesterday, the Pit was empty.

"Today's goal is similar to what we've already done," Tussy shouted from above. "But there will be some added dangers. As you know, in Ponderay, you'll be dealing with the Silver Sea. It's no summer vacation. There are strange creatures in the water, and with an Imbalance, they'll turn against whoever enters their domain. They'll try to stop you from reaching the top." She grinned, like she knew some sort of evil secret. "Watch your backs. Work as a team, *not* as individuals. And for the love of Ponderay, *don't* drown."

She blew her whistle, and in an instant, water started to pour from the sides of the Pit, rushing out of four giant holes like waterfalls.

"YES!" Birdie clapped her hands. "My Tile will help us win today for *sure*."

Leroy nodded. "It increases our odds by 76.7 percent.

But Slink has a Water Tile, too. Don't forget that, guys."

Albert smiled. Water was always good news for Hydra, with Birdie on their side.

Tussy blew the whistle again, and the same pillars as the day before rose from the ground, rushing high into the air as tall as the trees in Cedarfell. Water was already pooling around Albert's knees. It was *cold*. So cold his teeth chattered and his body started to shake.

"There are ten Tiles on the pillars again, but this time they are tucked into slots as they are in the Realm. The first team to collect the most will win this round," Tussy shouted. "There's no time limit! We'll compete until all Tiles are collected. Then we'll start Round Two. I don't care how tired you get. Balance Keepers, are you ready?"

Albert, Birdie, and Leroy exchanged glances. "READY!"

Across from them, Hoyt, Slink, and Mo shouted their answer, too.

"Good luck." Tussy grinned. She flipped a switch on the camera overhead, then blew her whistle. "BEGIN!"

Hydra circled up at once, and Albert started shouting out commands. "Leroy, go ahead and start climbing. Get a good vantage point. See if you can figure out what secret stuff Tussy was warning us about in Lake Hall yesterday. And get some Tiles, if you're able!"

"Aye, aye, Captain!" Leroy shouted. He flipped his hat backward and waded away into the now waist-deep water.

Birdie looked at Albert. "I can sense something in the water."

"Go check it out," Albert said. "I'll just start collecting Tiles."

"Good luck!" she shouted. She turned and dove into the water, disappearing beneath the silver surface.

"Here goes nothing," Albert said to no one.

The nearest pillar was about ten feet away. He was naturally a good swimmer, but with such cold water, Albert felt like he couldn't breathe. Even with the thick neoprene outfit Tussy had given them, all of Albert's limbs were starting to go numb, and he was sure he was going to turn into a giant Albertsicle any second now. The water had grown chest-deep. Just as Albert was about to dive under, something in the water touched his ankle. "Ouch!"

It felt like an electric *pop!* Almost like that time his younger half brother had shocked Albert after rubbing his fuzzy socks on the carpet for too long. He looked down, trying to see what was beneath the silver waves, but the water was too choppy.

The feeling left Albert's foot a little numb. Still, Albert swam faster. He reached the closest pillar and started to climb. It was difficult, soaking wet and trembling, and a few times, Albert's hand slipped.

He pictured a giant hair dryer blowing all the water away and warming him back up. Wasn't there some kind of heat symbol he'd learned about in the Black Book? It was a Warming symbol. Like a flame.

Albert focused hard, and sure enough, the chill eased up a little. The pillars were made of a softer rubbery substance today, which made them slippery. He found all the right hand and footholds, and didn't waste time on the climb. He knew the holds would disappear in seconds like they had last time.

It was almost too easy when Albert reached the top. He found the Tile sticking up from the slot—it reminded him of his mom making toast for breakfast—and grabbed it. He waved it in the air and there was a *CLANG!* signaling the point for Hydra.

Then the pillars started spinning. It started soft and gentle, like yesterday's slightly demented merry-go-round, but in seconds, they increased to breakneck speeds. Albert felt like he was on the top of a race car spinning out of control. He crouched low, just like he'd done yesterday, and pictured the Balance symbol in his mind.

Don't fall, he told himself. *If you fall in the Realm, you won't get a second chance.*

"Albert!" Birdie screamed from below.

"Yeah!" Albert screamed back, excited she was cheering him on. But then she screamed again, and he realized her voice wasn't excited at all.

She was warning him.

Albert looked around. There was Hoyt, a few pillars away, mirroring Albert in a crouch position. Hoyt grabbed a Tile for himself. And then Mo, right after, gaining Argon another point. Leroy was nowhere to be seen, probably lost in the mess of pillars.

A flash of color appeared in the water below, something thrashing back and forth. "What in the heck is that?" Albert had time to say.

Then something big and blue leaped out at him, soaring through the air so fast that Albert didn't have a chance to move.

"HAMMERFIN!" Hoyt shouted.

The shark was enormous, twice the size of the ones Albert had seen before in aquariums, and had a head shaped like a giant hammer. The Hammerfin smashed into Albert's pillar just as Albert leaped.

As he fell, he heard the shattering impact. *BOOM!*

Albert splashed into the water and came up sputtering for air. Where the pillar had been was only empty space. Or maybe not . . .

The pillar began to reform, rising out of the waves like a stretching hand.

"In Balance, the Hammerfins regularly destroy pillars in Ponderay as a way to keep the ecosystem in check. But out of Balance, they'll apparently try to destroy *you*, too," Tussy said. Albert glanced at Tussy and realized she was probably speaking from experience.

Something grabbed onto Albert's shoulders and spun him around. He screamed, expecting to see the open jaws of a Hammerfin. But it was only Birdie.

"Are you okay?" she asked.

Albert shook water from his eyes. "Just a little shocked is all. Sharks, Birdie. There are *sharks* in the Pit."

"We should get out of the water." Birdie nodded. "There's also other things. Like giant stingray things." She lifted up a swollen, red hand. "It shocked me like a jellyfish. I can't feel a thing."

"I think that's what got my ankle earlier," Albert said. He could still feel a little bit of numbness there. "I've got to move. Climb with me?"

"Let's go!" Birdie said, and together they swam, reaching the spinning pillars side by side. It took some work, swimming as fast as they could to grab hold of a pillar, but finally Albert and Birdie made contact with one.

They started climbing just as Leroy crashed into the water beside them. He was wrestling with one of the giant sharks. It snapped and gnashed its jaws, and for a moment, Albert was terrified for his friend's life.

"Leroy! You're insane!" Birdie shouted.

But Albert thought it was *awesome*.

Higher and higher he climbed. The wind whipped Albert in the face, making his eyes burn and his cheeks feel numb. Birdie fell, careening into the water. Overhead, Professor Flynn was shouting Albert's name, cheering him on. He was exhausted, and freezing cold, and there were so many things going on that it was hard to focus on any Tile symbols.

He reached the top of his pillar and grabbed a Tile, then put all the strength he had into hauling himself on top. The bell clanged, signaling another point. But then there were two more right after, for Argon.

How are they doing so well? Albert wondered, just as Hoyt grabbed the sixth Tile for Argon. Which could only mean one thing. Tussy blew her whistle, and Albert knew they'd lost.

"No way," Albert groaned.

The pillars slowed to a stop, and Tussy announced Argon as the winner of Round One.

Albert climbed down from his pillar and joined Birdie and Leroy in the waves. They were both out of breath and looking just as dejected as Albert felt. Across the Pit, Hoyt and his teammates were busy celebrating. It made Albert's heart clench and his stomach feel like it was twisted with thorns. How could Hydra lose like this, twice in two days?

"Round Two is similar to Round One," Tussy said into the MegaHorn. "But instead of collecting Tiles, you'll be putting them back into the slots."

"Why'd we take them out in the first place then?" Hoyt shouted. "Seems like a waste of time to take them out just to put them back in."

Tussy gave him a look that could kill, but if he was being honest, Albert was wondering the same thing. Hoyt might be happy to have won the first round, but he looked as tired as Albert felt, and if Albert could be done *now*, he'd much prefer that.

"Because, Mr. Jackson," Tussy shot back, "while we don't yet know the system behind the Tiles in the Ten Pillars, we're assuming that each Tile belongs to only one Pillar, and that somehow the Tiles have been switched around—that that's what's causing the Imbalance."

Albert could only think of one explanation for that. The traitor had to have switched the Tiles around by hand. Who was it? And how did they get inside the Realm undetected?

"Seems like a lot of effort based on a guess," Hoyt mumbled under his breath.

"Do you have any better ideas for what might be causing the Imbalance, Mr. Jackson?" If it was possible for Tussy to look meaner than she already did, she has managed it in this moment. It seemed to scare Hoyt enough. He just shook his head.

"Good." Tussy continued. "For Round Two, you'll each have five Tiles."

She tossed two black bags into the Pit—one to Hydra, and one to Argon on the opposite side. Albert waded forward in the water and grabbed the bag before it sank. Inside were five large blue rectangular Tiles. Albert saw, across the Pit, that Argon's Tiles were orange.

"The first team to get all five of their Tiles into the slots will win," Tussy said. "Move fast, work as a team, and don't forget to watch your backs. You never know when the creatures will attack!"

She blew her whistle, and the Pit sprang to life. Argon reacted instantly, the three teammates separating in the waves.

Birdie grabbed four Tiles from the bag. "We should climb pillars and plug in these Tiles, one right after the other."

"Sounds good to me." Leroy nodded.

"Let's move!" Albert tucked two Tiles into his waist-band. Birdie took one, Leroy took the last one, and Hydra dove into the waves.

With a little help from the Water symbol, Albert made it to a pillar in record time. He grabbed ahold of the slip-pery side and started to climb. In just a few minutes, he reached the top. He got onto his knees, struggling to combat the wind, but a quick thought of the Balance symbol and he was able to stay upright.

He plugged his Tile into the slot, and the bell went *CLANG!*

Seconds after, it clanged again. Albert saw Mo leap back into the waves.

"One point for Hydra and one point for Argon!" Tussy shouted into the MegaHorn. "The competition is neck and neck!"

Suddenly, the pillars began to spin *faster. How is this*

even possible? Albert thought. He squatted on his pillar, clutching the sides for dear life.

All around him, Balance Keepers were toppling overboard and crashing into the waves below.

Except for Hoyt. He was racing across the tops of the pillars, using his Speed Tile—he ran and leaped just as fast as they spun. When he made it to a Tile-less pillar, he plugged in a Tile. The bell clanged.

Albert felt a fire ignite inside of him. "Two can play at this game!"

He focused on the Speed symbol. There was the familiar buzzing in his legs. Albert stood, took a deep breath, and leaped.

He landed on the next pillar. There was already a Tile plugged into this one.

"Go, Albert!" Petra shouted from the stands, and Farnsworth barked along with him.

A Hammerfin shot out of the water, nearly crashing into Albert, but he was quick. He leaped to another pillar, then glanced back to confirm his suspicion. The Hammerfin had destroyed the pillar he'd just left. It crumbled into the water below, only to immediately rise up again, Tile still in place. But there was no time to waste. He cleared his thoughts and leaped again.

His mind was silent. He was all body, moving in a blur as fast as Hoyt was.

Finally Albert landed on an empty pillar. He plugged

his second Tile into the slot and whooped as the bell clanged.

"Two points for Hydra!" Tussy shouted.

The bell kept clanging as Balance Keepers plugged Tiles into slots. Birdie got one, and Mo right after her. Hoyt got another, and the score was 4–3, in Argon's favor.

If I can get to Leroy or Birdie and get another Tile, I can speed this up, Albert thought. He saw Leroy on a pillar across the Pit, and aimed for him, leaping and leaping across the spinning circle.

Just when Albert felt like he couldn't go any longer, something smacked into him in midair.

"I don't think so, Flynn!" Hoyt shouted.

They were balanced together on top of a pillar. Albert pushed, and Hoyt shoved, both of them trying to knock the other overboard.

"Look out!" Mo shouted.

Neither Albert nor Hoyt had time to react. A Hammerfin smashed into them from above.

Albert felt an explosion of pain in his skull, and his ears were clanging like a bell. He saw his dad's face in the crowd before he crashed into the cold water, Hoyt landing on top of him.

Water filled his lungs.

Everything started to go black, when an image popped into Albert's mind. He clung to it: a water droplet, just like Birdie's Tile.

In seconds, Albert felt better. He didn't need air, not while his Master Tile was harnessing this power. From here, he could see Hoyt sinking to the bottom of the Pit.

Had the Hammerfin knocked him out?

I could go back up now and win this, Albert thought.

But something tugged at his mind. It was a voice that reminded him of his mother's, telling Albert to do the right thing no matter what. With the image of the Water Tile still in his head, Albert swam down and wrapped his arms around Hoyt's torso.

Once he had a good grip, Albert kicked hard on the ground, and shot out of the water, carting Hoyt and himself upward.

Noise erupted into his ears the second Albert surfaced.

He pumped his legs, trying to keep himself and an unconscious Hoyt afloat. Albert was so tired he couldn't even find his voice to shout for help, but it turned out he didn't need to try for long.

The bell went *CLANG!* Albert heard Tussy's voice in the MegaHorn.

"Argon wins this round!"

"YEAH!" Slink and Mo shouted from across the Pit.

The pillars sank into the floor. The water receded into holes in the ground. When it was gone, the creatures were nowhere to be seen. There was just the soft, springy ground that Albert set Hoyt down on. The orange platforms appeared, ready to hoist the Balance

Keepers out of the Pit.

"Guys, over here!" Albert called to Argon. Hoyt was just coming to, and he didn't look happy to see Albert.

"Wh-what happened?" Hoyt groaned.

"You were knocked out by a Hammerfin," Albert told him. "You'll be okay."

It was only then that Slink and Mo noticed their teammate. They ran over and helped load Hoyt onto the orange platform.

Birdie and Leroy joined Albert on their own platform. As it started to rise, Albert looked into the crowd. Professor Flynn stood up to leave, and the two of them locked eyes. Professor Flynn nodded once. There was pride in his eyes for what his son had done. Albert nodded back, and Professor Flynn disappeared into the crowd.

Albert turned to his teammates. "I'm sorry, guys. We would have won if I hadn't dove down for Hoyt."

Leroy clapped him on the back. "You made the right choice, dude."

Birdie nodded. "I'm not so sure he would've done the same for you, Albert. What you did was really something."

Their platform reached the top, and Hydra stepped off.

"We should go to the Library and win some rounds of Tiles," Leroy said as he wrung out his baseball cap. "That will cheer us all up."

Slink and Mo helped carry Hoyt away. Tussy went

with them, and the crowd followed. Even almost conscious, Hoyt was the celebrity of the Pit. Albert half wondered if the guy was faking it. Still, Albert had to admit to himself that jerk or not, Hoyt was solid competition this term.

He had started to follow his friends out of the Pit when a hand closed over his shoulder, pulling him to a stop.

He whirled around, eyes wide. It was Trey. Albert thought he'd left with Professor Flynn.

"A quick word, Albert?" Trey raised a brow.

"Uh, sure." Albert motioned for his friends to go on without him. Birdie didn't look like she wanted to leave, but Leroy whined about playing Tiles and pulled her along.

Albert turned back to Trey.

Trey rubbed his chin, a strange look in his dark eyes. Almost like he was in pain. And wow, he looked exhausted. He pulled Albert deeper into the shadows of the Pit room. "I shouldn't be doing this. Your father would have to fire me as an Apprentice if he knew, but technically, since I'm no longer training you . . ."

Albert was dying to know what Trey was so worked up about. Maybe he would explain what was going on with him lately, why he seemed so frazzled.

Trey sighed and ran a hand through his hair. "I overhead Tussy talking during lunch the other day. She said Professor Asante is pretty much assuming at this point that Argon will become Ponderay First Unit."

Argon was already way ahead, with twenty-three points to Hydra's sixteen. It wasn't looking good.

"So you're saying me and my team have to up our game if we stand a chance of regaining Asante's confidence," Albert whispered.

Trey nodded. "You've now got less than six days to pull ahead."

Albert gulped. "We're doing our best."

"Try harder," Trey said. He turned to leave, but seemed to think better of it, and stopped. "A hint, Albert, if you want to get ahead? Professor Asante's study is often empty at night. The key isn't hard to find, if one looks high enough."

With that, Trey turned on his heel and marched away, carrying with him the scent of something strangely familiar, spicy and sweet all at once. But Albert was too curious about what Trey had said to take much notice.

CHAPTER 11

The Happiest Place on Earth

After lunch, Albert, Birdie, and Leroy went down to the hospital wing to check on Hoyt.

"I don't see why we're wasting our time," Birdie grumbled as they signed their names on the check-in sheet for visitors. "He's not going to say thanks to you or anything, Albert."

Albert laughed. "I wasn't expecting that. And besides, I *might* have been hoping to catch a glimpse of the news on the surface while we're down here."

"Oh, that makes sense," Leroy said. He scribbled his name onto the sheet. "I was wondering if you'd gotten a concussion, too."

They all laughed, but with a glare from the cyclops nurse, Albert and his friends quieted down.

The hospital was emptier than it had been last term. Albert guessed the Pures training for other Realms weren't being worked as hard as they were for Ponderay. The Pit was always dangerous, and Albert was thankful that he hadn't yet ended up in one of these beds.

One girl on the left was having her arm stitched up. A boy to her right held an ice pack to his face. He smiled and waved as Albert and his friends passed.

The very last bed on the right was occupied, and the curtains were drawn.

"That must be him," Birdie whispered.

Albert peeked around the curtains. Sure enough, Hoyt was inside, sound asleep. He was surrounded by piles of plush white pillows, and there was a get-well-soon balloon beside his bed. *He looks all right*, Albert thought. Hoyt suddenly opened his eyes and sat up. Albert ducked away just in time.

"Nurse!" Hoyt shouted from behind the curtains. "I need another blanket! And bring me something to eat!"

The cyclops nurse rushed past Albert and his friends, grumbling about Hoyt being perfectly fine.

"He's totally milking it," Birdie said.

"Milking what?" Leroy asked.

"It's an *expression*, Leroy," Birdie said, and the two of them began to banter.

Albert tuned them out. His attention was on the tiny, old-fashioned television in the corner of the room. He motioned for his friends to follow, and they all sat down in front of the TV.

Leroy positioned the bunny-ear antennas and started it up. He flicked through channel after channel, trying to find something besides black-and-white fuzz. Albert remembered being in here last term, when Birdie had been injured in the Pit. The three of them had settled down in front of this very screen to watch piles of ash cover up New York City.

Today, Albert's stomach filled with lead as the screen flickered to life, and the news report on California began.

There was a woman on screen, huddled beneath an umbrella that had seen better days. It was upturned so the wires stuck out all over the place like a dead bug's legs.

"Turn it up," Albert said, and Leroy cranked the dial so they could hear the woman's voice.

"I'm standing an hour from the coast in Los Angeles, in front of the entrance to Disneyland," the woman shouted into a soaking wet microphone. *"What is normally the happiest place on earth is now a ghost town. Vacationers have fled the park in fear of the oncoming hurricane."*

"Hurricane?" Albert said. "My dad was right. It's getting worse by the second."

"Maybe you should try and call your mom," Birdie suggested.

The screen showed a glimpse of Disneyland. The rides

were shut down, and the main street with all the shops was closed. The cobblestones were covered in at least six inches of water. It ran like a river down the middle of the road.

"Reports are coming in all around. The highways are packed with evacuees, but where can they go? Hotels are shutting down. Gas stations are running out of gas. It's as if the apocalypse has come. . . ."

The image changed, showing a highway with a line of honking cars. It was pouring rain, and the sky was so dark it almost looked like night, but the clock in the corner of the screen said it was only noon in California. The screen switched to show a place called La Jolla Shores. Its rocky cliffs could barely be seen through the torrential downpour. A lifeguard stand tumbled over into the sand, and a flock of wet seagulls huddled beneath it in hopes of shelter from the storm. There were marinas with sailboats' masts cracked in half, and giant yachts that had capsized.

The screen went back to the reporter, who now looked like someone was spraying her in the face with a fire hose. *"It's estimated that by nightfall, wind speeds will have reached one hundred thirty miles per . . ."*

Suddenly a gust of wind ripped the umbrella away from her. It flew through the air and smacked into the camera.

The screen flickered. Then it went black.

"*Omigosh,*" Birdie gasped.

"Whoa," Leroy said. "What just happened?"

"The Imbalance happened," Albert said. "And it's only going to get worse."

Dread filled him as he stared at the empty screen.

CHAPTER 12

Caught Red-Handed

Normally Albert wasn't a desperate person.

He excelled at lots of things (unless you counted school). Growing up, he'd *loved* the forest outside of Herman, and hiking, climbing, and running. These were things Albert just knew how to do.

So when he came to the Core the first time, well, it simply clicked for Albert. After he had figured out his Master Tile, of course.

But so far, this term was different.

Albert knew just how intense it could be inside the real Realms. And if Hoyt and his cronies got to be the ones to enter Ponderay, things probably wouldn't bode well for the fate of the world above. After seeing the news report, Albert's only thought was that it was time to work harder. Really put everything out there, so that when the end results came, Albert would know he'd done his absolute best to win.

When darkness fell in the boys' dorm, Albert and Leroy tiptoed past the scattering mess of tents and hammocks. Farnsworth and his flashlight eyes led the way.

They snuck out the door with ease, locking it behind them as they disappeared into the dimly lit tunnel beyond.

"We'll have to be quick," Albert whispered to Leroy as they walked. They stuck to the shadows on the edges of the wall, just in case someone came around.

They passed the statue of Frog Man, and even though Albert and Leroy had seen it a million times, the thing still made them shiver and hasten their pace.

"Birdie's meeting us in the Main Chamber," Albert whispered to Leroy.

There was a *creeeeak*ing noise behind them.

Albert and Leroy dove into the shadows and Farnsworth shut off his high beams. They waited as footsteps came closer.

An itch prickled Albert's nose, but he didn't dare move to scratch it.

The footsteps were almost upon them. Albert was about to turn to Leroy and tell him to run, when a person shuffled into view.

It was only a Core Cleaner, sweeping the floors. Albert and Leroy waited as she cleaned up, and when she was on her way, they both relaxed.

"I thought it was a Professor!" Leroy whispered. "We would've been busted for sure."

"Yeah." Albert nodded. "Let's hope Birdie hasn't been spotted."

They made it to the Main Chamber without any more incidents, and Birdie was waiting for them as planned.

"Let's go!" Albert stage-whispered, waving Birdie over. She was wearing all black, and she even had gloves on her hands.

"What do you think we're doing, Birdie? Robbing a bank?" Leroy muffled a laugh.

Birdie punched him in the shoulder, and he almost toppled over the railing of the bridge. Albert caught him just in time.

"It's just a precaution," Birdie whispered. "Let's move, boys."

Being out in the middle of the night was scary. The blue flames were dim, some of them completely melted away to purple embers, and there were strange, long shadows on the walls.

Leroy took the lead, using his Synapse Tile to navigate to Professor Asante's office.

They made it to the end of a wide tunnel, and there stood the door, old and wooden, just waiting for them to go inside.

There had to be tons of books in there, loads of secret information about Ponderay that couldn't be found in the actual Library. All Albert had to do was get Leroy inside. He'd be able to skim through any book in seconds, and maybe they'd have a chance in the Pit tomorrow.

"Trey said the key was up high," Albert whispered. "Farnsworth, a little light, please?"

Farnsworth wagged his tail and looked up, illuminating the ceiling in bright light.

And there it was.

An old brass key, dangling from a hook above the doorway, so high that only Professor Asante herself would be able to reach it.

"There's no way we'll be able to get that thing," Birdie said, shaking her head.

But Albert wasn't worried. He smiled, then reached up to grab his Master Tile from around his neck. "You're forgetting I have this."

"Then get on with it." Birdie nudged him. "The longer we stay here, the more chance we have of getting caught."

"Impressive reasoning skills," Leroy said, smiling.

"Okay, give me a second." Albert closed his eyes and pictured the Black Book. Hundreds of pages, thousands and thousands of Tile symbols.

What would he use for this?

It came to him, the only clear image in his mind. The Weightlessness Tile, the same one he'd used in Calderon last term to cross the swamp.

Albert focused on it, and soon he was floating a few inches off the ground.

"It never gets old." Birdie clapped her hands lightly.

Albert had to really concentrate to get himself to rise higher and higher. He was still rusty, but after one failed try that ended up with a squished tail and an apology to Farnsworth, Albert floated to the ceiling and snatched the key.

He landed softly, then inserted the key in the lock. It clicked open easily. A minty smell wafted its way down the hall, alerting Albert's senses. The door swung inward with a creak, and Birdie and Leroy shuffled inside. Albert went last, but not before stopping to cast a glance over his shoulder.

In the darkness, a shadow moved. Something that looked tall and thin and human.

The shadow turned and started heading toward Albert.

Albert practically dove inside the dark office, taking the key. He shut the door behind him, quickly locked it, then paused to catch his breath.

"Wow," he heard his friends say.

Albert looked up, and his own jaw dropped.

They were standing in the middle of a massive cavern, the walls lined with old wooden bookshelves. The desk in the middle of the room was piled high with stacks and stacks of paper.

But that wasn't the coolest part.

There was a thick black curtain taking up an entire wall. A cool blue glow peeked out from the edge of the curtain. Albert was *dying* to know what was behind it.

He took a step forward, eyes wide.

"What do you think it is?" Albert asked.

"I can sense water," Birdie said. "But I'm not sure."

"A good guess, Miss Howell," a voice called out from the darkest corner of the room.

Leroy screamed like a banshee. Albert and Birdie bumped heads, and Farnsworth growled, his fur standing on end. His eyes flashed a brilliant blue, illuminating the source of the voice.

There was a squealing sound, and Professor Asante emerged from the darkness. Albert gasped. She was in a *wheelchair*. The spokes glittered blue in the light of Farnsworth's eyes, and as Albert looked closer, he realized Professor Asante's leg was broken. It was wrapped in a thick white cast, and stuck out in front of her like a tree branch. What had happened to her inside Ponderay?

"What are you three doing in my office in the middle of the night?" Professor Asante asked. She raised an eyebrow.

"We're burned toast, dudes," Leroy groaned.

Albert was sure truer words had never been said.

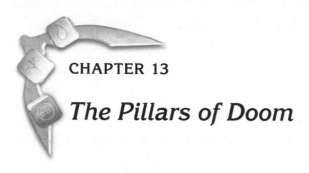

CHAPTER 13

The Pillars of Doom

"So you wish to discover the secrets of Ponderay?"

Albert, Leroy, and Birdie stood in the center of the room, while Professor Asante wheeled past them, parking herself in front of them. Seeing her like this, Albert's stomach whirled. Her injury was probably the reason for Professor Flynn and Tussy's whispered conversation in the Pit yesterday. What would happen to the chosen Balance Keepers, if someone as large and powerful as Professor Asante could end up like this after going into Ponderay?

Even sitting down in her chair, with her broken leg stuck out in front of her like a lead pipe, she was intimidating. And still taller than all three of them. She tapped her fingertips on her thighs. "I'm assuming that's why you broke into my office in the dead of night. I had a rough day in Ponderay, and now you three."

"We're sorry," Albert blurted out. He swallowed the lump in his throat and tried to sound a little more diplomatic. "We'll go back to our dorms. You can give us detention. We deserve it."

"Please forgive us, Professor," Birdie piped up, putting on her best doe eyes. "We were hoping to find an advantage we could use in the Pit, but we shouldn't have come into your office without asking."

Leroy just nodded and chewed on his lip, looking very much like a frightened rabbit that might bolt at any moment. Even Farnsworth whimpered, using his paws to shove his ears over his eyes.

"You admit your crime and ask for forgiveness at once. Interesting." Professor Asante motioned to a plush leather couch in the corner of her office. "Take a seat, please."

Albert exchanged a glance with his friends. They all looked a little sick, so Albert and Farnsworth took the lead.

Professor Asante followed, pushing herself past the trio to a bookshelf in the shadows. Across the room, Albert thought he saw a yellow flash on the edges of the curtain, but it settled back to blue when he looked.

"She looks like she's going to eat us," Leroy whispered to Albert and Birdie.

"She's not a witch, she's not going to snack on our

bones," Birdie hissed. "But there's no telling what else she might do."

"Just wait a second, guys," Albert whispered, trying to calm them both down. "Maybe she'll just give us detention and then let us go."

Professor Asante seemed to find what she was looking for. She wheeled back over, the rusted spokes of her chair squeaking like mice. When she stopped in front of the trio, Albert saw a fat leather-bound book perched on her lap.

"You aren't the first students to go looking for answers about the Realms, you know," Professor Asante said. She actually sort of smiled. "I admire your bravery. I never was a rule-follower myself."

Albert, Birdie, and Leroy all breathed a sigh of relief.

Professor Asante raised an eyebrow. "Nevertheless, you will serve detention tomorrow morning, as punishment." She tapped the book, and dust floated up, dancing in the air. "But for now, we'll simply enjoy a private lesson about Ponderay."

The book was massive, even larger than the Black Book. Professor Asante flipped through the pages, and Albert, Leroy, and Birdie leaned forward, eyes wide. They saw a map of the Realm for the very first time.

The only similarity between Ponderay and Calderon was the ringlike shape that outlined both Realms. But while Calderon had forests and fields and spires,

Ponderay looked like the Grand Canyon.

"Most of the Realm is rocky and dry," Professor Asante said. "But don't let the desert look fool you. The air is as frigid as a scorned woman's heart. The wind will knock a grown man from his feet, and the nights are darker than anything you've ever known."

Albert shivered and pulled Farnsworth into his lap. Birdie wrapped her arms around herself. Leroy groaned and looked like he might be sick.

"Yes." Professor Asante smiled, tapping her fingertips on the map. "Ponderay has been known to strike fear in even the bravest Balance Keeper's heart. But there's beauty there, as well. The Silver Sea."

She moved her tattooed finger across the map, toward the center of the page. There was a wide circle, shaded gray. And inside of it, ten sketched pillars. They looked similar to the practice pillars in the Pit. But something told Albert these would be much, much taller.

"The Ten Pillars have been in place since the beginning of time," Professor Asante said, her voice carrying a touch of awe. "Imagine the pillars you've been practicing on in the Pit, and triple them in height."

Albert pictured the Empire State Building, how he had to crane his neck to see the top. Sometimes, the clouds would cover it. What if the Ten Pillars were that tall?

Professor Asante went on. "Just over a thousand years ago, Ponderay suffered a massive Imbalance. We sent our best Balance Keepers forth, in search of the Means to Restore Balance. But they did not succeed."

Birdie gasped. "What happened?"

"An earthquake off the coast of what is now California. It devastated the surface world. Many lives—human, plant, animal—were lost."

Farnsworth whimpered again, and the glow from his eyes faded. Albert scratched him behind the ears and hugged him closer.

"So how come it stopped?" Albert asked. "I mean, Balance had to have been restored eventually, right, or it would've kept getting worse. Earth would've been completely ruined."

"Smart boy, just like your father." Professor Asante nodded. She leaned back in her chair, the old seat popping and squealing in protest. "It was the Professors themselves, from all the Realms, who entered Ponderay. They barely made it out alive. But what they discovered was fascinating. And it may well be the answer to our problems in Ponderay today."

"What is it?" Albert asked. He was hanging on Professor Asante's every word.

Even Leroy didn't look scared anymore. He looked fascinated.

Professor Asante smiled, and flipped to another page in the book. This one held a close-up of one of the Ten Pillars, showing its rocky sides, the strange handhold divots; there was even a rough sketch of the top of the Pillar.

Just like in the Pit, there was a Tile on it, sticking out of a slot in the stone.

"As you know by now, we are assuming each Pillar has its own Tile," Professor Asante said. "I managed to make it to the Silver Sea myself and climb one of the Pillars to attempt to confirm this. And indeed, when I removed the Tile, it had a rectangle marked on its face. The Core Researchers and I think each Tile has its own unique marking. But I fell into the Silver Sea before I could remove any others."

Birdie gasped. "You fell from one of the Ten Pillars?"

Albert imagined how far of a fall that must have been. Professor Asante was lucky to be alive.

"The Ten Pillars, as of last night, were spinning at top speed, estimated to be around fifty-four miles per hour. The Core creatures, upset by the Imbalance, are reacting defensively. I was attacked by all of them at once. I'm lucky to be alive." She stared at her injured leg for a moment before continuing. "By now, the surface world is reacting as we assumed it would, with hurricanes the likes of which no one has seen since the last Ponderay Imbalance."

Albert gulped, and tried *not* to think about his family.

"So are the Tiles mixed up?" Birdie asked. "Is that what's causing the Imbalance?"

"That's what we believe, yes," Professor Asante answered. "But like I said, I was only able to scale one Pillar. I have yet to confirm our speculations."

"But why?" Birdie asked. "How did that happen?"

"The question is not why or how, Miss Howell, but *who*?" Professor Asante shrugged.

Albert nodded. "You mean someone's created the Imbalance." He thought about what Trey had said earlier.

Professor Asante nodded. "I'm afraid so." She stretched her neck and went on. "We are speculating that if we can remove the Tiles, and decipher a code they may have, such as color or markings, and match them back to their correct Pillars, then the Imbalance would be solved." She pointed at her broken leg. "I shouldn't have gone in by myself. And now I can't go back in at all, thanks to this useless leg."

"But who will go in now?" Birdie asked. "If you can't go, and the First Unit hasn't been chosen yet . . . Tussy can't go in alone!"

Professor Asante looked right at Albert before she spoke. He had a feeling she was about to deliver some horrible news. "Professor Flynn has volunteered to enter the Realm in my place."

Albert's entire body froze. "Wh . . . what? But he can't! He's . . . no!"

Professor Asante didn't offer any sympathy. "It's very noble, what Professor Flynn is doing. He's a brave man, and I have faith that he will be a great partner for Tussy."

With his dad's life on the line now, Albert had to know. "How exactly did you hurt yourself? Could it happen to my dad and Tussy, too?"

"Anything could happen." Professor Asante grimaced as she touched her leg. "I made it all the way to the Silver Sea. I was halfway up the first of the Ten Pillars when the Jackalopes got to me."

"Jackalopes?" Leroy blurted out. "Like the ones in Cedarfell?"

"But those aren't much larger than Farnsworth!" Albert added.

"Ponderay breeds creatures that are five times the size of what we have here in the Core." Professor Asante motioned over her shoulder, to the curtain that covered up an entire length of wall. "In class tomorrow, you'll witness that firsthand."

Birdie leaned forward. "Why couldn't you just borrow Jadar and fly to the top of the Ten Pillars? Then the Jackalopes couldn't reach you!"

Professor Asante chuckled. "That's a brilliant idea, Miss Howell, but a companion creature from one Realm cannot enter another. It would upset the Balance on its own." She sat back in her chair and sighed. "I fear I've already given you enough answers for tonight. It's time you were on your way."

Albert nodded, lost in thought. Professor Asante had

already given them lots of information, but nothing that would help them win in the Pit. And even though his heart was full of fear for his dad, he still had a job to do here. He put on his brightest, most charming smile and leaned forward. "Before we go, Professor, could I ask one more question?"

Professor Asante nodded, and Albert went on.

"If we wanted to be the very best that we could be as a team in the Pit, what would you suggest we do next time?"

"Yeah, I'd like to know your best advice," Birdie added, leaning forward. She nudged Leroy, who shrugged and gave his very best puppy dog eyes. Even Farnsworth wagged his tail like he was begging for a cookie.

Professor Asante sighed. "You're clever, Hydra, and I like your determination, so I'll offer you a single bit of advice."

She wheeled her wheelchair closer, coming to a stop just in front of the couch. "Remember what I said about the Means to Restoring Balance. You won't just be collecting Tiles in Ponderay. You'll have to put them back where they belong. You must be ready to work *as a team*. I cannot stress that enough. Argon is working well together, and it's moving them up in the leaderboard. Last term, I would have chosen Hydra as my champions. But this term"—she took a deep breath and nodded— "I'd be proud to have either."

"We'll get you on our side," Birdie said. "We'll do our best to make you proud."

"You don't need to make me proud," Professor Asante said. "You need to save the Core, and in turn, the entire world."

She turned to wheel away, but Leroy cleared his throat and spoke up. "I'm just wondering, why don't we already know the exact way to solve the Imbalance, with the Pillars and their Tiles? You said an Imbalance happened a long time ago. Don't we have, like, old journals or notes or something from past Balance Keepers who saved the world?"

Professor Asante's face was grim. "There are documents for every Realm, from centuries ago, that have been preserved by the Core Watchers."

"So why not just go and read those?" Albert asked. Leroy nodded in agreement.

"We cannot turn to them," Professor Asante said, her voice as serious as death, "because they have been stolen."

The room was totally silent. Albert's heart raced in his chest. It was the traitor.

There was no other explanation. It had to have been. The very same person who created the Imbalance stole the documents, so that no one would know for sure how to solve it.

Albert clutched Farnsworth as if he could ward off the

dark thoughts that were entering his mind.

What kind of person would want to do such a thing to the Core, and in turn, the entire *world*?

"You'd better be on your way. Tomorrow marks five days," Professor Asante said. "Rest up, Balance Keepers. You're going to need it."

Albert and his friends stood up to leave. They made their way slowly through the winding dark tunnels. Farnsworth led the way, and the padding of his paws was the only sound to be heard. Not a single member of Hydra said a word, but a silent message seemed to pass between the three of them.

They *had* to get better. For Albert's dad. For Albert's family. For the rest of the world. Next time they were in the Pit, they had to win.

CHAPTER 14

The Cave of Whispers

lbert woke early the next morning to the soft
blue gleam of Farnsworth's eyes.

"What time is it?" Albert whispered. "Go
back to sleep, buddy."

Farnsworth whimpered and flashed his eyes. Before
Albert could roll over, the dog dropped a slobbery envelope onto Albert's chest. *That* got his attention. Albert sat
up, suddenly wide awake.

"Is it from my dad?" Albert asked as he scooped up
the envelope. Sure enough, he saw his name scrawled on
the front in his dad's typical chicken-scratch handwriting.

This envelope was heavier than usual. As soon as
Albert opened it, an ornate golden key tumbled out,

landing with a soft thump on Albert's lap. It glittered a strange blue-green in the light of Farnsworth's eyes.

"What's this?" Albert held up the key.

Farnsworth whined again. The light in his eyes grew so bright that Leroy groaned and slammed a pillow over his face.

"All right, all right, I'm coming," Albert whispered. "As long as you take me to whatever door this key belongs to."

Farnsworth winked a knowing, glowing eye. Albert climbed out of bed, laced up his boots, and followed Farnsworth out the flap of the tent.

For this early in the morning, the Core was surprisingly full of life. Albert passed three Core workers on the way to the Main Chamber. They had hard copper miner's hats on, like the Path Hider's, and were busy looking at a blueprint of one of the tunnels. A group of Core Cleaners scrubbed the statue of Frog Man.

"Good morning." Albert smiled and waved as he passed by the workers and marched out into the Main Chamber. The first thing he noticed, much to his dismay, was the glowing red 5 on the clock. *As if I really needed the reminder.*

Professor Bigglesby, an ancient dwarf who had a disturbing obsession with Core weaponry, stood on one of the bridges in the center of the room. He had a gleaming golden sword in his hand, and was practicing slicing and jabbing at the air.

"Up so early, Mr. Flynn?" Professor Bigglesby said, as Albert stepped onto the bridge. He swiped the sword past Albert, narrowly missing his shoulder. Farnsworth howled and raced across to the other side.

"I'm just going to see my dad," Albert said as he dodged another swipe of the blade. "Any idea where he is?"

Professor Bigglesby nodded, then dropped to the floor and rolled, tucking the sword close to his body. "He's in the Cave of Whispers, most likely!"

Albert raced off after Farnsworth. As crazy as the old dwarf was, Professor Bigglesby had skills.

Once out of the Main Chamber, Farnsworth led Albert down an unfamiliar tunnel. Blue flames flickered on the walls, and the longer they walked, the colder it became. The ground sloped downward, so steep at times that Albert was almost sliding in his boots.

Finally, Farnsworth came to a stop at an old door. The wood looked as if it were cut right from the bark of a tree. It was as gnarled and wrinkled as Pap.

There was a keyhole in the door, just above an old-fashioned crystal handle that sparkled like a million stars. Albert pulled the key out of his pocket and stuck it into the lock. It was a perfect fit, and almost like magic, the old door swung inward with a creak.

Farnsworth scurried inside, and Albert chased him into the darkness.

Albert couldn't even see his own two feet. It reminded him of his first time inside the Troll Tree, only now, Albert didn't feel the fear that he had back then.

"Okay, lights on," Albert said to Farnsworth. He was about to scratch Farnsworth's head and rev up his high beams, when suddenly, light shone at the end of the tunnel, beckoning Albert forward.

He took a few more steps. The path grew brighter and brighter as he went, and by the time the tunnel widened and Albert stepped into open space, his jaw was hanging nearly to his toes.

"Holy Calderon," Albert gasped.

The Cave of Whispers was completely covered, from floor to ceiling, in crystals. It was like Albert had just stepped inside a kaleidoscope. Every time he blinked, the colors of the gems flickered and changed. Some of them were the size of boulders, while others were as tiny as Farnsworth's eyes. But all of them, every single one, was so beautiful it was like Albert was staring into the stars. *More like a galaxy*, Albert thought.

In the middle of the cave, atop a large square purple crystal, sat Professor Flynn. He wore his emerald Professor's coat, and from here it almost looked like he was a part of the cave.

"Dad!" Albert called out.

His voice exploded across the cave. Suddenly the crystals began to tremble and shake. Smaller ones crashed down from the ceiling, and the colors flashed so brilliant and blinding that Albert had to shut his eyes and look away. The cave rumbled and groaned until the echo of Albert's voice faded to silence.

When Albert opened his eyes, Professor Flynn was crossing the floor to meet him.

"You have to keep your voice down," his dad said gently.

Albert nodded. When he spoke, he kept his voice softer than the ruffle of a bird's wings. "The Cave of Whispers?"

Professor Flynn nodded. "It's brilliantly designed, when you think about it. Noise isn't allowed here. If it gets too loud, the cave rebels. It's the perfect place to come when all you want to do is think. It doesn't allow for much more than that."

He smiled and waved Albert over. Together, they crossed the cave floor. Albert felt like he was walking on a rainbow. With each step he took, the colors changed. Sometimes he was walking on a green patch, other times he was walking on red or blue or magenta. All of it was mesmerizing.

Professor Flynn took his seat on a giant crystal, and Albert sat beside him. Farnsworth raced around the cave, leaping over crystals and gems, and snapping at them as their colors changed.

"You know lots of secret Core places," Albert mused. "What else is there?"

Professor Flynn's eyes sparkled with a boyish charm that Albert only noticed when they were inside the Core. It was like his dad was happier here, more himself than he ever could be on the surface. "Telling you would ruin the surprise. Someday, we'll visit every room in the Core together. Maybe even discover new ones."

Albert's heart swelled. "I'd like that."

"Despite the Imbalance you're here for, it's good to have you in the Core during the holidays. You're experiencing life the way I do here, year-round. The Float Parade is soon, and the Core . . ." Professor Flynn's voice trailed off, and he smiled like he'd caught himself about to spoil a delicious secret. "Well, there's much you'll discover soon."

The last time they'd been together alone like this, it was Albert's first time in the Core. His dad had taken Albert to the Cave of Souls, a place that held balls of light and fire that represented the souls of every Balance Keeper to ever pass through the Core.

Albert had taken Birdie and Leroy there just before they returned home. They'd been fresh out of the Calderon Realm, still full of the overwhelming joy that came from setting an Imbalance back to normal.

"Any more news on Ponderay?" Albert asked. He didn't mention that just last night, he'd been caught sneaking into Professor Asante's office. He also didn't mention that all he'd been thinking about since last night was how terrified he was for his dad's life.

Professor Flynn sighed. "Not yet, I'm afraid. Professor Asante's been injured, so we've taken another step in the wrong direction. Tussy can't go in alone. It's too dangerous. And on that note, I do have something I need to tell you. . . ."

"I already know you're going into the Realm." Albert cut his dad off before Professor Flynn could say anything else. "I'm scared for you, Dad. But I know you're doing the right thing."

Professor Flynn looked exhausted, but still, he gave Albert his best smile. "It's what you would do, huh, kiddo?"

Albert laughed. "You're exactly right."

His dad nodded. "I wish I didn't have to go in. But right now, California is in a complete state of emergency."

"I saw the news yesterday," Albert said. "Hurricanes. What's next? Earthquakes?"

Professor Flynn shrugged. "We cannot be sure, until the Realm decides to react further."

"I'm worried about Mom and the kids," Albert said. His chest felt constricted, and all he wanted to do was call and talk to them. "What if they aren't okay?"

"Pap heard from your mother just yesterday. They're trying to head back to New York, but flights have been canceled indefinitely," Professor Flynn said. "She's a smart woman. She'll figure out a way to keep the family safe."

"I hope so," Albert said. He imagined the determined look that was always in his mom's eyes, and he drew on that for strength. "Tussy is training us well. We'll be ready in just a few more days. If we're not, I'm afraid of what she might do to us. She's the scariest girl I've ever met."

They both laughed softly, careful not to disturb the silence. Farnsworth had chosen a spot in the far corner of the cave. His eyes were on full blast, but they blended right in with all the twinkling gems.

"The Core is amazing," Albert said. "I just can't believe there's someone that wants to harm it. Why?"

Professor Flynn put a hand on Albert's shoulder. His grip was warm and strong. "People are afraid of what they can't control. Do you remember when you first got your Tile?"

"How could I forget?" Albert asked. "That was the craziest day of my entire life."

He thought back to his very first day in the Core. Albert had dove deep into the Waterfall of Fate in search of a white Tile, only to come up with one that was unlike any other in the Core. At first, Albert had been disappointed, and a little afraid.

No one seemed to know what the Master Tile did. People looked at him differently while it hung from his neck.

"I guess what you're saying is, sometimes people freak out when they're faced with the unknown. Right?" Albert asked.

His dad plucked a stray strand of hair off of the lapel of his jacket. "You didn't see it that way. You saw it as a problem to solve. You did what you had to do, and came out stronger in the end. That is my hope for *all* Balance Keepers, for this Imbalance and all future Imbalances. That we will come together and save the Core before it's too late, rather than giving in to our fear of what could happen if we fail. I'm afraid that this traitor—whoever they are—wasn't feeling up to that task."

Albert reached down and closed his fingers over his Master Tile. It had saved his dad and the old Calderon First Unit in the Realm of Calderon last term. Maybe it could save the Core this time, too.

"Do you think I'll ever go into a Realm again?" Albert asked, a little too loud. "We've been so awful in the Pit lately. It's humiliating."

The crystals around the room buzzed and morphed from one color to the next, making Albert's head dizzy. It was beautiful, but also frightening in its own way, just like the Realms.

"In time, kiddo," Professor Flynn said. He plucked a tiny orange crystal from the floor, and held it out to Albert on his palm. It flashed like the flames of a roaring fire. "Reminds you of Calderon, doesn't it?"

"Definitely," Albert said. He could picture Calderon Peak, the King Fireflies buzzing and spitting flames, the Sea Inspire roiling with poison before Albert dove in and released the silver eggs to set it all back to normal again.

Professor Flynn smiled. "You were great there, kiddo. Greater than anyone I ever could have imagined." He flipped the crystal over, and on the other side its color was deep, starlight silver. It reminded Albert of what he knew of Ponderay.

Professor Flynn continued. "That was *you*, Albert, not the Realm of Calderon, that made you succeed. You'll do great anywhere you go. You're a Flynn, and you're destined for more than just *one* thing."

Professor Flynn tossed the crystal, and Albert caught it. It was warm and cool all at once. He tucked it into his pocket for safekeeping.

"I hope you're right, Dad," Albert said.

Professor Flynn reached into his pocket and produced a golden Medallion. "Before I forget, do me a favor and call your mom soon? She's left seventeen voice messages with Pap. Leave it to her to be in the middle of a hurricane with a crazy aunt and three kids, and still be worried about you on the other side of the country."

"She's got the determination of a Balance Keeper, that's for sure," Albert laughed and took the Medallion. He felt a little bit lighter, knowing that his mom had at least been able to call. She was okay, for now. "Thanks, Dad."

Professor Flynn nodded and put his arm around Albert's shoulders.

"Dad?" Albert asked. "Promise me you'll be safe tomorrow, in the Realm."

"I promise," Professor Flynn said.

They sat together for a little while longer, father and son in silence, watching the Cave of Whispers morph around them like a living, breathing thing.

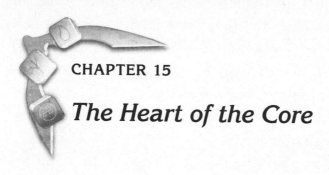

CHAPTER 15

The Heart of the Core

Albert was making his way back through the Main Chamber, dreaming about going back to sleep, when Leroy practically ran into him. Birdie dashed up a moment later.

"Albert!" Leroy panted. "Where have you been? We got a note—detention. Now."

"I got one, too," Birdie added. "We're supposed to meet Professor Asante here."

Albert groaned. "Perfect timing."

As if on cue, Professor Asante rolled up to the edge of the bridge with a clipboard balanced on her lap. Farnsworth barked a greeting.

"Just on time," Professor Asante said. "Someone push me along, please. Down tunnel three."

Albert and his friends exchanged glances. Professor Asante was *huge*, and they were all still basically half asleep—there was no way they'd be able to push her. So Albert, with all the energy he had left, used the Strength symbol to push the Professor along.

They headed into tunnel three and before too long, stopped at an iron door.

There was a glowing orange button on the wall, sort of like an elevator button. Professor Asante tapped the button, and sure enough, when the iron door slid open, there was an elevator waiting for them.

Or, sort of an elevator. It looked more like a big metal cage, but the four of them piled inside. Leroy was squished up against the back with his face pressed against the bars of the cage.

Down and down the elevator went, passing through a tunnel of slick stone that glittered black from natural coal.

"You'll be cleaning the Watcher's room this morning," Professor Asante said. "It'll be good discipline. A little hard work always does the job."

Albert's muscles were screaming, and he knew his friends were exhausted, too. This wasn't going to be fun. The elevator jolted to a stop.

"Go on, then, don't just stand here." Professor Asante pressed a button, and the door slid open. "Tussy will be waiting for you inside." She waved them away with her abnormally large hand. "See you in class in one hour. Don't be late. Off you go." The door slid shut behind them and carried her away.

They turned and stepped away from the elevator. Before them was another tunnel with blue flames, the same as most places in the Core.

"Good riddance," Birdie huffed. "She is totally creeptastic."

"At least she doesn't wear a snake across her shoulders like Lucinda does," Albert said.

"She almost ruins my appetite," Leroy said, "and that's saying something."

The three of them headed down the tunnel, which, as usual, stopped at a closed door. Albert turned the handle and pushed.

Tussy sat just inside on a stool, reading a fat leather book. Her hair was up in a bun, revealing the cuts on her face. Albert wondered if this girl ever *wasn't* hurt.

"Ah, my favorite troublemakers," Tussy said, closing the book. She stood up and waved them toward her. "Follow me."

The trio followed Tussy down a narrow hallway, their footsteps echoing like the beats of a drum. Albert sighed. This was going to be another lame detention, scrubbing floors until his hands were chapped and raw.

But then the hallway opened up into a wide cavern. And Albert felt his jaw drop toward his knees.

There was a *huge* boiling lava pool across the room. It glowed with a color so intense that Albert half wondered if someone had stolen the sun and placed it in this very room. Orange and yellow bubbles popped and oozed at the surface, and the room was so hot that Albert's head spun.

About ten adult Core workers sat in the chairs around the lava pit with clipboards in their laps. Some of them were wearing worker's scrubs and sticking long thermometer-shaped instruments into the lava. Albert expected them to melt to nothing.

But when they pulled the tools out, everything was intact.

"Seventeen cranks to the north," one of the men said, squinting at the thermometer.

All the people in chairs nodded and mumbled things, and then started scribbling away onto their notepads.

"What is this place?" Birdie said, her voice just a whisper.

Tussy smiled. "This is the Watchers' Cavern. These are the people that keep things on the surface in check. They've been working with Professor Asante and me to try and decipher the Means to Restore Balance in Ponderay."

Leroy rubbed his glasses on his shirt. "So they're, like, Core Researchers?"

Tussy burst into laughter. "Of course not. They're

Watchers. Big difference. They can sense things about the Core, things that normal science can't. They've studied it for years. They're able to observe the surface world and the Realms. They can tell us how bad an Imbalance is getting."

"Through lava?" Albert asked. "And giant thermometers?"

Tussy smiled that sharklike smile. "Those are called Readers. They're able to monitor the Core's activity. How hot it's getting, how hard it's working. And that's not lava over there." Her voice lowered, and she stared at the glowing, bubbling pool with a gleam in her eyes. "That's the Heart of the Core."

Suddenly, Albert felt like an invader. This place was sort of sacred, like the Cave of Souls and the Cave of Whispers.

Tussy motioned for the three of them to follow her to the corner of the cavern, where a gleaming stalactite stuck out of the rock like a giant fang.

"You'll be cleaning, as usual detention requires." She gave them mops and let them fill up buckets of water from a rusted old sink in the back of a supply closet. "Keep your heads down. And stay quiet. Don't bother the Watchers. They're under a lot of stress right now, and the last thing they need is three young Balance Keepers spying over their shoulders."

She turned to leave, when a loud *SQUELCH!* erupted

from the center of the room.

Suddenly the Watchers were on their feet, gathered around the edge of the pool.

"Stay here," Tussy said. There was shock in her eyes, something Albert hadn't seen from her before. She rushed over, and Albert couldn't stop himself. He followed, Birdie and Leroy on his tail. What he saw made his heart sink all the way to his toes.

Swirling through the brightness of the Heart of the Core was a vein of black sludge, as dark and slick as oil, and as foul-smelling as the garbage piled on the streets of New York City. A Watcher stuck one of the Readers into the dark bubbling substance. It melted the tool away, sucking it under in an instant.

Everyone gasped.

"Impure," one of the Watchers said.

"Impossible," another echoed.

"Inconceivable," said a third.

Tussy turned to Albert and his friends, her face a mask of calm. But her eyes told the whole story. "Go back to your dormitories."

"But what about detention?" Albert asked, shocked.

"Detention is the least of your worries now." She looked over her shoulder as the black goo snaked its way through the golden Heart of the Core.

Whatever that meant, it wasn't good.

CHAPTER 16

The Creatures of Ponderay

Tussy dismissed them from detention then—at least that much was good. Birdie and Leroy headed back to the dorms to get some more rest, but Albert knew he would just have nightmares if he fell asleep.

He wished more than ever that his mom could know the world of the Core. When Albert had had nightmares as a little boy, his mom would rush to his room and stay there until the bad dreams faded away. He could almost imagine her voice now, whispering to him that everything would be okay. Suddenly all Albert wanted to do was talk to her. His dad had said she was fine, but with the Heart of the Core turning black, Albert felt an overwhelming need to check on his mom.

He found the Medallion his dad had given him and tucked it into his pocket. Then he sat up, snuck past a sleeping Leroy and Farnsworth, and left Cedarfell behind.

It was still pretty early; the Library was quiet and still. Albert's footsteps echoed across the hard floor as he made his way inside. Lucinda's shop wasn't open yet, and the torches weren't fully lit.

There was one person who *would* be awake, though.

The Path Hider. He hid the paths to the Core, but he also monitored all phone calls in and out.

The Phone Booth was a simple hole in the wall, at the very back of the Library. Albert slipped inside and smiled when he saw the phone. He'd forgotten it was an old-fashioned kind, with separate ear and mouth pieces. There was a slot in the cave wall where Albert inserted the Medallion. Then he pressed the earpiece to his ear and waited.

Static buzzed on the other line. At first, Albert thought the Path Hider wasn't going to answer. But just before he put the phone down, he heard him speak.

"Recipient of your message, please?" the Path Hider asked.

"Hey," Albert said. "It's me again. Albert Flynn. Um, how are you?"

Albert heard gears whirring and steam hissing on the other line.

"Young Mr. Flynn," the Path Hider said. "What are you doing up so early? Preparing for the oncoming doom of the Core, I presume?"

"What? No, I was actually just hoping to talk to my mom."

"Of course," the Path Hider said. "Destination?"

"California," Albert said. He gave the Path Hider his mom's cell phone number. "If she doesn't answer, is there any chance you'd refund my Medallion?"

The Path Hider cleared his throat. "Money spent is money spent."

Albert sighed. "I figured you'd say that."

"Do come and visit with me sometime soon. There's much to discuss, much to learn. Perhaps you could bring Lucinda along with you."

Albert wasn't too keen on the idea of hanging out with some creepy dude in a miner's cap and a woman who had a fascination with giant hissing snakes, but he shrugged and said, "Yeah, maybe sometime."

"Your three minutes start now," the Path Hider said, and the static changed to a ringing.

Albert leaned against the wall and waited. After three rings, his mom picked up.

"Hello?"

"Mom!" he gasped. "Are you okay?"

"Albert!" his mom said. "I'm so glad you called."

Hearing her voice washed the tension away from

Albert's shoulders in an instant—the sound was so warm and familiar.

"We're trying to drive farther north. Aunt Suze's house is flooded from all the rain." The line crackled and cut off for a second. "But it's fine, Albert. We're fine. Are you okay? Are you having fun?"

Albert instantly recognized the tone in her voice. She was trying to make things seem better than they actually were, for his sake. He drew a blank. What was he supposed to say to her? *I called you because I'm having nightmares like I did when I was a little boy and I miss you so much it hurts. Oh, and I'm afraid for your life, because if I don't figure out how to beat Argon in the Pit, then I might not be able to save Ponderay and the surface from the Imbalance in time.*

"I'm fine, Mom," he said instead. "I just wanted to make sure you guys were safe."

"We're going to be all right," his mom said. It was like she was saying the words more to herself than Albert. She *was* afraid, and that made Albert scared, too.

"I saw the news reports," Albert said. "You have to get out of there, Mom. Fast."

There was a buzzing noise on the line, the signal for a minute already having passed.

"We are, Albert," his mom said. "We've been driving for two days."

"But they said the largest hurricane in over a century is about to hit," Albert said.

His mom's voice was deadly serious. "It's already here." She paused, and Albert heard her take a deep breath. "Are you sure you want to hear this, Albert? I don't mean to worry you."

If you only knew, Mom. "Yes, I just want to know what's going on out there," Albert replied.

"Well, just last night, three navy ships off the coast of San Diego went down. The waves are getting so big that they've started evacuating everyone, Albert. The entire state of California is emptying out by the minute. The rains are heading as far north as Oregon."

Oregon? That's where Birdie's family lives, Albert thought.

"I'm scared," Albert admitted. A lump formed in his throat, one that he couldn't just swallow away. Just last night, that happened? It had to do with the Core's heart turning black, he just knew it. Things were getting worse, and fast. He imagined the news report he'd seen in the hospital, of the streets filled with honking cars and buses, people trying to get to safety before it was too late, but that was a whole day ago. And now with his dad in Ponderay, miles from safety . . . Albert sighed. It wasn't just his family at risk. There were millions of other families out there whose lives were on the line. And if the Imbalance got any worse, then it would spread to the entire world before long.

"I have to go," his mom said. "They're rerouting traffic again."

Albert wanted so badly to tell his mom the truth, but the secrets of the Core had to remain locked away. Instead, he simply said, "Stay safe, Mom. Please. I love you. So much."

A bleating siren sounded in the background, followed by more honks from cars. "I love you too, Albert. Make sure to call me on Christmas, okay?"

"I will," Albert promised. "I'll see you soon."

"I'm counting down the days," his mom said. She started to say something else, but the connection was lost.

"Please insert another Medallion to continue your conversation," the Path Hider said.

"I'm all out." Albert sighed. "And she's gone anyway." He rested his forehead against the cool cave wall. "Hey, you've been around a long time, haven't you?"

"Depends on how you look at it," said the Path Hider.

"Is there any chance we're not going to fix the Imbalance this time? I mean, the Core has always been saved, but maybe someday, we won't be able to fix the problem. Maybe someday, an Imbalance will win."

The Path Hider took a while to respond. When he finally answered, his words left a strange, empty feeling in Albert's gut.

"There's always a chance that evil will prevail. Only time will tell, Albert Flynn."

With that, the line went silent.

*   *   *

Albert made a quick stop back at the dorm, and then he and Leroy headed to Professor Asante's classroom. Birdie was already sitting right in the front row with an open notebook in her lap and a sharpened pencil poised for the attack. When she saw Albert and Leroy arrive, she waved them over.

"It's so empty in here," Birdie said, looking up at them. "Normally we'd be fighting for a spot."

She was right. It was only ten or so Pure kids besides Hydra and Argon. It just felt strange, not to have a classroom full of kids and chaos. Albert sat down beside her and looked over his shoulder. Behind them, Hoyt was flipping through the pages of his book. Normally, he'd be busy shooting spit wads at the backs of people's heads.

Birdie leaned in and whispered, "When Hoyt got here, he didn't say anything at all about the last Pit competition. I figured he'd be shouting our loss to the world."

"Maybe he's changing," Albert said.

"Was that a joke?" Leroy asked. "Because if it was, I *so* missed the punch line."

"Not at all," Albert said. He looked back at Hoyt, and their eyes met.

Albert stiffened. *Here it comes.*

But Hoyt just stared back at Albert. Then, amazingly, he turned his attention back to the book in his lap without saying a word.

Two adult Core workers entered the room and sat down. Normally adults weren't in class, but Albert guessed, because it was an emergency term, anyone was welcome to learn more about the affected Realm. Sometimes, people felt better about things when they could learn as much as possible.

"This morning was intense," Birdie said. "Have you guys come up with any theories yet?"

"I have a theory," Leroy mused, adjusting his hat, "that the Heart of the Core is sick. And that black stuff was a virus. I think it's going to get worse as long as the Imbalance stays around."

"He's probably right," Birdie sighed.

Albert nodded in agreement. "Whatever's going on, it's giving me the heebie-jeebies. And Hoyt's behavior isn't helping. I feel like he's just waiting to pounce on us." Albert felt a shiver run through him, which made him think of the phone call with his mom. He relayed the information to his friends.

Birdie's and Leroy's faces paled when Albert mentioned the sinking ships, and how the rains were spreading all the way north to Oregon, but there wasn't time to discuss the matter any further.

Tussy came into the room, pushing Professor Asante in her wheelchair. Her leg was still in its cast, and students had to dodge out of the way so they didn't get whacked in the face.

"All right, class, settle down!" Professor Asante said, clapping her large hands. "Although I dislike the reason we have to have this session today, I do love the subject matter." She snapped her fingers, and Tussy pushed her toward a giant black curtain similar to the one they had seen in Professor Asante's office.

Everyone seemed to sit up a little straighter. They were all dying to know what secrets lay behind it, especially what was causing that eerie blue glow. Albert had come up with all sorts of theories for what it was hiding: another Realm, another Pit, maybe even some sort of icy cold lava lake they could swim in.

Professor Asante smiled, holding her tattooed arms wide. "Ponderay is a magnificent Realm. Today you'll witness that firsthand."

Tussy pulled a thick black cord at the far side of the curtain. Slowly, the curtain swept aside.

A giant, glowing blue aquarium appeared.

"Wow," Albert breathed.

Giant was an understatement. The aquarium took up the entire wall, and the water it held was a glittering, silvery blue, so bright and beautiful that Albert wondered if it was real.

But of course it was. This was the Core, and incredible things were an everyday appearance.

"The creatures that thrive in this tank are very rare. They weren't stolen from Ponderay. They were brought here because of illnesses or injuries, and will be rehabilitated into the Realm as soon as the Imbalance is solved."

Professor Asante snapped again, and Tussy went to work, passing out books to the students and workers in the room. There were the Ten Pillars on the cover of the book. It seemed to be the sign of Ponderay.

"Flip to page seventeen," Professor Asante said. "First, we'll study the Hammerfin."

Albert didn't need to look at the drawings in the book—Hydra and Argon knew the Hammerfin all too well already. Still, he read through the stats.

It was like a hammerhead shark on the surface world, only three times larger.

It could smash a pillar with the force of a wrecking ball.

Suddenly, Albert was excited to get a chance to actually study the thing up close in an environment where he wasn't just trying to stay alive.

"You've seen the artist's rendering." Professor Asante smiled. "Now let's witness the real thing."

Almost as if in response to her words, a black-blue blur shot across the aquarium, coming into view. People gasped. Some screamed.

"I can't believe we were in the water with that thing," Birdie whispered.

The Hammerfin's body was all muscle and sinew, and its fins spanned as wide as Professor Asante was tall.

"The Hammerfin's best defense mechanism is to use its powerful body to leap from the waves, and its head to smash," Professor Asante said.

"But it's a shark!" a redheaded girl shouted from the back of the room. "Doesn't it, like, eat people?"

"Man, I love sharks," Leroy said.

Albert balked. "*You* love *sharks*?"

"But you're, like, afraid of everything!" Birdie added.

Leroy shrugged. "Not sharks, dudes. They're cool."

Too shocked to say anything, Albert laughed and turned back to the lesson.

Professor Asante tapped the aquarium glass. The Hammerfin opened its mouth, and where Albert expected to see razor-sharp, lethal teeth, he only saw gums. It was like an old man without his dentures in. Albert smiled as he remembered Leroy wrestling the great beast in the Pit.

The room erupted into laughter and the Hammerfin swam away.

"I love all the Core creatures." Birdie smiled, scribbling notes on the pages of her book.

"Wait until you see the rest," Leroy mused, and flipped his book to the next page. "I'm sure they're even better."

He was right.

Over the course of several hours, in lieu of a Pit competition, Professor Asante showed them the rest of Ponderay's creatures. They studied Lightning Rays, a yellow stingray-like creature with a bird's beak. Its wing-span was four feet across, and its tail was twice as long, ending in a razor-sharp prong.

"The Lightning Rays won't kill you," Professor Asante said, motioning to the ray as it sped back and forth in the aquarium, dancing beneath the water. "But if you threaten it"—she rapped the glass with her knuckles, and the ray flashed a shockingly bright orange—"its shock will provoke an intense paralysis."

"It's incredible," Birdie sighed.

"You just like it because it has a bird's beak!" Leroy whispered.

"I knew I felt something sting me in the Pit yester-day!" Albert was glad now he'd only encountered one.

Next they studied Jackalopes.

Professor Asante was right—the Jackalopes in Cedar-fell were miniature compared to the one sitting in Professor Asante's office now. Tussy brought it out on a leash. It was about the same size as a horse. Its antlers were as large as an antelope's, twisting and curling like pointed ribbons.

"You're used to seeing Jackalopes in the forest of Cedarfell," Professor Asante said, "but these creatures' natural habitats are caves within the Ten Pillars them-selves. Don't make the mistake of being fooled by their big eyes and soft fur—the creatures are anything but gentle to anyone who invades their territory."

Albert believed Professor Asante, but just barely. This Jackalope hopped alongside Tussy with its soft brown eyes wide. It had a wrap around its back leg, and was limping slightly. All the girls in the room made oohs and aahs. Even some of the boys joined in. Albert was itching to stand up and get a closer look at the creature.

"Can we pet it?" Leroy blurted out. Albert and Birdie both whirled around to look at him. Leroy had never shown much of an interest in the Core creatures. That was two of them in one day.

He shrugged. "He reminds me of a horse I used to ride when I was a kid. He's kinda cool."

"One at a time." Professor Asante nodded.

The handful of students and workers took turns going up to the Jackalope, careful not to scare it. The animal seemed a little flighty, like it wanted to hop away, but it couldn't with its injured leg. When Leroy went up, the Jackalope sniffed him all over, its giant nose working overtime. By the end of Leroy's turn, he may as well have been the king of rabbits. The Jackalope wouldn't leave his side.

"What was that all about?" Birdie asked, when Leroy returned to his seat.

He shrugged. "Beats me. But I like Jackalopes. I think I want one."

"Good luck finding one for adoption around here," Albert said. "I'm pretty sure every single Pure kid and worker in the Core is wishing for one too, right about now."

By the end of class, everyone was buzzing about the creatures of Ponderay. Albert enjoyed getting a closer look at some new Core creatures, but he thought Farnsworth was cooler. *A dog with headlights for eyes? Beat that!*

"Class is dismissed," Professor Asante said. The students passed in their books. The Core workers said thanks for being allowed a tiny glimpse at Ponderay. Tussy took the Jackalope back to its home, which turned out to be in another secret area of the Core that only Professors and Apprentices had access to.

Everyone was ready to file out of the room when suddenly, the door swung open.

Professor Flynn made his way through the crowd. He was breathless and his face was red, and just like Tussy, he, too, was covered in fresh cuts and bruises. He looked like Ponderay had put him through the ringer just since Albert saw him in the Cave of Whispers this morning, but at least he was *safe*.

Albert sat up straight. *What's he doing here?*

Professor Flynn stopped in front of Professor Asante's wheelchair and leaned down to whisper into her ear. Albert looked around, at all the faces of his fellow students and the Core workers. Everyone had stopped what they'd been doing. They were all staring at his dad.

Finally, Professor Flynn turned, straightened out his

emerald jacket, and spoke. "I have a quick announcement to make."

Birdie nudged Albert and mouthed, *What's happening?*

Albert shrugged. He didn't know what was going on, either. He leaned forward and listened as his dad spoke.

"In light of recent events with Professor Asante's injury and other—" Professor Flynn glanced at Professor Asante. She shook her head almost unperceptively and Professor Flynn continued, "—and other . . . developments in the Core, my fellow Professors and I have decided that it is of the utmost importance to remind you of how *dire* our situation is. Unfortunately, as of this morning, the Imbalance has escalated further. We've moved into a third phase."

Whispers spread throughout the room.

Professor Flynn continued. "In a completely unexpected event, the Pillars have switched directions—they are now rotating counterclockwise, and at even greater speeds, now reaching seventy miles per hour. This has understandably confused the creatures and they've become even more hostile. The hurricane on the surface has hit full strength. Streets and homes and businesses are flooding. Power has been lost due to increasingly high wind speeds, and"—he swallowed, hard, and made eye contact with Albert—"there is a whirlpool in the Pacific Ocean. It is sucking up everything in its path, destroying entire ships and navy tankers."

Whispers buzzed like locusts. Birdie reached over and squeezed Albert's hand.

Professor Flynn went on. "As a result of this, competitions in the Pit are going to be extremely grueling from this point forth. Preparation is key. And now I must deliver the bad news."

"The bad news?" a Core worker asked from the back. "Isn't what you've said already bad enough, Professor?"

Professor Flynn frowned. "I'm afraid not. The Core Watchers have decided that our original timeline will no longer suffice. We believed we had seven days, which would leave us with five days at this point. But now, after much deliberation, the Watchers have given us a total of two days. In forty-eight hours' time, we will crown a new First Unit as our victors, and they will enter Ponderay."

Albert's heart froze. *Forty-eight hours? That was nothing.*

Murmurs sounded all around, and Professor Asante clapped her hands to silence them. Leroy and Birdie both looked as sick as Albert felt.

Professor Flynn pulled out a small roll of parchment. He unfolded it. "And lastly, I have the Ponderay standings." He took a deep breath, and Albert thought he saw his dad's shoulders droop. The whole room was suddenly as silent as a grave.

Albert felt the eyes of his classmates on him and his team. When his dad spoke, his voice sounded cold and empty. "Argon is in the lead by nine points."

Albert already knew Hydra was losing, but hearing his dad say it out loud, in front of everyone, was humiliating. Albert put his head in his hands. Leroy started chewing on his thumbnail, and Birdie punched her fist against her book. Farnsworth whined, and Albert had to hush him before he went into a full-out howl.

"YES!" Hoyt shouted from behind them.

A few people looked genuinely happy about the standings. Others gave Albert, Birdie, and Leroy apologetic glances and mutters. But Albert didn't care about how everyone else felt. His eyes were on his dad.

Professor Flynn wouldn't look at Albert. Was his dad ashamed? Was he embarrassed, of Albert? Was he angry with Albert for not doing as well as he had last term?

"In further news," Professor Flynn said, rustling the paper in his hands, "I want to remind everyone that hope is not lost. We have two talented teams competing for the First Unit spot. Good luck to you both, Argon and Hydra. Be brave, Balance Keepers. You have two days left."

His eyes went right to Albert's. He nodded, and in that moment, Albert knew his dad still believed in him.

Now Albert just had to prove him right.

CHAPTER 17

The Battle Royale

After lunch, Hydra technically had free time, but neither Albert, Leroy, nor Birdie seemed to be able to think about anything other than Ponderay.

"We've got to win in the Pit tomorrow," Albert said. "If Argon goes into Ponderay, I'm afraid of what might happen. They've never been in a Realm before, not like us."

"So let's go practice," Leroy suggested.

Birdie and Albert practically choked on their surprise.

"You want to go practice?" Birdie asked.

Leroy shrugged. "Why not? I bet Argon's been practicing. We should, too."

"He's right," Albert said as they changed directions and headed toward the Pit. "And, Leroy? I like the determination."

"I'm always determined," Leroy said as he took the lead. "It's just this whole forty-eight-hour thing that's getting to me."

They passed by the clock in the Main Chamber. It had switched to counting down the hours rather than days. The glowing number *48* stuck in Albert's mind, even after it was far behind them.

As soon as they stepped through the door into the Pit room, they realized how wrong they were about thinking they could get some practice time in alone.

Argon was already in the Pit.

Hoyt, Slink, and Mo sat at the bottom on the spongy floor, talking and laughing. Albert sighed. *So much for some nice private time for Hydra to really focus on teamwork.* He turned to leave. Birdie and Leroy followed, but before they'd escaped unnoticed, Farnsworth barked a greeting down at Argon. Hydra's cover was blown.

Three heads snapped upward, and three sets of eyes locked onto Albert, Birdie, and Leroy.

"Well, what do we have here, boys?" Hoyt called up from below.

Albert clenched his fists, sure that Hoyt was about to sneer and make some typical, bullying remark about him and his friends.

But instead, Hoyt stood up and smiled. A *real* smile, not the sneer that seemed to be permanently sewed onto his face. "We've really been looking forward to seeing you three today."

Albert nearly choked on his own laughter. Birdie just stood there, looking like she'd seen a ghost. Leroy let out a sound that went something like, "Wha-huh?"

Slink and Mo laughed, and Hoyt continued. "We've decided that we're tired of old, boring competition with you three. This is getting repetitive, every day in the Pit."

"So what do you want, Hoyt?" Birdie asked, finally finding her voice.

Hoyt's eyes glittered darkly. "We want to have some *real* fun. Let's make it count, Hydra. Let's raise the stakes."

Albert took a step forward, his toes on the very edge of the Pit. "You mean you want to bet on who wins?"

Hoyt nodded. "You and I both know, Flynn, that a little friendly competition never hurt anyone. And besides, there aren't any Professors here today to stop us."

"He's playing at something," Leroy warned, but Albert shushed him.

This was the perfect opportunity to put Hoyt in a corner. Albert couldn't punch him again, not like he'd done last term, without getting weeks of detention, or ultimately, an expulsion. And besides, Albert wasn't really about that. But he'd play. He couldn't back down now.

"We'll play your game, Hoyt," Albert said. "Your team against my team. No Professors, no crowd. Just the six of us. Now. But first, I want you to swear that if you lose, you'll stop picking on me and my team. And you'll leave the new Core recruits alone next term. You'll stop being a bully to everyone."

Hoyt tipped his chin up. "I like your fire, Flynn. I'm game. But if my team wins, Hydra has to swear not to practice outside of Pit hours beyond this session. We don't need you getting any extra opportunities to get ahead like you did for Calderon."

Albert looked sideways at his friends. They formed a tight circle and kept their voices low.

"Sounds like he plans to humiliate us in front of everyone if we lose," Leroy said. "And then take the stage in Ponderay and save the day."

"So we won't lose," Birdie hissed. "I'm sick of looking so pathetic in front of their team. We were crowned a *First Unit* last term, you guys. Next term, the new recruits will be looking to us for answers. This should be nothing! We're strong, and we can win this bet, easy."

"I don't know about this," Leroy said. "I think we should just go. We might just be setting ourselves up for failure."

Birdie grabbed his shoulders and shook him lightly. "Leroy! Where's your sense of adventure? Suck it up and get ready to rumble, because we're totally doing this!"

Albert nodded, drawing on Birdie's strength. "Professor Asante told us just last night that she's looking at Argon differently. She almost seemed like she wanted to pick them." He looked right into Leroy's eyes. "We've got the guy with the Synapse Tile on our side. We need you, bro. We can't win this without you."

Leroy's chest puffed out, just the slightest. "If we lose, I'm blaming you guys for the untimely death of my cool factor."

"You got it, man," Albert said. He turned and looked down at Argon. "We're in. Let's do this."

Hoyt rubbed his hands together like Hydra had just fallen right into his trap.

No one saw the dark shadow in the corner of the room.

Someone was watching them.

There wasn't a whistle this time. There was no one in the crowd to cheer the teams on, no video camera to record them for Professor Asante to watch later. It was eerily silent as Hydra's platform took them deeper into the Pit, finally stopping on the floor.

Albert, Leroy, and Birdie stepped off. Albert took the lead as they marched to meet Argon in the center.

"All right, boys," Hoyt said, his thin arms wrapped over his chest.

"That's boys *and* a girl," Birdie growled.

Hoyt nodded. "Boys and a girl."

Slink and Mo met him at his sides. Together, they looked like a bunch of prep school boys in matching orange T-shirts, not like the Pit masters that they'd some-how become.

Hoyt went on. "I'm guessing the Pit will set up the

same competition as last time. Grab as many Tiles as you can, and then we'll plug them back in during Round Two. We'll add up the first-round and second-round scores. No breaks, and no stopping to rest. Anything to add to that, Hydra?"

"No playing dirty," Albert said, forcing himself to remain calm.

Hoyt laughed, a sound that echoed across the Pit.

"We don't play dirty," Slink said. "Right, guys?" He looked sideways at Mo and Hoyt. Hoyt glared at Slink for a second, but when Slink took a step forward, Hoyt took a step back.

"No, we don't play dirty," Hoyt sighed.

Albert realized something just then. Slink was the biggest guy on their team, and easily the strongest. Maybe Hoyt had a little fear in him, after all. Mo noticed Albert watching closely. He stepped protectively in front of Hoyt, as loyal as a dog.

"Enough chatter. Let's do this," said Mo.

"Good luck." Albert put on his best fake smile. "You're going to need it."

The two teams lined up at opposite sides of the Pit. Albert could almost feel a charge of life in the air. They were *willingly* hanging out with Argon, practicing during free time.

Hoyt crossed the Pit and punched a red button on the wall.

Almost instantly, the Pit started to take shape.

As Hoyt had guessed, it was similar to practice just the day before, with giant rubbery pillars and handholds that Albert knew would disappear within a few seconds of grabbing on to them. There was still the freezing, ice-cold water that started to fill up the Pit floor. The pillars began spinning, starting slow at first, then accelerating to speeds that could rival a runaway train.

Great waves rocked the waters, so Albert, Birdie, and Leroy held hands, making a human chain.

"There's no creatures in here today," Birdie mentioned. "I can't sense them."

"Maybe it's because the Professors aren't here," Leroy said. "Like, it's them who set the creatures loose."

"You ready, Hydra?" Hoyt shouted from across the Pit. "Remember our bet!"

Albert could see flashes of Hoyt and his team as the pillars spun by.

"We'll win," Birdie said to Albert, with a look of complete and utter determination in her eyes. Even Leroy was leaning forward, like he couldn't wait to dive forth and make Hydra's name known.

"READY!" Albert cried.

The chaos began.

Albert didn't waste any time giving out his orders. Today they were going to win fast, and shut down Hoyt's bullying for good.

"Let's all climb!" Albert shouted over the roar of the

waves and the wind that had picked up around them as the pillars spun. "Get as many Tiles as you can. Let's move fast. Don't be afraid to take chances."

"Got it." Birdie laughed like a maniac and dove into the water.

"She's crazier than that Guildacker of hers!" Leroy shouted. "See you on the other side, bro."

He and Albert separated and dove into the waves. For Birdie and Albert, it wasn't impossible to navigate the tough waters. But Leroy was struggling. Albert could hear him shouting, see him fighting the waves.

Albert's heart sank.

No amount of points was worth endangering his best friend. Albert grabbed Birdie's hand. They both turned back, then each stretched out a hand to Leroy.

Poor Leroy looked like a wet rat, his hair stuck to his face, his glasses askew. "Just leave me to drown, huh, dudes?"

"Hey, we came back!" Albert said. "Hang on to us!"

Leroy held on tight to both Albert and Birdie. Together, they used the power of their Tiles. With the natural swimmer's strength that came with Birdie's Water Tile, and the power of the Master Tile, they were able to haul Leroy across the angry waves.

They were almost to the spinning circle of pillars. Albert reached out, thinking he'd be able to just grab one and hang on for a wild ride. But suddenly the pillars changed their direction. A massive wave slapped Albert in the face.

"What the heck?" Birdie yelled. "What's going on?"

"I think they're mirroring the Realm," Albert realized.

Leroy nodded. "Like the Pit knows the Ten Pillars have switched directions. Let's try again."

They started swimming again.

Hoyt laughed from somewhere above. He'd already managed, somehow, to start the climb. Slink and Mo were still in the water, splashing about as they, too, tried to grab a hold and start the climb.

"The pillars are moving faster than yesterday!" Albert said. "How did Hoyt get onto one so fast?"

Leroy chewed on his lip while they all treaded water, fighting to stay afloat. "Can you swim, like, dolphin-fast?"

Birdie's eyes lit up. "Heck, yeah."

Albert thought on it, then smiled. "I can manage it, if I use Speed and Water at once."

Leroy explained his reasoning. "We've got to move in the same direction as the pillars are spinning. Get close enough that we can reach out and grab ahold, once we're at a good-enough speed alongside the pillars."

"That's genius, Memory Boy!" Birdie shouted. "Let's move on three."

Albert pictured both symbols in his mind, merging together.

"One," Leroy said. (Albert pictured the Water symbol.)

"Two . . ." (Albert pictured Hoyt's Speed symbol.)

"SWIM!" Leroy shouted.

Albert and Birdie took off, toting Leroy along between them in a Superman position. Albert could feel the water running across his body at top speed, forming bubbles against his skin.

Faster and faster they swam, passing Slink and Mo not once, but twice. The wind was on Albert's face. He let out an excited cry, but it was cut short when he saw Hoyt way overhead, waving a Tile in the air.

He can't win today. He just can't!

"That's . . . fast . . . enouuuuuugh!" Leroy shouted, water spraying him in the face.

Albert and Birdie exchanged glances.

"Leroy first!" Albert shouted.

Birdie nodded, and they swam closer to the pillars, the wind and waves picking up. "Get ready."

Leroy was spitting water and trying to see clearly, but he nodded like he understood.

They angled him closer, and as a pillar swept by, they gave Leroy a good shove. Albert imagined the Strength symbol to give Leroy some extra oomph.

It was like slow motion, watching Leroy stretch his arms, trying to grab a hold as a pillar spun by. His fingers stretched. His glasses were coated in water droplets, and his mouth was set in a hard line. The pillar was close enough that Leroy was able to grab a hold. The pillar carried him away like a floating buoy.

Albert had to trust his friend to find the strength to start the climb.

"Let's move!" Albert shouted to Birdie.

They started their swim again, chasing the pillars like dolphins in an ocean storm. In seconds, they'd picked up enough speed to catch onto pillars of their own, and from there, it was everyone for themselves.

The second Albert was on his pillar, he traded the Water symbol for Strength, and started scurrying his way up.

Today he was running on more than the desire to beat Hoyt for himself. He wanted it for his friends, for the bet he'd made on their behalf, for the safety of the surface world and Ponderay below.

He wanted it more than anything in the entire Core.

He reached the top and grabbed a Tile. A bell sounded, announcing one point for Hydra.

Now I just have to jump to another pillar while this thing is moving.

Albert looked up. Across from him, Slink grabbed a Tile. The bell clanged, a point for Argon.

On and on it went. Clang after clang, point after point, until all ten Tiles were taken. The Pit calmed, but the pillars didn't stop spinning entirely.

"It's time for Round Two!" Hoyt shouted from across the Pit. He leaped from a pillar, did a front flip, and landed in the waves beside Slink and Mo.

Albert joined Birdie and Leroy, and they compared Tiles.

"I got three," Albert said. Birdie held up one, and Leroy held up another.

"That's five for us!" Leroy said.

Birdie squealed with excitement. "That means Argon has the other five. We're tied! We still have a chance to win this!"

Albert felt the familiar buzz of adrenaline that came from being one step closer to winning. But the competition wasn't over yet. They still had to beat Argon in the second round.

He turned and looked across the Pit, past the spinning pillars. "We're tied!" Albert shouted to Argon. "Forget about a new set of Tiles. Whoever plugs in their five Tiles first is the winner!"

"You're going down, Hydra!" Hoyt shouted.

The second half of the competition began.

Both teams dove into the waves. Hydra swam with a fury they hadn't before. Albert and Birdie held Leroy in between them, and in a matter of seconds, they'd managed to fling him onto a pillar.

Suddenly, the direction changed again.

"Hang on, Leroy!" Albert shouted.

Leroy's fingertips were white, but somehow, he managed to keep his grip even as the momentum from the direction change threw him around like a rag doll.

Albert and Birdie avoided the tidal wave that came toward them. They separated, and Albert's heart was pounding like a jackhammer by the time he hauled himself onto his pillar. He climbed, breathlessly, toward the top, and with one final burst of energy, pulled himself up. But he couldn't get to his feet. Not with the wind, and not with how fast the pillars were spinning.

Even Hoyt was having trouble. He tried to make the leap from one pillar to another, but the wind knocked him off course, and he was catapulted into the side of the Pit.

Albert closed his eyes and perched on top of his pillar like a bird. But he couldn't think of a single Tile symbol that would help him here—Speed, Strength, Balance. Nothing would help him defeat the wind.

He tried to jump anyway. All that he accomplished was getting a fat bloody lip and a big splash into the waters below.

The fight went on.

Thirty minutes passed.

The teams were neck and neck. Hydra and Argon had each plugged three Tiles into slots.

Somehow, doing the same pattern over and over again, Albert, Birdie, and Leroy were keeping a steady scoring pace. They were working as an efficient team, but if they wanted to win, they'd have to really pull ahead.

They'd have to do something crazy.

Clang! Albert looked up and saw Mo plug a fourth Tile in place.

"We're not moving fast enough!" Albert shouted to Birdie as they swim in circles, trying to launch Leroy onto another pillar again. "If they plug in their fifth Tile before us, they win!"

"What are we supposed to do, sprout fins or wings?" Birdie shouted.

"I don't even know if that's possible!" Albert shouted back.

They launched Leroy onto his pillar, and Birdie shot ahead and grabbed on, too.

"I'll stay here with him and we'll work on this Tile together," Birdie shouted as they sped away.

Albert found his own pillar. He was exhausted. Albert climbed with everything he had, using Strength, but his mind was growing weak now. His limbs were trembling like leaves, and he just couldn't stay focused on the Master Tile symbols.

"Give up now, Flynn!" Hoyt shouted from his perch on a pillar.

It gave Albert just enough fury to climb up, plug in Hydra's fourth Tile, and slide back down into the water.

Now they were even again. Albert dove into the waves where Birdie and Leroy were waiting, the Tile still in Leroy's hand.

"Come on!" Birdie cried out.

"We'll finish this together!" Leroy shouted.

But Albert had other ideas. He had the Master Tile, and the power to finish this before Argon could. "Give me the last Tile!" Albert shouted. "I can do it!"

Birdie looked nervous, but she tossed it to him. He caught it and tucked it in his waistband.

He tried to swim fast. He pictured the water droplet in his mind, but it kept flickering, like those times the power started to go out in his mom's apartment, and the TV screen wouldn't keep a clear picture.

No. I can't give up now, Albert thought. *I have to win*. He clenched his teeth so hard he accidentally bit his tongue and tasted blood. His hands were throbbing from gripping the pillars so tight, and his lip was swollen beyond belief.

Albert was *just* able to get his Master Tile to harness the power of the water droplet, when he saw a flash of orange overhead. He looked up as Hoyt, Slink, and Mo stood on the tops of three pillars. They were all holding hands, using one another for support.

Albert gasped as they leaped as one unit.

And landed, somehow, on three separate pillars.

They stooped down, and Hoyt plugged in the final Tile for Argon.

Clang!

The pillars suddenly stopped spinning. The wind died down, and the water began to disappear, draining into the bottom of the Pit.

Albert gasped, all of the strength going out of him, as

he saw the glowing leaderboard overhead, on the rocky side of the Pit.

Hydra had nine points.

Argon had ten.

Hoyt's team had won, and Hydra had lost the bet.

Five minutes later, the Pit was back to normal, and Hydra and Argon made their way out. Everyone was so exhausted that Argon hadn't even celebrated with their usual whoops and hollers.

"Remember our bet" was all Hoyt said to Albert as the two teams separated.

Albert nodded, lost in his thoughts, as Argon took the pathway down from the Pit and faded away into darkness.

Albert was shocked, not because of the loss, but because Argon had done something Hydra hadn't. They'd figured out how to work as a real team with the way they'd linked up arms and done the final steps together. Hydra had worked together in the water, but not on the pillars. With their victory today, Argon had proven themselves worthy of defeating the Pit, fair and square, no lying or cheating necessary.

Albert left the Pit in a daze, with Birdie and Leroy hot on his heels. Farnsworth didn't even run. His ears dragged across the dusty floor, and his eye lights were dimmer than a dying candle.

Hydra didn't speak, not even after they'd all gone to

their dorms, changed clothes, and met back up in the Main Chamber.

It was Petra who found them, sitting silently on the edge of the Ponderay stream, staring at the glowing numbers on the clock. Time was nearly up.

"Come on," Petra said. He forced Hydra onto their feet. "You need a morale boost."

The group headed to Petra's secret float room, where they helped him patch together a few final touches on the Guildacker. Farnsworth perched on top of the float, gnawing on one of his favorite blue bones.

"I just don't get it!" Birdie was saying. "We've done everything we could've done last year. How are they beating us?" She slammed her fist on the Guildacker's head, and a gold coin fell off, clattering to a stop on the stone floor far below.

"Oops, sorry, Petra!" Birdie climbed down and scooped up the coin.

"No worries," Petra called from the wing. "The parade isn't for a few days. I've got time to fix things."

He was lacing together more of that crazy moss, wearing thick black gloves so it wouldn't affect his skin. Leroy was glaring at the moss like he wanted to stab it. Apparently, he still hadn't forgiven it for his balloon hand last term. Birdie was back on top of the Guildacker, and she suddenly groaned and punched its head. The misplaced coin wasn't sticking. Leroy noticed her struggle to fix it, and climbed up to her. He patiently showed her how to do it the right way.

It struck Albert, as he watched his friends working together from below, that he loved these people, and he didn't blame them for losing today. That was when something sparked to life in Albert's mind.

Something that hadn't really hit him yet.

"They're good," Albert said. "Apparently, even better than us."

"Don't say that! You're just panicked," Birdie gasped, but Albert was as cool as a cucumber. He'd come to terms with the loss. He'd sat there in silence for hours, analyzing what had happened. And now he knew.

"It's true, guys." Albert leaned forward onto his knees and sighed. "We did a good job today. Really good, and we all know it. And we were good last term. Great, actually."

"The best," Birdie and Leroy said together, and Petra nodded along.

"But not this term," Albert said. "Things have changed. Hoyt might be a pig-faced jerk, but his team's got skill. They've improved a *lot*. Maybe, if we can forget about trying to *beat* them and just focus on doing the best we can as a team, playing to our strengths like we did in Calderon, maybe it'll make a difference."

It made perfect sense. In the Pit, all Albert had been doing was stress, stress, and stress some more. To him, it was about proving a point. Beating Hoyt's team just so he could be a winner.

But that wasn't the way it should be.

Being a Balance Keeper was about bravery and having heart, working together as a team, even when it seemed impossible to win or keep going. It wasn't about pride. It was about teamwork.

"Maybe we just need to start fresh," Albert said. "Let's go to the Pit tomorrow and forget about winning. Let's just have some fun and enjoy being Balance Keepers."

"Albert's right," Petra squeaked. His face was covered in oil and sweat, but his smile was as bright as ever. "You guys need to stop worrying so much. Just have fun. I'd do anything to be a Balance Keeper."

"I'd do anything to be such a good sculptor." Leroy smiled, popping the last of a peanut butter and jelly sandwich into his mouth.

Petra put the finishing touches on the Guildacker's wings. They glowed magnificently. It was so realistic that Albert almost thought the float might fly away into the Main Chamber.

"Yeah, you're amazing Petra," Albert added, and Birdie also sang his praises.

"Thanks, guys." Petra's face instantly grew red. But he recovered quickly. "So, I love hanging out with you guys and all, but if I were you, I'd go get some rest. You're going to need it toni—I mean tomorrow," he quickly corrected. His face grew red all over again.

"Do you know something we don't, Petra?" Albert asked. Petra had that mischievous gleam in his eyes.

"Nope! Don't know anything!" Petra gave them a quick thumbs-up, then disappeared beneath the float to work on the gears. "See you later!"

Albert shrugged. Maybe Petra was as weird as he'd always been and they'd just gotten used to him. It made Albert smile.

Farnsworth led the way back, scurrying across the Main Chamber. Even with today's loss, and the impending doom of Ponderay, Albert noticed a change in the Core. Everyone was gearing up for the big Float Parade. The Core workers were on towering, wobbly copper ladders, stringing lights and garlands across the chandelier and the steaming pipes overhead. It was a welcome distraction to everything going on in the Imbalanced Realm.

Even the CoreFish was out tonight, giving kids free rides on its back in the streams below, making clicking noises like a happy dolphin. Overhead, Jadar soared across the crowd, screeching with glee as he chased a giant purple butterfly.

"He's adorable," Birdie sighed, watching her companion as they crossed over a bridge.

"Adorable? More like adoraNOT," Leroy yelped.

CHAPTER 18

The Core Hunt

That night Albert finally got the good sleep he'd been so desperate for. His eyes closed as soon as his head hit the pillow. He had no dreams, just blissful, beautiful sleep . . . and it was soon ruined by the bright beam of a flashlight right over Albert's face.

"Farnsworth," he groaned, putting his arm over his eyes.

"I'm not your dog, weirdo!" a boy's voice said. Someone nudged Albert's shoulder. "Get up!"

Albert opened his eyes, and saw that Jack was standing over him. He was wearing all black, and he had camo paint on his face, making him look like some kind of soldier.

"What time is it?" Albert said, wiping the sleep from his eyes.

Across from him, a dark-haired Pure guy who Albert remembered was training for Belltroll last term, Rick, was waking up Leroy.

"It's time for the best tradition of the season," Jack said, hauling Albert out of bed.

"I thought the Float Parade wasn't for another couple of days," Albert said.

Jack smiled, his eyes bright like he knew a secret. "That's a great tradition, but this one is *secret*. Usually, it's for Pure Balance Keepers only. But since you and your team came all this way, you get to join in the fun."

"And," Rick said, arms crossed over his chest, "it's dangerous."

"Oh, perfect," Leroy groaned, pulling a sweatshirt over his head. "Danger is *just* what I was hoping for at three o'clock in the morning."

The boys laughed, and Albert and Leroy had no choice but to follow them out into the darkness of night.

The Library was dark and cold when they arrived. Albert could almost imagine the whispers of all the thousands of books around him, the stories just waiting to be read. Some of the torches on the walls were still flickering, but most had gone out. Lucinda's Core Canteen was dark, with a chain-link barrier pulled down so sneaky Balance Keepers couldn't go inside and steal things when she wasn't looking.

They made their way toward the back of the Library,

filing inside the Tiles competition room.

"If it's a game of Tiles, then things are about to get interesting," Leroy said.

The room was already packed with Pure Balance Keepers when they arrived. Birdie sat with a cluster of girls in the corner, her feet covered in fuzzy pink bunny slippers. They even had floppy ears.

"Nice footwear." Albert nudged her with a wry grin as he came up next to her.

"Hey, they're not as goofy as that bed head you boys are sporting," Birdie said with confidence, as Leroy helped her to her feet.

The conversation fell silent as the Apprentices appeared. Trey was in the lead. Albert smiled and waved. Trey didn't wave back. Instead, he appraised Hydra with a strange sort of stiffness in his posture. It was like he was uncomfortable to even be near them.

"Seriously, what's his problem?" Birdie hissed.

Albert shrugged. "Beats me."

"What you're about to enter into is extremely secret," Trey said, and though he was talking to everyone, Albert felt like he was aiming the words right at Hydra. "Due to special circumstances, a few surface Balance Keepers will be joining us this year. If you feel like you can keep this secret, raise your Tile in the air."

Everyone did as he asked. Albert lifted his Master Tile high. Trey's eyes fell onto it, and he glared, then looked back at everyone else. "All right. Now swear on it."

"I swear!" Albert, Birdie, and Leroy said together.

Trey, Tussy, and Fox, the male Apprentice for Bell-troll, all raised their own Tiles as well.

"Good," Trey said. "Now get ready for the best night of your lives. This is the Core Hunt."

The room filled with whispers. But when Trey held up a hand, everyone fell silent again.

"Tussy, the box, please," he said.

Tussy held out a box wrapped in thick white cloth. When Trey unwrapped it, everyone was standing on tiptoe to get a better look. Albert gave himself a little advantage, using Flight Vision (which looked like a bird's wings), to help him see over the crowd.

The box was old and wooden, not much larger than a textbook. Trey opened the lid and dust filled the air, dancing like little fairies. "In this box," he said, "are fifty Tiles. Special ones, with powers you have yet to experience."

He angled the box just a little, and now Albert could see inside. There were lots of Tiles, indeed, all different colors. He wanted so badly to get up and go to the box to see better. Albert didn't have much use for the special Tiles, not with his Master Tile, but Birdie and Leroy could really benefit from them. Trey snapped the lid shut.

Tussy stood a little taller. Her scratched and bruised face was proud, and Albert realized that even at three in the morning, she seemed ready for action. He wanted to be like Tussy, someone who looked, at all times, like a champion of the Core.

Tussy raised her voice. "Whoever finds this box will own these Tiles for the remainder of this term. And believe me. You'll want these Tiles on your side in the training Pit. I'm looking at you, Hydra and Argon."

Trey handed the box to Tussy, who handed it off to Fox. The tall Apprentice left the room with the box cradled in his arms like an infant. Everyone watched him leave with hungry eyes.

When the door closed behind Fox, Trey called their attention back to the front of the room and nodded at Tussy.

"There are no real rules," Tussy said. "If you choose to play dirty, then so be it. Just please, don't kill anyone. There's already enough drama going on in the Core to add a death to the list."

Everyone exchanged nervous glances and anxious laughs.

"You'll stick to your Pit teams," Tussy said. "Be creative and smart in your search. The box could be anywhere in the Core."

"What do we do when we find it?" Birdie asked.

Trey laughed. "You run like the wind, and hope no one tackles you for it. Whoever gets the box back to this room first wins. Oh, and don't get caught by any Professors. Detention, for anyone out past dark, as always."

The Balance Keepers sat around waiting for at least twenty minutes, while Fox hid the box of Tiles somewhere inside the Core. Someone tried to start up a game of Tiles, but nerves were high, and the game fizzled out. Plus, no one wanted to compete against Leroy. It was a losing battle from the start.

"I can't believe they've been doing this game all along, and we never knew," Birdie said to the boys.

Leroy shrugged. "It makes sense, though, that full-time Core people would have their own special traditions."

"He's right," Albert said. "It's pretty cool of them to let us join in. Finally, we'll get to have some real fun."

Fox came back. There was a glow of mischief in his eyes. "It's time."

Trey nodded, then surveyed the room. "Balance Keepers, are you ready?"

"Ready!" Albert, Birdie, Leroy, and the rest of the room called out.

Even without the regular amount of students, their voices were still as loud as the roar of an army, and suddenly it hit Albert: the Core *was* an army, with soldiers training to defend their homes both here and on the surface. Whoever had set the Imbalance was going to have a difficult time winning in the end.

While everyone else ran off to search the Core, Albert, Birdie, and Leroy stayed in the small room strategizing.

"We could go check the Pit," Birdie offered. "I bet they'd place the box in some sort of extreme Balance Keeper challenge."

"We could," Albert said. "But don't you think that's

where everyone else might go?"

Leroy nodded, leaning back onto his elbows. "It's where everyone will look."

"So then we should look in the last place they'd expect us to." Albert chewed on his bottom lip. Leroy was grinning like a maniac. Albert sensed that Leroy already had the answer; he was just waiting for Albert to catch on. He tried to think like someone with a Synapse Tile would.

"The Library!"

Birdie nodded. "Of course! They'd put it right here. While everyone else is out scouring the entire Core, it's probably just sitting on a bookshelf somewhere close by, waiting for us to grab it."

Leroy laughed. "Maybe my smartness is rubbing off on you guys." Farnsworth growled and tugged at Leroy's bootlace. "But of course you've always been the smartest one, little guy."

They set off through the Library with Farnsworth's eyes guiding their way. The rows of shelves towered as tall as the pillars in the Pit, old oak and metal somehow melded together. There had to be at least thirty rows, and as they walked past them, Albert couldn't help but picture ghosts or ghouls hiding in the shadows.

"Maybe we should check somewhere besides the shelves," he said.

"Like the tallest part of the Library?" Birdie asked.

That highest place in the Library wasn't a bookshelf at all. It was the rock-climbing wall with the zip line that Albert loved so much.

The three of them headed that way. Albert didn't need his Tile powers for climbing the familiar rock wall, and Birdie was right on his heels. Leroy, having gotten braver at this kind of thing since last term, was even laughing as he scaled the jagged surface.

Albert reached the top first. It was just a few feet across, room for a couple of kids to sit on top and dangle their legs over the side. The box wasn't here.

"Dang," Albert said. "Well, it was worth a try."

Birdie came up behind him and sat down, breathing hard. "You know what we have to do now, right?"

Albert grinned. "If you say zip line back down, I'll be your best friend."

Leroy came up behind them. "She already *is* our best friend, bonehead."

Birdie grabbed the T-shaped handle of the zip line and held on tight. "See you on the other side, boys!" With a giggle and a bend of her knees, she leaped from the top of the wall.

The zip line made a *zing!* noise as it carried Birdie away. When she reached the bottom, she turned a crank that sent the handle all the way back up.

"Go on then, Leroy." Albert nudged him.

Leroy swallowed, hard. "If I die, return my glasses and hat to my mother. And make sure there's cake at my funeral."

"Chocolate or vanilla?"

"Both," Leroy said. "And strawberry, for good measure."

Leroy bent his knees and leaped. "Yeehaw!" He was so long and lanky that his feet touched the ground way before Birdie's had, and from up so high, Albert was pleased to hear that Leroy was actually laughing.

He *had* gotten braver, that was for sure. Last term he never would've done that.

Albert waited for the crank to bring the zip line handle back. Up so high, he felt like he was on Calderon Peak, back in the Realm. He looked around the darkened Library like he was a king and all the books were the people of his kingdom.

The handle made it up to him. Albert had turned, grabbed ahold, and prepared to jump, when a shadow caught his eye.

It was someone ducking into the rows of bookshelves far below. It looked like a man, the figure tall and strong. But the figure was alone. It couldn't be someone competing in the Core Hunt. They'd be with a team.

Albert shivered. For days now, he'd felt like he was being followed or spied on. Could the shadow be the same person?

There was only one way to find out. He turned, clutching tight to the handle, and leaped from the rock wall.

CHAPTER 19

The Book of Bad Tiles

"I know I saw someone go back here, guys," Albert said, as he and his friends walked down the final row of bookshelves. They had all been empty so far, and Albert was starting to feel like a fool for ninja-rolling around the darkened corners with Leroy.

"There isn't anyone in here except for us," Birdie said, reaching out to catch Leroy as he tripped over his own feet.

Leroy brushed himself off and straightened his shoulders and hat like nothing had happened. "Dudes, if there was anyone here but us, Farnsworth would've barked. Right, buddy?"

Farnsworth yipped, his little tail wagging as he walked in front of them, a fearless leader.

"You're probably right," Albert said. "But I can't shake the feeling that someone's been spying on us. And what's up with Trey lately? He seems like he hates us now."

"He helped you the other day, by telling you about Professor Asante's office," Birdie replied.

Albert thought on that. "Yeah, but he also didn't think to warn us that she might be in there waiting to catch us!"

Leroy nodded. "Statistically speaking, we should have thought of that ourselves."

They reached the end of the last row of shelves. And that was when Albert smelled it.

Mint and cloves.

He'd smelled the minty scent before, in the hallway outside of Professor Asante's office. And the first night he'd come back to the Core. And again, just now. Albert shelved that into his mental library for further investigation.

"If I were a box of Tiles," Birdie said, plucking a book from the shelf, "where would I hide?"

Albert yawned and stretched his arms and his neck, staring up at the tops of the shelves. Just then, Farnsworth decided to mimic Albert, stretching his little furry back so that his eyes shone into the rafters of the room.

A glint of something silver caught Albert's eye.

"Look!" Albert pointed. "There's something up there! On the top shelf, in between those two big books!"

"No way," Birdie gasped, scooting in closer to Albert so she could see where he was pointing. She squinted hard. "I think there *is* something!"

Leroy yawned. "I'd love to help out and all, but if it requires climbing up a super-old, super-rickety bookshelf that's 57.07 feet high, then no way. You two go ahead. I'll stay here with Farnsworth and stand guard."

Birdie tapped the bill of Leroy's hat. "You're coming, Memory Boy, and that's final."

Seven minutes later, Albert, Birdie, and Leroy reached the top of the bookshelf. They had all almost fallen not once, but twice, catching their boots on the corners of old books. Leroy was whining like a toddler, but Albert loved it. The climb made him feel alive, and he lived for the thrill of the chase. He stopped climbing when he reached the shelf on which he'd seen the flash of silver.

Dust filled his nostrils as he reached up, stretching to try and grab what was hidden there.

"Can you get it?" Birdie asked.

"I'm not tall enough. I could maybe use the Stretch symbol—" Albert suggested, but Leroy stopped him.

"It's time to be a man and use what my mama gave me." He nodded down at his long arms as he clutched the shelf. "These babies were made for this moment."

Albert shrugged, then scooted aside so Leroy could do his thing. It took a few tries. There was a book in the way, a heavy old one that tumbled over the edge of the shelf, narrowly missing Farnsworth as it crashed onto the ground far below.

"Sorry!" Albert, Birdie, and Leroy called down.

Farnsworth growled and immediately started to gnaw on the book.

Finally, Leroy yelped. "Got something!"

His legs were shaking, and he was only holding on to the shelf with one hand, but Albert was filled with pride, watching his friend do something so dangerous. Slowly, Leroy removed an old, wooden box from the topmost shelf.

"Careful!" Birdie warned. "Don't drop it."

Leroy winced. "Someone take it, or I'm totally gonna!"

Albert reached out, snagging the box just in time. It was covered in dust, and he sneezed, but refused to drop it.

They headed back to the ground slowly. It was dangerous work, but Albert gave himself a little help with a Balance symbol and his Master Tile.

His feet touched the ground. Birdie and Leroy landed beside him, and Albert set the box on the floor between them.

"A little light, Farnsworth?" Albert asked. He couldn't wait to see what Tiles were inside. Birdie and Leroy were going to have a blast using them in the Pit.

The dog shone his high beams onto it. When they all looked down, their eyes widened.

It wasn't the box they were expecting it to be.

This box was old oak with silver accents, something that was probably beautiful once. But half of it was blackened, almost as if a part of it had been burned in a fire.

"What the heck is that?" Leroy gulped.

"It's definitely not the box Trey was holding," Birdie added.

"There's only one way to find out," Albert said, as he reached down, slowly. "Let's open it."

His fingers shook as he lifted the tiny locking mechanism on the box. It popped open, and the lid rose without a sound.

A small leather journal sat inside. It was soft, supple leather, black as oil. Albert lifted it out carefully. The box was old, covered in dust when they'd found it. But the journal looked fresh, almost as if someone had opened it recently.

"Should we read it?" Albert asked. His voice was a whisper, and he didn't quite know why.

"Of course we should," Birdie said, nodding. "There's *loads* of secrets in journals. One time, I read my mom's journal. It was hidden in her nightstand, and I found out that . . ."

"Birdie." Leroy cut her off. "This isn't social hour."

Albert couldn't explain why. But he felt a strange sense of darkness blooming in his chest as he held the journal. He flipped open to the first page.

It was full of Tile symbols, much like the Black Book.
But these symbols were very, very strange indeed.

"This one shows you how to silence a person, even
if they're screaming at the top of their lungs," Leroy
pointed out. The symbol was a hand covering a mouth.

"And this one," Birdie said, tapping a symbol that
looked like a handheld mirror, "will fool someone into
thinking you look like their most trusted friend."

Albert pointed at another symbol, one that gave its
user the ability to lie with perfect ease. Suddenly his
stomach lurched.

These weren't normal Core powers. These were useful
things, very useful, but only to someone with a certain
type of wickedness in their heart.

He dropped the journal back into the box and slammed
the lid shut.

"These are bad symbols," Albert whispered. "Can't
you feel it?"

It was like the air around them had grown cold, like
they were sitting in the bottom of the training Pit.

Birdie shivered, then pointed at the box. "Who does
it belong to?"

No one answered, because no one knew.

"We should destroy it," Leroy said. "I don't want that
journal falling into the wrong hands. Could you imagine
if someone like Hoyt found it?"

"That's true," Albert said. "But most Balance Keepers

can only do what their Tile allows them to do."

Birdie gasped. "Unless they have one like yours, Albert. Just imagine the possibilities. That could be really, really bad." Her eyes were wide with fear.

Albert knew it was possible, and suddenly a memory resurfaced in his mind. Last term, when they'd found the Black Book, there had been a page torn out of the back. Did it have something to do with this journal? Could the person who ripped out the page in the Black Book also be the person who owned this journal? And could that person actually have a second Master Tile?

Albert shivered at the very thought of it.

The Professors hadn't seen a Master Tile in centuries. Surely, if they had, they would've said something to Albert. It wasn't a big secret. Everyone in the Core knew about his Tile. Everyone was amazed by it.

"I don't believe there's someone out there who'd want to use these horrible symbols," Albert said. He motioned to the black box.

"Except for the person who set up the Imbalances," Leroy whispered.

His words hit Albert right in the gut. Had they just come across evidence that could help the Professors discover their enemy? Then another thought occurred to Albert, one that he felt guilty just thinking, let alone saying aloud. "What if one of the *Professors* was the one who created the Imbalance? Think about it. They're the most talented people in the Core. They know everything about the Realms."

Birdie shifted from one foot to another. "I don't think so, Albert. They defend the Core."

"But it's the perfect cover," Leroy said. "No one would suspect them."

Birdie held up a hand. "We're jumping to conclusions. Right now, we need to focus on this Book of Bad Tiles."

"Birdie's right," Albert said. "The book exists. Someone wrote these things in it. Someone knows how to use them. Hey, maybe we could even catch them in the act and save the day."

Albert had meant it as a joke, but suddenly Leroy stiffened. "We could," he whispered.

Leroy and Birdie leaned in to hear his plan.

Leroy explained that there was a pair of special Tiles in Lucinda's shop. They were Homing Tiles, sold at a very high price. One Tile was to be worn around someone's neck at all times. The other Tile was to be hidden with whatever someone wanted to track. When the Homing Tile sensed the object or person moving location, it would alert the Tile that was around the wearer's neck.

It was the perfect plan. From what Leroy had gathered, no one had come to check out those top-shelf books in months. If motion was detected, it was likely it would be the owner of the blackened box retrieving their secret treasure.

"I can start playing more Tiles competitions again,"

Leroy suggested. "We all know I'll win, and we could save up enough coins to buy the Homing Tiles from the shop."

"That's brilliant, Leroy!" Birdie clapped her hands. "Albert, what do you think?"

Albert shuddered. The right thing to do would be to take the box to his dad's office. He could feel it. But with all of the trouble going on inside the Core, maybe handing over this box would just cause more stress for the Professors. Albert remembered the Path Hider's warning, from their first day back.

Trust no one.

Albert trusted his dad, wholeheartedly. But he didn't want to bog Professor Flynn down with more troubles.

"We can try the Homing Tiles," Albert decided. "But if anything else goes wrong, we should turn the box in."

"This is like a total sting operation!" Birdie giggled.

"A what?" Leroy's eyes were wide.

"You know, like those cop shows, where they set up the criminal and catch him in the act."

They fantasized about saving the day, outsmarting the person causing all of the Imbalances. Leroy climbed back to the top of the bookshelf, dust dancing around him, and put the box with the Book of Bad Tiles back where they'd found it. He even covered it up in dust again, so it looked like no one had touched it.

"We'll get the Homing Tiles soon," Leroy promised. "And we'll settle this once and for all. Imagine going into the Realm and settling the Imbalance, then catching this guy in the act when we get back. We'd be heroes for sure, dudes."

They laughed as they headed from the shelves with smiles on their faces and hope in their hearts.

They didn't know that someone had seen everything, watching from the shadows in silence.

Farnsworth led the way back, with his little paws padding on the hard floor. They'd barely made it out of the Library when shouts rang out from the hallway. The double doors burst open, and Balance Keepers sprinted inside.

It was Hoyt, Slink, and Mo. Hoyt held the box over his head, laughing as a few other teams chased him, trying to steal it before he reached home base. But Argon made it, winning the Core Hunt. Another thing to raise Hoyt's ego. It was so big by now, Albert wouldn't be surprised if it burst.

Hydra stuck around as the Apprentices came back and announced Argon winner. Everyone left, ready to get a few hours of sleep before the Pit tomorrow.

On their way back through the Main Chamber, Albert stopped to glance up at the countdown clock.

The glowing number *36* shone down on him, as red as blood.

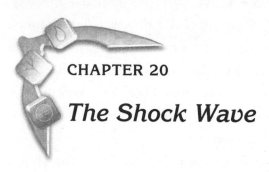

CHAPTER 20

The Shock Wave

The next day, it seemed that luck was finally on Hydra's side. When they arrived in the Pit and rode their platform down, everything looked as it normally had in the days before. It was the same towering ten pillars, same freezing-cold water and dangerous hurricane-worthy wind.

Professor Asante was present for this competition, sitting on the edge of the Pit in her wheelchair, a notebook in her lap, a pen poised and ready to scribble furiously. There was a massive crowd today. It seemed that every Pure and worker in the Core had come to watch the competition. Albert swallowed a lump in his throat.

Even his dad was there watching, which made Albert happy. As long as Professor Flynn wasn't in Ponderay, he was safe. Trey sat beside him. As was usual lately, Trey was furiously flipping through a stack of papers. *What's all that about?* Albert wondered. Petra was in the very front row, and today he was wearing a blue shirt to match Hydra's, though it looked like he'd written the logo himself. Farnsworth raced across the edge of the Pit and leaped into Petra's lap.

Tussy sat beside Petra, and when she saw Hydra arrive, she stood and walked to the edge of the Pit. Albert noticed that her shoulder was bandaged. Her hair was messy in that just-been-to-the-beach sort of way that girls always seemed to covet. Albert had a feeling the state of Tussy's hair wasn't a fashion statement, though, and he was right.

"Balance Keepers—as you know, since Professor Asante injured her leg, Professor Flynn and I have been entering Ponderay in her place, seeking to learn more about the Means to Restore Balance." Tussy lowered the MegaHorn, as if her arm needed a rest from just holding it up. She took a deep breath and continued.

"Early this morning, we made it farther than Professor Asante did." Tussy shot a quick glance at Professor Asante and quickly added, "Though we couldn't have made it this far without her efforts before us."

Professor Asante nodded and Tussy continued.

"This morning, we made it across the Silver Sea and summited two of the Pillars."

There was a gasp in the crowd. Albert shared a look with Birdie and Leroy. No wonder Tussy was tired. And his *dad* had actually been on *top* of the Ten Pillars? He suddenly had an image of his dad's sparkling green jacket flying out behind him like a cape in the winds of Ponderay. It was a funny and scary image at the same time.

"Professor Flynn and I further confirmed something Professor Asante and the Watchers had suspected—the Tiles on top of the Pillars are marked. The two we found each had a different symbol than the rectangle Professor Asante found—we are now confident that each of the ten Tiles has a different symbol." She held up one of the Pit Tiles, which now had a blue triangle on it, then quickly lowered it, again like she hardly had strength to hold it up. Professor Flynn took over.

"On a hunch, Tussy and I traded two of the Tiles in their Pillar slots, and we think we felt the rotations of the Pillars slow just a bit. That's all we were able to do, though, before the creatures became so aggressive we thought it best to turn back. The work is too much, and far too dangerous, for only two people."

Leroy leaned over to Albert. "Maybe them switching up two Tiles is why the tremors off the coast of California have calmed this morning."

Albert nodded, eager for them to go on.

"We are now assuming," his dad continued, "that each Tile is marked with a symbol that somehow matches each Pillar, and that correctly placing each Tile in its appropriate Pillar will stop the spinning. We believe this matching of Tile and Pillars is the Means to Restore Balance."

There was a murmur in the crowd, a collective sigh of relief. Albert felt a weight off his own shoulders—at least now they knew what they'd have to do if they entered Ponderay.

"Your challenge today, Balance Keepers, is to gather the Tiles on top of each pillar and put them into the matching slots, eventually stopping the spinning. The team who matches the most Tiles with pillars will win, earning ten points. We've marked each Tile, as well as each Pillar. However, since we still don't know how the Ten Pillars are marked, we're not telling you how we've marked these Pit pillars. You'll need your best observation skills in Ponderay to figure that out—it would be wise to start using those skills now." Professor Flynn took a deep breath. Albert could tell he, too, was exhausted from his time in the Realm. He knew from last term that Professors' and Apprentices' bodies weren't fit to handle too much time in the Realms. They were both bound to the Core, and as a result, lost a great deal of their strength once they entered the Realms.

"As Professor Asante, Tussy, and I have discovered, the conditions in Ponderay are brutal—time will be of the essence. You'll have seven minutes to collectively match at least five Tiles today. If you fail, the Pit and the clock will reset, and you'll begin again."

"How is that helpful?!" Birdie asked under her breath, loud enough for Albert to hear. "They'll completely exhaust us!"

Albert just shrugged. It looked like they better get used to being exhausted.

Tussy, who had sat down, handed Professor Flynn her whistle. He took another deep breath, brought the whistle to his lips, and blew it. The competition began.

Water filled the Pit, and Albert had the sinking suspicion that the Core creatures were already beneath the surface, ready and waiting to stop any Balance Keeper from completing their task. Normally, Albert took the lead. But this wasn't just about strength or skill. Today, this was about logic.

Birdie was already on it. "I say we gather the Tiles and then put them in different pillars and hope it works out."

. . . Or maybe Birdie *wasn't* on it.

"That'll take forever," Albert said. "We've only got seven minutes. Leroy, you're our Boy Einstein. What's your plan?"

"I know exactly how to start," Leroy said, a huge grin on his face. He wiped off his glasses as water splashed around them in the wind. "The pillars have very, very tiny marks, on their sides, here at the bottom, in colors and shapes. I saw them before the pillars started spinning, right when we got here. It'll be difficult now to decipher the marks at the speed those pillars are moving. But we can do it."

Birdie and Albert just stared at Leroy. Not a minute into the challenge and he'd already figured out the system for matching Tiles—unbelievable! Albert wondered why he himself hadn't decided to just picture the Synapse symbol 100 percent of the time so he could share Leroy's mad mental skills. He made a note to use that symbol more often. For now, he sprang into action.

"I say we do what we did the other day. Use Birdie's Water Tile and my Master Tile to get up to speed, and allow Leroy to see the colored markings on the sides of the pillars. Sound like a plan?"

"Yes! And then we can all climb up and match the colored Tiles to their correct pillars!" Birdie exclaimed. She put her arms around the boys' shoulders. "You two ready to rock this?"

Leroy nodded. "I thought you'd never ask."

Albert looked at the clock. A minute had already passed. It was time to speed things up.

They set to work, swimming up to top speed, Albert with his Master Tile and the water droplet symbol in his mind, Birdie with her natural Water Tile abilities. They did exactly what they'd done the last time they were in the Pit. Albert swam on one side, and Birdie swam on the other, with Leroy in the middle. They were like a pod of dolphins racing as fast as their fins could take them.

They were almost close enough to a pillar for Leroy to make out the marking when a fin appeared in the waves. It was a Hammerfin, and the creature chased Hydra round and round the Pit. They lost almost a full minute trying to avoid the giant creature. Finally, the Hammerfin seemed to lose interest and they got back to swimming as fast as they could go in hopes of deciphering which symbols were on each pillar.

"Go, Hydra, go!" Petra cheered from above. Some people joined in with him, while others rooted for Argon. Farnsworth howled, and Albert saw a familiar flash of blue as his dog's eyes lit up.

Focus, Albert. Instead of launching Leroy onto a pillar like last time, when Hydra got close enough, Leroy simply looked for the colored marking on the pillars' stony side.

The first pillar was a yellow triangle.

The second was a blue rhombus, and the third was a purple circle.

On and on Albert and Birdie swam, carrying Leroy to each pillar so he could decipher and remember their individual marks. Leroy plotted them on a map in his mind.

"I love your Synapse Tile!" Birdie shouted to Leroy, as Tussy yelled *five minutes left.*

Suddenly, there was a flash of color, and Birdie yelped.

"I think a Lightning Ray just got me! I can't feel my left foot!"

Her speed slowed a little, and Albert was forced to take on more of the weight. The disruption distracted him and he looked around to see what Argon was doing. *Where was Hoyt? How far ahead were they? Had Argon figured out how the pillars were marked yet?*

But Albert silenced his mind and told himself this was about Hydra, not the other team. Today, he committed to focusing *only* on the task and his teammates. Nothing else mattered.

By the time Tussy had yelled out *four minutes left*, Leroy had managed to note down all of the colored markings on the pillars.

"Time to climb!" Albert shouted to his friends.

They treaded water as the pillars spun by. Hoyt, Slink, and Mo were blurs at the top of the pillars as they passed at breakneck speeds.

Albert and Birdie took off with Leroy in the middle again, and launched him onto a pillar. Then they started the climb.

Albert's hands and feet seemed to know what to do on their own. They found all the right holds, and in record time, he'd summited the first pillar.

"Three minutes left!" Tussy shouted.

We're running out of time! Albert thought. Nerves seeped their way into his system, but he shook them off and hauled himself up and onto the top of his pillar. He rose to a crouch. The wind blasted him in the face, and threatened to knock him overboard. But he wouldn't let it.

Today, Hydra was going to win.

Across from him, Birdie summited, and Leroy soon after. They all looked at one another.

"Grab a Tile!" Albert shouted.

They all grabbed the Tiles from their pillars. Across from Albert, Hoyt climbed on top of a pillar and grabbed a Tile of his own. He held it in the air and waved it around, a look of pure elation in his eyes. Then his face fell as he realized he had no idea what to do with the Tile—Argon still hadn't figured out how the pillars were marked. Albert smiled.

He turned to where Birdie was crouched on a pillar across from him.

He closed his eyes and pictured Hoyt's Speed Tile, and when he opened his eyes, Albert didn't hesitate. He rose to his feet, sprinted across the top of his pillar in two strides, and leaped, landing on Birdie's.

"Now let's get to Leroy!" Albert shouted.

He grabbed Birdie's hand, and with all the determination they could muster, the two of them leaped. They rolled to a stop on Albert's pillar, then rose to their feet and leaped again, landing on Leroy's.

Hydra was back together again, and they had three Tiles.

"Now what?" Birdie asked Leroy.

"We'll match the corresponding Tiles to their pillars. Let's see what we've got."

They all crouched down together and braced themselves on hands and knees to help stay balanced against the raging winds. Their Tiles were marked. One of the Tiles was a blue rhombus.

"I know exactly which pillar that is!" Leroy said. He tapped his head and grinned like a champion. "It's three pillars to our right!"

Together, Hydra stood, linking arms like they had seen Argon do the last time in the Pit.

They readied themselves to leap, when a splash sounded from below. A Hammerfin, larger than they'd seen so far, leaped from the waves.

"Jump!" Albert screamed.

On the count of three, they leaped. The Hammerfin annihilated the pillar they'd just been on. They barely made it onto the next pillar. Leroy tumbled overboard, and it took quick reflexes, and a quick thought of the Strength symbol, for Albert to keep his friend from falling.

Birdie helped haul Leroy back up.

"Thanks, guys," Leroy said. "You ready to leap?"

"Ready," Albert and Birdie said.

They checked to make sure their Tiles were still tucked safely into their waistbands. Then they grabbed one another's hands and leaped.

Leroy called out when to jump, and they followed his orders, jumping far and wide until they had made it to the pillar that had the blue rhombus marking on its side.

"You're sure it's this one?" Birdie asked.

Leroy nodded. "Sure as sugar, dudes."

"What does that even mean?" Albert asked, but Leroy shook his head. Birdie pulled out the Tile from that pillar's slot—it was a red heart—and then Leroy slammed the blue rhombus-marked Tile into the slot.

Ding!

"One Tile for Hydra!" Tussy shouted into the Mega-Horn. Somewhere in the crowd, Farnsworth howled with pride. Petra shouted another cheer, and Professor Flynn stood up and fist-bumped the air.

That was all Hydra needed. They'd figured out the markings and now they were going to win. Albert almost didn't notice it—but as soon as they'd placed their Tile into its slot, the spinning pillars slowed. It was hardly a change, just a tiny drop in the wind, but it was there.

The competition bore on. Pillar after pillar, Tile after Tile and slot after slot, Albert, Birdie, and Leroy began to match it all up.

Argon was so confused that once, Albert saw the three of them down in the waves below, fighting like a trio of angry cats. They had no idea what to do, and hadn't matched a single Tile—hadn't even tried.

Hydra had matched five Tiles when Tussy shouted the

one-minute mark—at least they could rest easy knowing they wouldn't have to start over. They didn't have to worry about Argon either—they had all but given up.

As the crowd began to count down from ten, Albert held up the last Tile they had in hand, a pink squiggle. Leroy motioned that the pillar they stood on shared the same marking. By now, the pillars had slowed to carousel-like speeds.

"You do the honors," Albert said, and handed Leroy the Tile.

Leroy slammed it down into the slot on their pillar.

Ding! Ding! Ding!

"Hydra wins by a landslide!" Tussy shouted, just as the clock ran out.

The crowd went wild. Their cheers were louder than Albert had ever heard in the Pit, in all his past competitions. Birdie and Leroy wrapped Albert in a hug, and the three of them joined in the cheers with their hearts racing wild.

They'd actually done it. They'd earned ten points, which meant . . . Hydra was in the lead, 35–34. By *one* point, they were finally beating Argon on the leaderboard.

As the pillars slowed to a stop, and the water and wind died down and the creatures disappeared, Albert caught his dad's face in the crowd.

Professor Flynn practically glowed with pride. He

smiled at Albert, and in that moment, everything else faded away.

I knew you could do it, kiddo, Albert imagined his dad saying.

It made Albert happier, and prouder, than any win ever could.

Lunch that afternoon was the best meal Albert had enjoyed so far this term. He sat beside Tussy as she went on and on about the day's competition. The other Balance Keepers at the table were all leaning forward, eyes wide, ecstatic about the news.

"It's about time you guys showed Argon who you really are," one of the Pure girls, Cecily, said. She had light blue eyes and dark hair, and Leroy couldn't look at her without turning as red as a beet. "How did you win, anyway?"

Today, the Whimzies had served chocolate cake for dessert, topped with strawberries and cream. A great way to celebrate Hydra's win, and as Albert looked at his friends, he knew exactly how they'd pulled it off.

"We worked as a team," Albert said. Birdie smiled and patted him on the arm.

"We stopped focusing on winning and starting focusing on using *all* our skills to get the job done. But Leroy was the real hero today," Birdie said. She nudged Leroy. "Right, Leroy?"

"Cake," Leroy mumbled, eyes going wide as he looked at Cecily and then looked away just as fast. "Good cake."

Everyone laughed.

The conversation went on. Professor Flynn stood up to lead the Core song as lunch came to an end. The song was half over, and Albert's heart was swelling with pride for his team.

That was when the ground shook. It started as a tiny tremble, like maybe the Core was shivering.

But then, all at once, a shock wave ripped through Lake Hall. The water swelled, causing a few of the docks to almost capsize. People screamed. Plates fell from tables and glasses shattered. The lights flickered until all the blue flames went out. The room was in complete and total darkness, save for the blue brightness coming from the companion creatures' dock. Farnsworth's eyes were two bright beams of cool, calm blue, the only thing besides Albert's friends that kept Albert from running in fear in that moment. With a tremor so intense, the origin of the shock wave couldn't have been that far away from where they were sitting right now. *What was happening to the Core?*

The tremors continued for more than a minute, an eternity for such things. Great rocks fell from the ceiling, barely missing the dock the Professors sat on.

Finally, the shock wave stopped, but the screaming didn't, not until Professor Flynn stood up and shouted, "SILENCE!"

His voice was so loud, so full of order, that everyone shut his or her mouth at once.

Farnsworth turned his eyes to Professor Flynn, bathing him in a blue spotlight. Everyone in the Core watched him, waiting for a command.

Albert was shaking, and Birdie was, too. Leroy was frozen still, cake crumbs all over his face. But Professor Flynn looked calm, cool, and collected.

"Everyone, take a moment to look around you," Professor Flynn said. "Look at the person to your left, and to your right."

Birdie reached out and took Albert's and Leroy's hands, and held on tight. All around Lake Hall, people were doing the same, some with arms wrapped around one another, some holding hands. A few people had even begun to cry, and some of them had bumps and bruises, a few nasty cuts. Hoyt had scurried under his table to hide, and was using Slink and Mo as a protective barrier on either side of him.

"Are you guys okay?" Albert asked his friends.

Birdie and Leroy were both pale as the moon. They nodded without saying a word.

Professor Flynn continued on. "These are your friends, your family, and we are all here to face this together. Everything is going to be all right."

He waited for another moment, allowing people to seek comfort in the silence before he spoke again. Albert's heart was still racing, his head wobbling from the shock wave. *What had happened? Was this the Imbalance, or something else?* A terrible thought came to his mind. *What if the shock wave also happened on the surface?* He thought of his family, and his skin felt clammy all over.

"Apprentices, please escort the Balance Keepers back to their dorms. Core workers, escort any of the injured to the hospital wing, then return to your barracks. Professors, meet me in my office, please."

He clapped his hands, and everyone did exactly as he said.

More turtles arrived than normal, carting everyone back to dry land within a matter of seconds. Once on the other side, Albert, Leroy, and Birdie followed Trey in a single-file line, the Pure students going with them.

Everyone was quiet the whole time, voices hardly rising above a whisper.

The tunnel back to the Main Chamber had been hit pretty hard. Torches had fallen from the walls. Some large boulders had crashed from the ceiling, and a stalagmite had cracked in half. They had to take turns helping one another over the wreckage.

"There's nothing to worry about," Trey said, as he led the terrified students along.

"Nothing to worry about?" Hoyt shrieked. "We almost died back there!"

"You're a Balance Keeper, Mr. Jackson," Trey said,

turning to look Hoyt right in the eye. Hoyt cowered and shook like a dog. He started inching backward like he wanted to hide behind Slink and Mo.

Trey turned to address the rest of the group. "You must be brave, if not for your own sake, then for everyone else's. Everything is fine. It was a minor tremor. Now let's move along. Keep up, students." He turned and continued down the hall.

Albert followed. Trey was trying to cover something up, he knew it. It was what a good leader needed to do, in that moment, but that didn't stop Albert from shaking. What had happened to cause the shock wave? Was it going to happen again?

Had anyone been hurt? Had anyone (he was afraid even to think about it) *died*? Again, he thought of his family and everyone in California. Had they felt it on the surface?

They came out into the Main Chamber. A giant roar erupted, and Jadar swooped down from the rafters, landing in front of Birdie with his leathery wings outspread.

Some students—Hoyt included—screamed and dove out of the way. Faced with *real* fear, the guy was becoming a real scaredy-cat. Albert just shook his head.

Birdie rushed forward and hugged Jadar's neck.

"I'm okay," she said. "I'm okay! Are you?"

Jadar practically purred with relief.

"Miss Howell," Trey said, a warning in his voice as

he stood off to the side, eyebrows raised. "Please remind your Guildacker to keep his voice down. He's scaring the students."

"He's sorry." Birdie patted Jadar's head. She looked down at Albert and Leroy. "I'll see you guys as soon as we're allowed to, okay?"

Albert and Leroy nodded, then waved as Jadar took to the sky, soaring down the tunnel toward Treefare. Tussy took the girls in that direction, while Trey escorted the boys down their tunnel to Cedarfell.

When they got there, Albert's stomach lurched. Some of the trees had cracked in half, their great boughs like shattered limbs. Massive stones had fallen from the ceiling, crushing hammocks and tents like they were nothing but bugs. Acorns littered the floor, and all of them had cracked in half. Their fizzy liquid had spilled like blood.

"Stay here until an announcement is made," Trey said. "Anyone who leaves without permission will lose their Balance Keepers status immediately."

He looked pointedly at Albert before he turned on his heel and marched from the forest, slamming the door to Cedarfell behind him.

"What's he so worked up about?" Hoyt said. He marched forward and started ordering kids around. "Let's get this mess cleaned up, boys!"

One of the Belltroll First Units, Elliot, barked out a laugh. "Now you're going to act all big and brave? If I remember correctly, you practically peed yourself when that shock wave happened, Hoyt!"

Some of the guys laughed and circled around the two boys.

"What did you just say to me?" Hoyt growled.

The two of them started a war of words, and Albert tugged Leroy along down the path into the woods. He couldn't take Hoyt's nagging voice right now. He needed some peace and quiet. Some normalcy. They sat down at the campfire, and a few of the other boys joined. Slink got a fire started. Albert was surprised not to see him lingering by Hoyt's side as usual.

"That was intense," Leroy muttered, as he and Albert sat down at the fire pit.

"It felt like the Core was ripped apart," Albert said.

"Hydra!" a voice called from behind them.

Leroy and Albert turned to see Petra rushing toward them. He held a tiny box in his hands, and he was breathless, as if he'd just run halfway across the Core.

"Petra—you're not supposed to be here—" Albert started to say.

"Can I speak to you in private for a second?" Petra asked.

Albert and Leroy joined him off to the side, behind a fallen tree. Its leafy canopy was splayed across the forest floor like a wall.

"There's no way for me to say this without upsetting

you guys," Petra said, looking at his toes. "I heard what you said in the Library the other night. I saw everything about the Book of Bad Tiles."

"You *what*?" Leroy gasped.

Albert sighed. "I wondered if someone was sneaking around. Was that you I saw lurking in the shadows, when I was on top of the rock wall?"

Petra shook his head. "Nope, I don't know who that was. I didn't get there until you were by the shelves."

So there *had* been someone else in the Library that night. Albert knew it. He just had to figure out who it was.

Petra continued. "Look, I'm sorry for spying, but I've always wanted to know what the Core Hunt was all about. I followed you guys, and I was going to see if you wanted help looking for the box of Tiles, and then . . ." His words trailed off as he held out the tiny box in his hands. "When the tremor happened, I was in the Library. Lucinda ran out, and I sort of snuck into her shop and took these."

"You stole from Lucinda?" Leroy asked. His jaw dropped.

"Petra, what got into you?" Albert added.

"Of course I didn't steal them!" Petra looked taken aback. "I left a handful of Medallions on her desk. I'd been saving up to buy some extra stuff for the float, but this was worth it."

He pressed the box into Albert's hands. Albert raised an eyebrow, and Petra nodded eagerly. Albert opened the lid on the box.

One yellow Tile sat inside. Its symbol was simple, a circle with a dot in the center, like an eyeball.

"This is a Homing Tile," Leroy gasped.

Petra nodded. "I already hid the other one in the box with the Book of Bad Tiles. Now you can catch the owner in the act!"

Albert stared at the yellow Tile. He scooped it up and held it out to Leroy. "It was your plan. You can wear the Tile."

Leroy grinned and slipped it over his head. It landed with a clink over his Synapse Tile. "Thanks, Petra."

Petra nodded, then took a step closer and lowered his voice. "You guys said you can't trust anyone. But you can trust me. You are the only friends I have in the Core, and I would never do anything to jeopardize that." He rocked back and forth on his heels. "Plus, I'm your biggest fan."

Albert chuckled and clapped Petra on the back. "We're a fan of you too, Petra. Thanks for getting the Tiles for us. We'll let you know if they detect anything."

"I've got to go see if the Professors need me now." Petra grinned, then turned and scurried away into the woods.

Albert and Leroy joined the other boys back at the fire.

All the boys traded theories about the shock wave, but

no one seemed to know what had caused it. *What had happened to the Core?*

The question stuck in Albert's mind, even as free time passed, and Trey didn't return. Soon the red birds of Cedarfell began to sing their evening song.

Albert returned to his tent and began flipping through the Black Book, but he couldn't focus on studying Tile symbols. All he could picture was the Core, falling apart from the inside out. Gone forever.

A half hour later, the loudspeaker clicked on. Albert perked up—maybe his question about what had happened would finally be answered.

Professor Flynn's voice rang through the loudspeaker, covered up by a film of static. "Balance Keepers, please report to the training Pit at once. There's been some damage. Please proceed with caution."

Albert could hear the hint of fear in his dad's voice.

Whatever had happened to the Pit, it wasn't good.

Eleven minutes later, Albert sat beside Birdie and Leroy on the spectators' bleachers, looking down into the Pit. Or at least, what used to be the Pit.

It was now a pile of rubble, dust still hovering in the air. The edges had crumbled into the middle, making the entire thing look as if it had swallowed itself whole. There were strange, oozing globs of colorful goo pouring from the Pit's sides (what was left of them), so that it looked like it was bleeding.

The Core maintenance men were already there with blueprints and tools, trying to decipher what had happened and how the Pit had been destroyed like a giant foot stomped down on it. Professor Bigglesby hadn't been around much this term, but he was here now, clearly concerned. He stood with the maintenance men, and was using some sort of oversized copper binoculars to peer down into the rubble.

"The Pit has never been damaged like this before," Professor Flynn said. The MegaHorn made his voice loud, but without the Pit's depths, there was no echo. It was oddly disconcerting. "And while we're still working on figuring out what caused the shock wave earlier, our engineers have determined that the quake wouldn't have caused this level of destruction on its own. Someone used the chaos of the shock wave as cover-up for destroying the Pit. This was no amateur prank, no random act."

Professor Asante sat beside him in her wheelchair, dark eyes scanning the crowd of Balance Keepers. She whispered something into Professor Flynn's ear, and he nodded.

"We suspect someone knowingly vandalized the Pit to disrupt the training of our Balance Keepers, to prevent us from having the capability to protect the Realms."

Farnsworth growled angrily, as if he would protect

the Core all by himself if he could.

A murmur spread through the bleachers. Albert sat still and silent, taking it all in. But his stomach felt sour as if he might be sick, and he clutched Farnsworth so tightly the poor dog's eye lights went out.

Professor Flynn held up a steady hand.

"In the Core, we are family. If any of you have any knowledge, any information or evidence about who might be behind this, I urge you now to come forward, for your and everyone's safety. If you yourself have con-tributed to this chaos, I urge to you confess; we have seen enough destruction."

Heads moved back and forth as people looked at one another with questions in their eyes.

"Now is the time," Professor Asante said. "Come for-ward."

"This is bad," Birdie whispered. She groaned and put her head into her hands.

"The Book of Bad Tiles," Albert whispered back. "We have to tell my dad. I can feel it, guys. Whoever owns that is the one who did this."

Just then, Trey slipped away from the edge of the crowd and disappeared into the shadows, then out the door of the Pit.

"It's him, isn't it?" Leroy whispered back. "It's Trey. That's why he's been acting so weird. Following us. Glar-ing all the time. He knows we know."

And suddenly it hit Albert.

The minty smell that always accompanied the strange shadow. It had been on *Trey* when they'd spoken the other day, just here in the Pit. He gasped. "It could be!"

"Don't jump to conclusions," Birdie warned. "He's an Apprentice! There's no way he'd do something like this. Besides, isn't he our friend?"

Albert shook his head. "Not anymore. Not since we came back this term."

"Let's just stop and think for a second," Birdie said. "We can't just accuse a person without solid evidence. And I still don't think Trey would ever do anything like that. He'd never betray the Core. It's his entire life."

After a few more moments of waiting, the Professors nodded, obviously disappointed that no one had come forward, but resigned to moving on.

"From now on, everyone will be required to move in a buddy system. No more lone walkers in the Core," Professor Asante said.

People groaned, but Professor Flynn held up his hand again. "This is only for safety reasons, Balance Keepers. Someone is targeting our practice arena. Which means, in turn, they might target you."

The room went silent as everyone realized the real danger they were in, trapped underground with nowhere to run.

"I don't say this to frighten you. I say this to keep you on your toes. Be vigilant. Keep your eyes open, and watch your backs. Now, we were planning to have one more competition before choosing the First Unit midday tomorrow, but as the Pit is no longer working, and repairs will likely take too long . . ."

He swallowed, his voice falling into silence. And then his eyes turned toward Albert. Professor Flynn looked sad. Dark. Full of worry.

Professor Asante took the MegaHorn from Professor Flynn's hands.

"Our rulebooks don't mention the destruction of the Pit," she said. "The Realm of Ponderay needs a First Unit. Without the Pit to rely on, we will simply have to cease the competitions. We were supposed to have more time. But that has come to an end."

Tussy appeared, holding a miniature version of the leaderboard. Albert's heart went into his throat. Were they about to pick the First Unit? He tried to remember what the scores had been between Hydra and Argon, but suddenly his mind went blank.

Professor Asante took the scoreboard and turned it toward the crowd.

There were thirty-four points in Argon's favor, a whopping score.

But Hydra had thirty-five.

Which could only mean one thing, and it dawned on Albert just as Professor Asante turned to look at him and his friends.

"Hydra is now the Ponderay First Unit," she said. The

crowd's whispers rose like the voices of ghosts.

Albert should have felt like shouting for joy. He should have felt like dancing or singing or anything at all, but for some reason, the victory didn't feel complete. The resigned looks on Birdie's and Leroy's faces matched his.

They all turned to look at Professor Asante. She sighed, and the lump in Albert's throat told him that she wasn't done with the news. There was something else.

"I wish I could congratulate you, Hydra. I wish I could bestow this great honor upon you with confidence." She took a deep, rattling breath. "But under these circumstances, with the level of the devastation in Ponderay, and the danger of a traitor in our midst, and without you being fully ready . . ."

Now the lump in Albert's throat disappeared, replaced with a sinking feeling in his chest. He didn't like where this was going.

"The Professors and I have decided to appoint *two* teams to go into the Imbalanced Realm. Argon competed with great skill and determination. Their presence in Ponderay will only further our chances of restoring Balance. This is not the time to take risks. This is the time to be vigilant."

The brick in Albert's chest dropped solidly to his stomach.

"No." Birdie breathed out the word. "No!"

She tried to stand, but Albert and Leroy kept a tight

grip on her. It gave Albert something to focus on besides the shock that was now running through his veins.

Professor Asante turned toward Hoyt and his cronies, who were seated just a few bleachers below. Slink and Mo both leaned forward. Their eyes were as wide as saucers, and they had huge grins on their faces, like they couldn't believe this was happening. Hoyt, on the other hand, looked petrified. He was clenching and unclenching his fists and chewing on his bottom lip. It reminded Albert of the Jackalope in Professor Asante's room the other day: like Hoyt wasn't sure if he wanted to bolt out of fear, or stay here with everyone else.

Professor Flynn spoke. "Argon, you will be the other unit. Together, you six will enter Ponderay tomorrow and execute the Means to Restore Balance to the Realm."

Albert was surprised he didn't wake up just then. Surely, this was a nightmare, a really, really bad one. He almost asked Birdie to pinch him.

But when Hoyt turned toward Albert, and their eyes met, and Hoyt said nothing, *did* nothing, just stared back at Albert with the same shocked expression on his face that Albert surely wore right now, Albert knew.

This was real life.

They were going into Ponderay, together.

Whether Albert liked it or not.

CHAPTER 21

A Crash Course

That evening, Albert and many of the boys gathered their sleeping bags, which they were using in lieu of beds until the damage to Cedarfell was fixed, and grouped together around a fire. No one spoke. Instead, they all sat in silence, listening to the crackling of the flames. Hydra sat beside Argon, and for once, they didn't exchange words. They simply *sat*. The camaraderie of the moment made Albert feel a little bit braver, and helped to chase away the panicky thoughts that threatened to take over his mind.

Some while later, Tussy came knocking on the Cedarfell door—it was time for a crash course on Ponderay. Albert, Leroy, and Argon rose from the campfire circle and left without a word. "I'm really wishing for those original seven days right about now," Albert whispered to Leroy as they headed down the tunnel to Professor Asante's office.

"Me too, bro," Leroy whispered back. "Me too."

Their footsteps echoed eerily down the empty tunnel as they walked. Everyone else in the Core had been confined to their quarters, even the Core workers. When they got to Professor Asante's office, her door was wide open. Farnsworth scurried inside and barked a greeting.

Birdie stood in the corner of the room looking very small. When she saw the boys, she rushed to their side. There were dark circles under her eyes. "I feel sick," she whispered.

"Me too," Leroy said with a gulp.

"It's just nerves." Albert shook his head. "I don't think anyone in the Core is feeling too good right about now. Well, except Farnsworth."

The little dog wagged his tail in reply.

Tussy called everyone to sit down on the couches in the corners. Albert, Birdie, and Leroy sat on the couch on one end of the room. Hoyt, Slink, and Mo stood on the opposite side, up against the bookshelves.

Even though no one was speaking, Tussy clapped to get their attention.

"All right, listen up Balance Keepers. You must take this lesson seriously tonight. The Core Watchers have confirmed that the quake from earlier was the Imbalance escalating to Phase Four."

Albert looked at Leroy. Weren't three phases enough? How many were there going to be?

Tussy continued. "The Pillars have changed direction yet again, and are still spinning at top speed. They've also moved outward, farther apart from one another— their circle is getting bigger. The Watchers think that that movement was what caused the shock wave earlier today."

"Oh man," Leroy muttered, "what's that doing to the surface?"

Tussy looked down and took a breath in and out before answering. "I'm afraid the rains and hurricanes have spread from California into surrounding states." She glanced at Birdie with an uncharacteristic soft expression.

"My family's in Oregon!" Birdie said. "We have to do something!" Albert saw her eyes begin to well up with tears.

"That's why you're here, Balance Keepers. The Realm needs you desperately and you must prepare. I'm going to get the Professor. Stay here," Tussy commanded. She left the room in a hurry.

"Are you okay, Birdie?" Albert asked.

She shrugged. "I guess so. I'm just ready to get into Ponderay and get this over with."

Leroy put a hand on her shoulder. "Me too. We'll do it. We'll stop the Imbalance."

"This has never happened before," Hoyt said from the corner of the room. "Two teams, going into a Realm together. It should have been Argon."

"Well it's not, moron! It's both teams." Birdie growled. She leaned forward like she wanted to snap at him, but Leroy and Albert held her back.

Slink held out his hands. "We're okay with it, Birdie. We're just shocked, is all."

Birdie's face grew red the moment she realized Slink was talking to her. She looked at her toes. *What's that about?* Albert thought.

Slink continued speaking. "It's a lot to take in. *Right*, Hoyt?" He nudged Hoyt, who mumbled *sure* and crossed his arms.

"We want this Imbalance solved just as badly as you guys do," Mo said. "Can we at least agree on that?"

Birdie's shoulders sagged. "Fine. I guess you're right."

"He is," Leroy said, "and no matter how much we can't stand each other, we'll have to make it work."

Slink and Mo both nodded in agreement. Hoyt still sat there, just staring into the distance.

"Hoyt?" Slink said. He leaned toward him, and Hoyt suddenly snapped his head up.

Albert realized something he hadn't before. Hoyt might pretend to be their fearless leader, but sometimes,

Hoyt seemed *afraid* of the other guys. Lately, he acted like he was afraid of a lot of things.

"You guys haven't been to a Realm before, but you've done some great work in the Pit," Albert said. "If we can learn to put aside our differences, we might be able to knock this Imbalance out of the park." He gave a nod of thanks to Slink and Mo, who both returned it at once. They were turning out to not be so bad. If Hoyt could get it together, this might work out to their advantage in the Realm.

"Let's just agree right now to act like teammates," Albert continued. "I'm in if you guys are."

He couldn't believe what he was about to do. Last term, he never would have dreamed of it. But Albert crossed the room and held out his hand.

Leroy followed and put his hand on top of Albert's. Slink stepped forward next and put his hand on the pile. Next was Mo, and finally, Birdie stepped forward with an exaggerated sigh.

"Let's do what we have to do, boys," Birdie said.

Hoyt came last. Albert watched closely as Hoyt lifted his hand.

Their eyes locked as Hoyt put his hand on the top of the pile.

"To Hydra and Argon," Albert said.

"To Hydra and Argon," everyone else echoed.

The door of the room swung open, and Tussy wheeled

Professor Asante inside. Everyone backed away, almost like they were embarrassed to have been caught agreeing on something.

"Well, isn't this a sight for sore eyes?" Professor Asante chuckled as Tussy wheeled her past the six of them. "I like what I'm seeing, Balance Keepers. Now get comfy, because you're about to get a crash review course on Ponderay. We have a lot to cover; you enter the Realm at noon tomorrow."

The six Balance Keepers exchanged looks—that was only eighteen hours away—but they settled down on the ground in front of Professor Asante's desk, all six of them in a line.

"Very good." Professor Asante nodded in approval. She motioned for Tussy to hand her a book from the bookshelf. Tussy brought one over, and Albert recognized it as the book Professor Asante had shown them when they snuck into her office.

"Ponderay is a very delicate Realm," Professor Asante started. "You've trained with replicated pillars. But the ones in the Pit were nothing compared to the real Pillars of Ponderay. The Ten Pillars will be three times as large. As you know, they'll now be moving faster than a tornado, and the creatures won't hesitate to attack. You've seen the Hammerfins and the Jackalopes. Don't forget the Lightning Rays. Their goal will be to defeat you. They almost never lose."

Albert swallowed, hard.

"No one will defeat Argon," Hoyt said, crossing his arms over his chest. When Professor Asante turned her angry eyes on him, he cleared his throat and said, "I mean, um, no one will defeat us. The, uh, six of us."

Albert couldn't believe his ears.

Professor Asante nodded. "That's more like it. From now on, while you are in Ponderay, you must *forget* the names Argon and Hydra. You are now part of a new team."

Professor Asante flipped to the middle of the book. The pages crinkled as she found what she was looking for. It was a map of the Realm, shaped in a circle just like Calderon was, only this one seemed bigger, and far more intense.

"The Ring of Entry, like all Realms, is where the tunnel will spit you out." Professor Asante pointed to the map. "That part will be the easiest. It's here, at the Canyon Cross"—she pointed farther toward the center of the map—"that things will start to get rocky."

It was like the Grand Canyon, but to get from canyon to canyon, there were rickety bridges and clusters of pillars that looked like they could crumble at any second. Albert gulped. They hadn't trained for that. What else would they face in Ponderay?

"You'll face the Path of Pillars there. You must pay attention to your surroundings at all times in the Realm, but especially in the Path of Pillars. Once you get past that point, you'll be well on your way to the Silver Sea."

In the middle of the Realm were the Ten Pillars. She explained the goal again, how all the Tiles on top of the Ten Pillars were scrambled, and would need to be reordered to set the Balance right.

"I only summited one of the Pillars, and Professor Flynn and Tussy only summited two, so we don't know the full extent of the challenge. I don't know the order the Tiles need to be in. Look for colors or symbols—maybe shapes—on both the Pillars and the Tiles. What I do know is that this task will be dangerous." Professor Asante took a deep breath. "We want you to be as safe as possible. Tussy, if you would, please."

Professor Asante held out her hand. Tussy scrambled over, holding something wrapped in red cloth. She set it onto the old desk with a *thwump*. Albert leaned forward, eyes wide, eager to discover what the object was.

Professor Asante unwrapped the cloth, and all six Balance Keepers gave a collective *oooooh*. It looked like a crossbow, only it was made of wood, like something from the days of knights and kings. Albert couldn't wait to get his hands on that thing.

"What is it?" he asked.

Professor Asante covered it back up with the red cloth. "This is a CoreBow, handcrafted by Professor Bigglesby. Very dangerous. Very useful. Now, because *you*,

Mr. Flynn, can use your Master Tile to take aim, I'll be appointing the CoreBow to you."

Hoyt sounded like he was choking on a lollipop. "What? But that's not fair!"

"Fair is a childish word," Professor Asante said. "You'll be using your Speed Tile to run and jump, possibly even the lengths from Pillar to Pillar."

"Of course," Hoyt said, recovering. "I was just trying to make sure everyone agreed with the plan. Since we're teammates and all."

Birdie looked like she was going to puke. Slink smiled at her apologetically, and she sat a little straighter after that.

Professor Asante went on to review all of the dangers:

Icy winds.

Water cold enough to give a person hypothermia in less than sixty seconds.

Bridges that could snap and send a Balance Keeper falling to his or her death.

Angry, Imbalanced creatures, from Hammerfins to Jackalopes to Lightning Rays.

And of course, the fact remained that if they didn't succeed in returning the right Tiles to the right Pillars, the entire Realm would basically crumble, and in turn, the surface world above.

No pressure.

After four hours of a grueling review of information,

Albert's head felt ready to explode. He hoped Leroy had logged most of the information with his Synapse Tile, because there was no way he'd be able to recall all that tomorrow.

"We'll meet in the Main Chamber at twelve noon tomorrow," Professor Asante said. "I suggest you get some sleep now—as much as you can."

"Yes, Professor," they all said.

As Tussy escorted them from the room, Albert had to laugh. "Argon and Hydra," he said. "Who would've thought?"

"Not me," Birdie said.

"Definitely not me," Leroy added. "All that's on my mind right now is getting one final night of sleep."

"Final night of sleep?" Birdie asked, as they rounded the corner and walked out into the Main Chamber. Hoyt had gone ahead and was standing on one of the bridges, peering into the depths of the water below. Slink and Mo stood off to the side, talking in hushed voices.

"It's a final night of sleep for sure," Leroy said, chewing on his thumbnail. "Because tomorrow, with those guys in the way, we're totally gonna die, dudes."

That was the phrase that stuck in Albert's mind the entire night long.

He couldn't sleep, not without picturing the world destroyed. All because Hydra and Argon couldn't solve the Imbalance in Ponderay.

Hoyt's annoying laugh plagued his dreams, and Albert woke up breathing hard, drenched in sweat.

Farnsworth whimpered beside him in the darkness.

"It's okay, buddy," Albert whispered, petting Farnsworth's soft fur.

Leroy was snoring in his bed across from them.

"At least one of us will be rested," Albert sighed, rolling over onto his stomach.

He climbed out of bed and grabbed the CoreBow, then slipped out into the dark woods.

Albert and Farnsworth walked deeper into the trees, skirting past the fallen branches and broken piles of tents. When they had gotten far enough away from the main camp, Farnsworth lit up the night with his eyes.

"Let's see how this thing works," Albert said.

He grabbed a short, fat stick from the forest floor and slid it into the open groove at the front of the bow. There was a trigger like a gun. Albert took aim, pointing the CoreBow toward a nearby tree.

"Here goes nothing," he said.

He squeezed the trigger. The stick shot out like a bullet. It exploded against the tree's trunk and splintered into a million pieces.

Farnsworth wagged his tail excitedly. Albert's fingertips buzzed. "That was incredible."

Behind them, a stick snapped. Albert spun around just

as Hoyt emerged from the trees. Farnsworth growled, but Albert put a hand on his head to silence him.

"What are you doing up?" Albert asked.

Hoyt shrugged. "Couldn't sleep."

The two boys stood there awkwardly for a moment. Albert figured now was as good a time as any to try and get Hoyt on his side. Maybe, if they could *try* and be friends, tomorrow might be a little easier.

Albert held out the CoreBow. "Want to try it?"

Hoyt's eyes flashed. He smiled, but quickly hid it away. "I guess so."

Albert watched as Hoyt shot the bow a few times. He wasn't great with aiming it, but Hoyt seemed to be having a good time. They took turns shooting sticks into the trees. Albert aimed at some of the acorns. He was pretty decent at this, even knocking a few of them down. They didn't exchange any words, but even so, Albert could feel some of the walls coming down between them.

After a while, Hoyt handed the CoreBow back to Albert. "We should get some sleep. Tomorrow's a big day."

Albert could hear the fear in Hoyt's voice. Since the tremor, Hoyt had been different—a little less of a bully, a little more of an actual human being with thoughts and feelings.

It was nice to see him this way.

"It'll be all right," Albert said, as the two of them

walked back toward camp. "The Realms are pretty cool, if you can get past knowing you're there because of an Imbalance."

Hoyt shrugged. "I wouldn't know."

"You will tomorrow," Albert said.

Hoyt stiffened.

Albert understood how it felt, the night before going into a Realm for the very first time, not knowing what to expect, not knowing if you'd make it back alive. "You don't have to be afraid," Albert said.

It was a mistake to say it, because suddenly Hoyt rounded on him. "I'm *not* afraid."

Albert held up his hands. "Right. Of course not. " He sighed and slung the CoreBow over his shoulder. "Well, I'll see you tomorrow."

Hoyt nodded, but he wouldn't look Albert in the eyes. "See you tomorrow, Flynn. I'm going to sleep."

Albert headed back to his tent with Farnsworth. Before he slipped inside, he turned and looked over his shoulder.

Hoyt hadn't gone to sleep like he'd said.

He was sitting against a tree and staring into the darkness. Albert guessed he'd be there all night.

CHAPTER 22

Entering Ponderay

People lined on both sides of the river in the Main Chamber. Others stood on the bridge, squished up against one another to get a good look. The Core workers were there, all the companion creatures, even the Whimzies from Lake Hall (minus their baskets of food). It seemed as if the entire Core had come to see them off.

The Professors were lined up closest to the door to Ponderay, with the Apprentices behind them. The countdown clock had switched from days to hours now. Its numbers glowed a big *15*.

Hydra and Argon stood together, wearing new featherlight suits that were designed to withstand the fierce winds and waters of Ponderay. They were all in matching silver. Professor Asante had given them back-packs, stocked with extra protective clothing they could wear when they reached the Silver Sea. She'd also sup-plied Leroy with a new pair of vision-correcting goggles he could put on later, so he wouldn't have to wear his glasses in the Silver Sea.

"I've never felt so nervous in my entire life," Birdie said, as she tugged at the long sleeves of her new jacket.

"I didn't even eat this morning," Leroy groaned.

"I ate *too* much," Mo said.

Slink shifted from one foot to another, stretching his arm muscles like he was gearing up for a fistfight. Hoyt stood beside him, staring absently into the river.

"Deep breaths, guys," Albert said. He stood off to the side with the CoreBow strapped across his shoulders. Somehow, the heavy weight of it against his back helped him feel a little safer, a little more like a real Balance Keeper should at this moment; not scared and trem-bling like a wet cat, something Albert had been doing all morning when no one was looking.

Petra arrived to say good-bye, and Leroy gave him the Homing Tile for safekeeping while they were gone.

"Keep an eye on it," Leroy said, as Petra put the Tile over his neck. "If anything happens while we're gone, it's in your hands."

Petra beamed. "You can trust me, guys."

The crowd began singing the Core song, getting

everyone geared up for the two teams to enter. It was louder than ever before, and Albert could feel his chest trembling with the sound.

"All right, Albert?" a voice spoke from behind him.

Albert spun around and nearly had his nose bitten off by Lucinda's giant black snake. It hung from her shoulders, hissing as she stroked it with her bejeweled fingers.

"Hey, Lucinda," Albert said. "I didn't know you'd be here."

She smiled and continued to stroke Kimber. "Of course, my dear. I wouldn't miss it for the world."

For a second, the two of them stood there awkwardly. Then Lucinda stooped to one knee and lowered her voice. "I brought you a gift."

She produced a white bundle of cloth from her pocket, eyes widening as she placed it into Albert's open hands. He unwrapped it carefully, unsure of what was inside.

When he saw the red Tile, he raised his eyebrows in question. It was a symbol he hadn't seen before, with four circles. It reminded Albert of the map of Ponderay.

"What's it do?" Albert asked.

Lucinda looked around to make sure no one was listening. But they were still singing away, distracted by trying to build morale for the Balance Keepers.

"It's a Chance Tile," Lucinda whispered. "If you find yourself in a moment where you've lost hope, its power will make all the difference."

Albert nodded. Lucinda took the Tile from his hands and strung it over his neck. It landed with a clink on top of his Master Tile. She also pulled out a copper device that looked like a watch. "And this is a Counter," she said, strapping it over Albert's wrist. "It will let you know how much time you have left, before it's too late."

Albert gulped, not wanting to think about what Lucinda meant by *too late*, but he gave Lucinda his best smile. "Thanks for all the help."

"Be brave, young Balance Keeper," she said, placing her warm hand on Albert's cheek.

As she faded back into the crowd, Professor Flynn approached. The moment was quick, for they had only seconds before the Core song was over.

"You did great in the Pit the other day," his dad said as he placed his hands on Albert's shoulders. "And you'll do great in the Realm. Remember to work as a team, and keep your wits about you. Don't forget to pay attention to your surroundings. Ponderay is a tricky Realm."

Albert nodded and looked into his dad's eyes. They were so similar to his, and for some reason, that thought settled Albert's twisting nerves. He was the son of Professor Bob Flynn, and he'd make it through today no matter what. "Thanks, Dad. I'll see you soon."

Professor Flynn nodded. "Promise?"

Albert nodded back. "I promise."

Professor Flynn squeezed Albert's shoulders. Then he

turned and headed back to where the other Professors stood.

As the song ended, Birdie and Leroy eyed the Tile around Albert's neck. They looked as nervous as Albert felt, and it only got worse when Professor Asante motioned for both teams to join her beside the door.

She looked at all six of them with a certain graveness in her eyes. "If you don't solve the Imbalance in fifteen hours, Ponderay will collapse. The world as we know it will be forever changed, and we will never be able to reverse it."

"We'll fix this, Professor," Albert said.

Beside him, Hoyt nodded. "He's right."

Well, that was odd.

Professor Asante spoke. "Remember, time is of the essence. The entire western coast is in dire need of a savior right now. You *must* be that savior. We cannot afford to slip up or falter—the fate of the world is in your hands. Be brave, Balance Keepers, and may the hope of the entire Core carry you through." She took a deep breath. "Are you ready?"

Albert, Birdie, and Leroy exchanged nervous glances.

"Yes, Professor," Albert spoke for them. Slink, Mo, and Hoyt nodded their readiness, too.

In the crowd, Farnsworth howled. Petra was holding him tightly.

"I'll be back before you know it, little buddy," Albert

said to Farnsworth. "Hang in there."

The river in front of Ponderay began to bubble and steam. The water churned, and suddenly it was rushing toward the door, building in height as a great wave crashed and exploded upon the old wood.

Albert closed his eyes, ready for the wood to shatter to pieces, but instead the river went silent and still.

A dark hole stood where the door to Ponderay used to be.

"I'll never get used to that," Leroy said, wiping water off his glasses.

"Here we go again," Birdie said.

Hydra held hands as they crossed over the border, and the Counter on Albert's wrist flicked on: fifteen hours.

Argon marched in behind them. Before they got too far, Albert looked back.

His dad's face was the last thing he saw. Farnsworth's mournful howl carried Albert and his teammates into the darkness.

The way to Ponderay was dark and cold. This was darkness so endless that no matter how hard Albert tried to make sense of his surroundings, nothing appeared. The glow from his Counter wasn't even able to penetrate the blackness. He had the feeling that if he were to trip over his own feet and fall, he'd fall forever, never to land, never to come back up again.

Albert felt Birdie shake off a chill beside him.

"It'll end soon," Albert said. Still, his friends' hands in his were the only things that told him he wasn't alone. "Remember, it was the same way when we entered Calderon."

"Was it this cold?" Mo asked.

"Yeah," Albert answered. Even with the new suits they wore, the tunnel was frigid. But Albert knew that if what Professor Asante had said was true, the cold would only get worse once they entered the Realm.

The longer they walked, the more the darkness faded, turning less black, a little grayer. The tunnel seemed to widen, and in the distance, Albert could see a pinprick of light.

"This is it," Leroy breathed from beside him.

"Round two," Albert said, and for some crazy reason, a smile suddenly broke onto his face. He lived for this danger, these wild moments in the Realms. They kept walking, one foot after the other, until suddenly the tunnel was simply gone.

"Holy . . . freaking . . . cake balls," Leroy said.

Hoyt laughed. "What are you even talking . . ." His words trailed off.

Everyone gasped, eyes widening like dinner plates.

They stood on the edge of a crumbling cliff. The Realm of Ponderay spread out before them—and below them.

CHAPTER 23

Canyon Cross

Calderon had been a struggle, a real challenge that tested the limits of Albert, Leroy, and Birdie from the second they stepped inside.

But from the edge of Ponderay, the Realm had a razor-sharp look about it that told Albert he was about to face the wildest ride of his life.

Albert looked left, then right. All throughout the Canyon Cross, as far as he could see, there were cliffs of a reddish brown color, like the Grand Canyon, only these had a far more sinister feel. Water sparkled at the bottoms of the cliffs, snaking through the entire Realm like a giant spool of silver thread that had unraveled.

Albert gulped. If he fell from one of those cliffs, the outcome wouldn't be good. They had to be miles and miles high. There would be no coming back from a fall at these heights.

Wind whipped past them, pummeling into Albert like it was trying to knock him off course. His teeth chattered and he wrapped his arms around himself, but it didn't seem to help. Overhead, the sky was a dark, angry gray, like the way New York City looked before a major snowstorm.

"There's the bridges," Birdie pointed out.

Across the Realm, miles away, Albert could see rope bridges crisscrossing back and forth between a few cliffs.

Others had small lines of columns connecting them. Those small pillars looked like they weren't more than a few feet across. *If the wind blows too hard while we're on one of those, we'll fall*, Albert thought. He shook his head as if to clear the thought away. *My dad said once that bravery was a Balance Keeper's greatest strength.*

"The Ten Pillars! Look!" Slink shouted, pointing just past Albert's head.

They were hard to miss.

Right in the middle of the Realm, just as Professor Asante had said, there was a giant, sparkling silver sea. It was a great circle of water, and standing in the middle of it, like ten skyscrapers, were the Ten Pillars of Ponderay.

From here, Albert could lift a thumb and cover them up.

But up close he knew they'd be even taller than Calderon Peak.

He looked at the Counter on his wrist. They had already reached thirteen. How was that possible? It felt like they'd been in the tunnel for seconds and hours and days all at once.

Albert guessed time was a funny thing in the Realms.

"We need to get moving," he said, turning to look at his team. Birdie and Leroy nodded, but Slink and Mo looked toward Hoyt for their answers.

He stood with his arms crossed, looking out at the Realm. The first chasm was just a few paces away. An old, rickety-looking bridge was the only option they had to get across.

"We should split up," Hoyt said. "You know, so that we can move faster."

Slink look a little unsure. Mo nodded, but Leroy caught on.

"You're just saying that so you'll have a better chance of saving the day and getting all the glory."

"We need to stick together," Albert said. "It's safer that way. Trust me, in the Realms, you don't really know what you're up against. Even when it's barreling toward you, staring you in the face."

"I wish I'd seen Calderon," Slink said. He smiled at Birdie. "What was it like?"

When Birdie realized Slink was talking to her, she

opened and closed her mouth like a fish out of water. Then she turned away.

"Can it, Slink," Hoyt snapped. "No fraternizing with the enemy."

Albert practically choked on laughter. "We're not the enemy, Hoyt! We're a team now, remember? What happened to all that talk last night in Professor Asante's office?"

Hoyt guffawed, then stepped closer to Albert, eyes set in slits. "You're no team member of mine." He poked Albert in the chest.

"Is that so?" Albert was instantly full of rage. He poked Hoyt back.

Birdie, Leroy, Slink, and Mo stood off to the side, staring with their mouths open.

Hoyt responded with a doglike growl. "If you do anything, Flynn, *anything* to screw this up for Argon, I'll . . ."

"ENOUGH!" Leroy shouted, throwing himself in between both boys. "We're not here so the two of you can act like little kids fighting over who gets the last cookie!"

Albert and Hoyt both looked like they'd been slapped across the face.

Leroy continued. "Now, we're going to start our journey across this Realm, and if anyone does anything to anyone, besides *helping them* like a real team, I'm going to kick you into the next Realm. Do you understand?"

Slink and Mo hid their laughter in their hands.

Birdie looked downright impressed.

"You sound like my mother," Albert gasped.

Leroy lifted his chin and stared down his nose at Albert. "Yes, well, someone has to be the voice of reason right now. I thought we'd worked out our differences yesterday. We're all here fair and square, and nothing about that is going to change. We won't save the Realm—or the world—if we go back to our old ways."

"We're already wasting time," Slink added.

Albert shook it off, then looked sideways at Hoyt. He didn't want to admit it, but everything Leroy said was true. "He's right."

Hoyt didn't look happy about it. He pulled the straps of his backpack tighter and sighed. "Let's just get moving."

He turned to the left, then started marching away. Slink and Mo traded worried glances. Then they followed Hoyt a few paces behind.

Albert sighed. "This is going to be a long trip."

"You can say that again." Leroy nodded.

"Let's move," Birdie said.

The three of them set out, following Argon to the only way off that cliff and onto the next one: the first bridge.

This was going to be a challenge, and Albert knew it the second they stood in front of the bridge. The chasm that it hung across, connecting one cliff to another, had to be at least a half-mile wide.

"Point five two miles," Leroy said, nodding, as he looked at the chasm.

Albert took a step forward and peered over the edge.

Wind whistled and snapped, and Albert's stomach got a little queasy just imagining the fall. He could hardly see the bottom. He knew a river was down there, but how deep was it? Would falling from this height kill a person, even with water at the bottom?

"This bridge looks like it's going to snap any second," Mo said. He stood at the entrance, one foot on the first wooden plank. "Where did it even come from?"

The bridge was a series of wooden planks, held together by old, fraying rope. It looked like something out of an Indiana Jones movie.

"Some of the earliest Balance Keepers made them, like, a thousand years ago," Leroy said.

"Great. So they're really old and weak," Hoyt said. Once again, the tremor of fear was back in his voice.

But now Albert didn't feel bad for him. He just felt annoyed.

"It held Professor Asante, Professor Flynn, *and* Tussy, didn't it?" Birdie suggested. "Surely it can hold us, if we go one or two at a time."

"There's only one way to find out," Albert said.

He took a step forward and put one foot onto the first plank. Then, slowly, his other foot.

There was a *creeeeak*. But the bridge held his weight. He took a step back onto solid ground. "All right. Looks like it might hold."

"Fine, let's get this over with then," Hoyt said. "It's no big deal." He shoved past Albert and onto the bridge. He started walking across, slowly at first, then at a more normal pace. Before too long, he used his Speed Tile, and was safely on the other side of the bridge, standing on the second cliff, waving his hands like a champion.

"I guess we should just do what he did," Albert said.

"Here goes nothing," Slink said. He gave Birdie a sideways glance before stepping onto the bridge. She gave him a tiny smile back. After a few minutes' time, Slink reached the other side without incident. Mo followed right after, and made it, too.

"Statistically speaking, the more people we send across the bridge, the more likely it is that the rope will fray. And whoever is on it will go down," Leroy explained.

"Thanks for the vote of confidence, man," Albert laughed.

"I'll go next," Leroy said.

He crossed like a snail, stopping every few seconds, looking back over his shoulder at Albert and Birdie. They cheered him on, and finally, nine minutes later, Leroy reached the other cliff.

"All right, you go, Birdie. I'll take up the rear," Albert told her.

Birdie took a few deep breaths, then straightened and looked at Albert with sheer determination in her eyes. "See you on the other side."

With that, she crossed, going at a faster speed than Leroy had. Birdie made it, and Albert relaxed. All his friends and teammates were safely across.

Now it was only him left.

He took a step onto the bridge, testing its strength. The boards creaked under his weight, and the rope swayed, causing him to feel a flutter of angry butterflies in his stomach.

It's just like the Pit Path, Albert told himself. *Keep moving, and you'll be there before you know it.*

For good measure, he pictured Hoyt's Speed Tile in his mind. There was the familiar buzzing in his feet, and Albert took off, whizzing across the bridge.

He was mere feet from the other side when he felt the gust of wind.

Before Albert could do anything at all, the ropes behind him popped, rocking the entire bridge like an ocean wave.

Then they snapped.

"ALBERT!" Birdie and Leroy screamed together.

Albert lost concentration, and the Speed symbol fizzled away. He was able to take a few steps, just before the falling bridge caught up to him.

This was the end. He was too scared to think, too scared to grasp onto a Tile symbol in his mind.

The bridge beneath his feet dropped. The CoreBow's weight on Albert's shoulders pulled him down. Just when Albert began to fall, a hand caught his wrist.

Albert looked up, breathless.

It was Slink!

"Come on," Slink said, groaning from the effort. "Climb."

With Leroy's and Mo's added strength, and a little last-minute Weightlessness help from Albert's Master Tile, they managed to haul him onto the cliff.

All four boys lay there on their backs, heaving for air. Albert almost let shock take him away, but he reminded himself that he was a Balance Keeper. And it was his task to help save the world right now. He had to stay in control, stay brave. He stood up, wiping down his sleek silver pants.

Albert held out a hand to Slink. "Thanks. You were really something, man. I owe you for that one."

"No problem." Slink shrugged, but his face broke into a glittering smile when Birdie pulled him into a hug.

"You saved him!" she squealed. "Thank you!"

Then she realized what she'd done, and backed away awkwardly. *What is going on with her?* Albert wondered.

"It was nothing," Slink said when Birdie pulled away. "Really, it was no big deal. Anyone would have done it."

Albert wasn't so sure. It's not like Hoyt had moved to help him.

"Of course it was nothing for him," Hoyt snarled from

behind them. "Slink's just a big bunch of muscles."

Slink looked down at his toes.

"That wasn't cool, Hoyt," Mo said, crossing his arms. "What's your problem?"

Hoyt took a half step back. "I don't have a problem."

Mo stepped closer. "Yes, you do. You're taking it out on us because you're upset about not being the only team here. Hydra made it too, and they destroyed us in the Pit last time. They're good, Hoyt, and we are, too. Accept it."

Albert was shocked. Mo had always been a guy of few words, and he'd always seemed closer to Hoyt than Slink. But Mo had just proved to Albert that he wasn't so bad after all.

Hoyt clenched and unclenched his fists, but he said nothing.

Leroy broke the silence when he pointed at Albert's Counter and said, "We lost another hour from that."

He was right. It was at twelve now. Time was moving way too fast.

Albert pulled his wrist away, then motioned for everyone to follow. "Let's just keep moving toward the center. Hopefully we can make it there before dark. I don't know about you guys, but I don't want to climb those Pillars in the pitch black."

Hoyt took the lead, as always, but this time he didn't keep his head held high. Slink and Mo followed, farther back than they had before, falling into step beside

Albert, Leroy, and Birdie.

Slink was a big dude, at least a foot taller than Albert. Mo had a permanent scowl on his face. They both *looked* scary, but Albert was starting to think he'd been totally wrong about both boys. And if they weren't so bad, maybe there was some good in Hoyt, too, deep, *deep* down. It had sure seemed like it last night, in the woods of Cedarfell.

"You okay?" Leroy asked. "That was scary back there."

"Yeah," Albert said as he kicked a red-brown rock. "I just lost my mind for a second. Fear got ahold of me. I could've used the Float symbol, or Anti-Grav, or something, but I just lost it."

"It's okay." Birdie patted Albert on the back. "Next time, you'll be prepared."

Albert hoped his friends were right, because the Ten Pillars were coming up soon. And he couldn't afford to screw up when it came to that.

CHAPTER 24

The Path of Pillars

The six Balance Keepers walked for the next hour. Even with the special clothes Professor Asante had given them, everyone was trembling against the ice-cold wind.

Every so often, they would stop. Leroy would scan the horizon, making sure they were still on course, using the Ten Pillars as their distant guide.

"Angle seven degrees to the north," Leroy would say, and when Albert, Birdie, Slink, Hoyt, and Mo stared at him like he was speaking Spanish, Leroy sighed and took the lead.

Albert felt as if he were in a dream world. The constant red-brown color morphed into one big blur. Ponderay's distant Silver Sea never seemed to get closer, no matter how far they walked.

They crossed bridges like the first one, but they were smarter. Albert used his Master Tile, giving himself super strength. Together, from opposite ends, Albert and Slink held the fraying ropes.

The wind couldn't be controlled, but everyone held on, using their practiced skills from the Pit. No one fell.

The journey into the heart of Ponderay was going smoothly, until they came to a cliff without a bridge—the start of the Path of Pillars. The canyon in front of them had hundreds of tiny pillars, miniature versions of the Ten Pillars, lined up in a row.

Leroy stopped at the edge of the cliff. "Well, this reminds me of the Pit, and that's not a good thing."

Hoyt peered over the edge. "We can make it across. We'll just have to go slow." He glanced at his chest. "I guess my Tile is useless right now."

Birdie cracked her knuckles. "We don't need Tiles to get across. We're Balance Keepers, and we've trained for challenges far worse than this."

"You're right, Birdie," Mo said. He stepped forward next to Hoyt. "But this is still going to be a challenge. The pillars aren't standing at even heights."

Albert looked back out at the chasm, and realized Mo was right. The pillars were probably too thin to comfortably jump and land on, just a foot or two in diameter. Some were three or four feet taller than the others, with four feet in between them.

"Now the real fun begins," Albert said, shivering.

Just as he said it, there was a great splash from far below. Something dark blue rocketed into the sky, and Albert recognized it at once, just as the Hammerfin smashed its face onto one of the pillars. There was an earth-trembling *BOOM!*

When the rubble cleared, Albert saw that the pillar had been obliterated into a bazillion pieces, and in its place was a too-large gap of nothing but air.

"Oh, *come on*!" Hoyt yelled. "We're supposed to put up with those things here?"

"I thought they were only in the Silver Sea," Birdie mused.

"Incorrect," Leroy said, pointing, as a dark fin flashed in the water far below. "Remember what they did in the Pit? The Hammerfins are supposed to destroy the smaller pillars, and let the Realm build new ones. It helps keep the Realm Balanced, sort of like natural tremors that are supposed to happen. The only problem is I don't see a new pillar being made in its place."

"There's *not* a new one," Albert said. He thought hard, focusing on the Flight Vision symbol. His eyes started to itch, and when Albert's Master Tile took control, his vision soared from his skull like it was on a bird's wings. He *zoooomed* across the chasm and went down, down, down into the depths, until he was looking at the surface of the water. It shimmered like it was made of melted silver coins.

Nothing sprouted, not even a tiny, pathetic little replacement pillar.

"Yeah, nothing happening down there, guys. Must be a side effect of the Imbalance. But we can handle it." Albert looked at Birdie and Leroy and gave them a thumbs-up. "Too bad we don't have Jadar with us this time, huh?"

Birdie sighed. "I promised him I'd bring back a souvenir."

"I have to admit, that ugly dragon-bird of yours would be able to help us here," Hoyt said.

"He's a Guildacker, and I'll take that as a compliment," Birdie said.

The more time they stood here talking, the closer the Counter got to hitting zero. Albert knew they needed to get across to the other side, but *how*?

It was Hoyt who made the decision. "Stay here," he said suddenly. His voice was determined and strong, and very different from how he usually spoke. "I'm going to fix this."

Before anyone could stop him, Hoyt turned and sprinted away from the group, disappearing in a cloud of dust in the direction they had just come from.

"Where's he going? Why's he going *back*?" Birdie shouted.

"We never know why Hoyt does what he does," Slink said, shaking his head.

Albert had to hand it to Hoyt. He *was* fast.

In less than five minutes, Leroy stood up and pointed. "Look!"

There was a cloud of dust coming back their way. Albert squinted, and before he knew it, Hoyt was racing toward them like he had just drunk a whole bunch of energy drinks. He had a big huge bundle of rope in his arms.

Hoyt dropped the rope in front of them on the cliff, like a big coiled snake. He twirled a pocketknife in his fingers. "We'll have to skip that bridge on the way back. Go ahead, thank me. I won't mind."

"You destroyed our way back?" Birdie screeched.

Hoyt waved a hand. "You got a better idea, Blondie?"

Birdie kicked the cliff, spraying a few rocks over the edge. "No."

"Then it's settled," Hoyt said. "We'll use the rope." He shoved Mo, who, after a pointed glare at Hoyt, stooped down and started to uncoil the rope.

"I really strongly dislike that guy," Leroy grumbled to Albert.

"You're not alone in that," Albert said, shivering as the wind picked up again, spraying red dust across the cliff. "But as much as I hate to admit it, I think Hoyt's right. If we use the rope to create a sort of overhead handhold across the chasm, we can grab onto it for balance when we land on each pillar, and use it as a monkey bar to get between pillars where the gaps are too big to jump across."

"Either that," Birdie said, tightening her ponytail so hard that she winced, "or we'll all go overboard."

"Do you want me to tell you the odds of us dying, dudes?" Leroy asked.

"No," Albert and Birdie said together.

They didn't need to be told. They already knew the answer couldn't be good.

"If we tie this end of the rope here," Leroy said, motioning to a large boulder nearby, "and then someone goes across and ties the rope around the top of that taller pillar on the other side, then we should be able to use it as we move along the uneven pillars."

"I like it," Albert said. He stared at the scattering of pillars. "I'll go first, and tie the rope. You guys cool with that?"

No one objected, not even Hoyt.

Slink stepped forward. "My dad is a fisherman in Florida," he said. "I know how to tie knots."

He grabbed the rope with his big fingers, which were surprisingly nimble, and showed Albert how to tie the strongest type of knot. They looped the rope around the boulder, and then Albert practiced the knot a few times with the other end of the rope. When he'd mastered it,

Slink nodded in approval.

"You're ready. Good luck," he said. He helped loop the rope up several times so that it could hang over Albert's shoulder.

"You need to move fast, Albert," Birdie said.

"Before the Hammerfins destroy more pillars," Leroy added.

Albert nodded. "Well, here goes nothing." He handed the CoreBow to Leroy. "Hang on to this for me."

Slink, Mo, Hoyt, Birdie, and Leroy stood on the edge of the chasm as Albert readied himself for the dangerous journey.

Albert's knees felt weak as he prepared himself to leap. The first pillar was only about three feet away, and was at even height with the cliff that Albert stood on now. It should be easy.

Just don't think about the drop.

Albert bent his knees, took a deep breath, and leaped. He landed on the pillar with ease.

"Yay, Albert!" Birdie cheered from behind him.

So far, so good.

"This isn't so bad," Albert said to himself. He leaped across more pillars, careful not to fall each time he landed. He'd made it halfway across when he got to the real trouble.

The next pillar stood about two feet higher than the pillar Albert was on now. To make that leap, he'd have to put in some serious leg power. Plus, the second pillar looked thinner than this one. If Albert didn't land right on the center of it, he could lose his footing and fall.

"Take it slow," Slink offered.

"But not too slow," Leroy added.

Birdie clapped her hands. "You've got it, Albert."

And I have my Master Tile, Albert thought. He pictured the Jackalope symbol, which looked like a Jackalope's outline. He imagined himself leaping high, but not *too* high, almost like the times he jumped over orange construction cones back in New York City.

The wind whipped him in the face, and the cold seeped into the fibers of his silver suit.

Just jump, Albert.

He conjured up the jumping Jackalope symbol in his mind, and put all of his concentration into not losing the image. He made sure he had a good grip on the loose end of the rope. Then Albert leaped, about two feet upward and four feet forward. The Jackalope symbol gave him the boost he needed. Wind tugged at his hair as he crossed the gap, and for a second, he was afraid he wouldn't make it. But Albert's feet landed on the pillar. Behind him, everyone cheered.

"One step closer!" Leroy shouted. "Just keep doing what you've been doing, and you'll reach the other side!"

The next pillar was trickier. Instead of higher, it was about a seven-foot drop, and even farther away. Albert would need to use Balance *and* the Jackalope symbol for this one.

He pictured the Balance symbol—a triangle with a sphere balanced perfectly on top. It was one that had become so familiar to him over the past two terms of training in the Pit *and* in the Realms. On top of that, he pictured the Jackalope symbol. He imagined the two symbols interlocking, becoming one.

Without hesitation, Albert leaped.

The drop was quick and terrifying, and he almost let go of the end of the rope. Albert's heart went into his throat, and as he saw the silver river below, he wondered what it would be like, falling into it from this height, hundreds of feet up.

He needn't wonder, because the Jackalope symbol carried him across, and again, Albert landed. He wobbled, close to toppling overboard, but a quick thought of the Balance symbol, and suddenly Albert felt so balanced he could have done a twirl without falling off the tiny pillar.

On and on he leaped, sometimes jumping higher, sometimes jumping lower, and once, which was incredibly tricky, Albert had to jump to a stray pillar that was far off to the right.

As he leaped, he could hear everyone else shouting for him, rooting him on. Albert thought he even heard Hoyt's voice in there, somewhere. It filled him with

confidence and spurred him forward as Albert made it
to the final pillar.

This one was the tallest of the bunch, standing several
feet higher than all the others. From up here, Albert felt
incredibly small. The pillar was wide enough that Albert
could at least stoop to one knee for a breather. He looked
around at Ponderay, at all the red and brown shades, and
the cliffs with their jagged edges that reminded Albert of
gnashing teeth.

To anyone else, Ponderay might have looked ugly, a
dark and desolate place. Albert thought it was beautiful,
though it wasn't without fault. Ponderay held the kind
of beauty that came with a warning, like a delicate rose
hiding sharp thorns.

Mess with me, Albert imagined Ponderay saying, *and
you might not leave with your life.*

He shook the thought away as his friends waved at
him from the other side.

"Tie the other end of the rope!" Slink shouted. His
voice was nearly lost in the howling wind.

Albert set to work. He had to lay on his stomach and
leaned over the edge of the pillar. The wind tugged at his
hair and prickled the skin on his face, and staring into
the endless drop below didn't help.

But on the other side of the chasm, Albert could still
hear his teammates urging him on.

Albert looped the loose end of the rope round and

round the pillar. He used the Strength symbol, and pulled the rope as tightly as he could before tying it off. He gave it a test tug, and the line held.

It stretched across the chasm, from the boulder on one side to the very last pillar where Albert stood now.

"It's ready!" Albert called. He waved his arms over his head, and his friends all prepared to make the journey across.

Albert stayed on the final pillar and watched.

Surprisingly, Leroy was the first to make the leap. He jumped onto the first pillar, his long lanky form as awkward as ever, but he'd done it. Albert's chest buzzed with pride for his friend. Leroy leaped to the next one to clear a space for Birdie.

Birdie went next, landing with ease onto the first pillar.

On and on they leaped, from one pillar to the next until Mo and Slink were on pillars, too. Once or twice, one of them over- or undershot, but the rope was there for them to grab onto until they found their footing. One by one, they crossed the gap the Hammerfin had created, using the rope like a monkey bar, and made it safely to the other side.

Hoyt was the last one on the opposite cliff. Albert watched, biting his lip, as Hoyt leaped.

The second Hoyt made it onto the first pillar, Albert noticed a flash of something bright yellow below, followed by a strange popping noise.

"LIGHTNING RAY!" Mo shouted from the middle of the group.

The ray was soaring from the waters below like a bird, its flapping sides outspread like wings. The ray was *massive*, almost as large as the King Fireflies had been back in Calderon.

Albert watched it all happen in slow motion. The ray soared up, far over their heads. When it reached top height, it did a flip in midair and dove downward, barely missing Leroy's face. It nicked him in the foot, and Leroy stumbled, the shock having paralyzed his foot.

"I'm gonna die!" Leroy cried out, wiggling his foot and about to topple off his pillar because of his panic. "I'm only eleven and I'm gonna die!" But he grabbed the rope in record time, and managed to straighten himself. Right then and there, Albert thanked Hoyt for coming up with the idea of the rope. It had just saved Leroy's life.

"Leroy, focus!" Albert shouted.

"Get it together!" Birdie yelled. Leroy whirled on his pillar, eyes wide.

"It's fine, Leroy!" Albert coaxed. "It's just a little numbness. It'll wear off soon. You have to keep heading my way, before more rays attack."

The next pillar for Leroy was a big leap. But he managed to make it, and Birdie, Slink, Mo, and Hoyt followed suit, landing on theirs. Hoyt was still a few pillars behind, though. It looked like it was taking everything he had just to make each jump.

Suddenly, another Lightning Ray leaped from the waves. It stung Hoyt in the hand, and he howled like Farnsworth at the pain.

Seconds later, the Hammerfins attacked.

Two of them bolted out of the water like rockets, speeding toward Hoyt's pillar so fast that no one could have done anything about it. Hoyt leaped.

Boom! Boom!

Rock and dust exploded everywhere. All six of them screamed, and suddenly there was a huge tug on the rope. When the dust cleared, Albert could see everyone straining to keep themselves on their feet.

There was nothing left in the space where Hoyt's pillar used to be, and nothing next to it, either. There was now at least fourteen feet of empty space, and right in the middle, Hoyt dangled from the rope with both hands, hanging on for dear life.

"I can't hang on much longer!" Hoyt shouted. "I can't feel my left hand! I'm slipping!" His feet dangled over the chasm below. If he fell, he would surely die.

"Someone help him!" Slink yelled.

Albert's entire body froze in fear.

They had to do something to help Hoyt, and *fast*.

Hoyt needed to scoot across the rope, but he was already slipping, the numbness from the Lightning Ray rendering his left hand useless. His fingers turned bright white as he tried to hold on.

There was a *pop!* A Lightning Ray rocketed from the waters below and went for Slink. He ducked, narrowly avoiding a paralyzed face.

More Lightning Rays followed, targeting the other Balance Keepers.

"Move!" Birdie shouted. In front of her, Leroy leaped, reaching another pillar, and Birdie followed. Slink and Mo followed, too, and Hoyt was left hanging on behind them.

"We have to go back for him!" Mo shouted. He turned and tried to leap onto his previous pillar, but a Lightning Ray got in his way. Mo's hand swelled to twice its normal size. He tried to leap again, but another ray leaped out of the water below and stopped him.

The Lightning Rays didn't want them passing, and they'd do whatever they could to prevent it. Just like Professor Asante had said.

While everyone else ducked and hopped and avoided Lighting Rays from their own pillars, Albert watched Hoyt.

They couldn't just let him hang there.

A gust of wind whipped through the air, and Hoyt's injured hand slipped. Mo tried to go back and help again, but this time a Hammerfin burst out of the water.

Mo had to jump onto Slink's pillar, and together, the

two boys barely fit. Mo's pillar had been smashed to bits.

"Come back!" Hoyt screamed. "Don't leave me here! Don't leave me, please!"

He dangled by one hand for a moment, before gaining his grip again. His eyes met Albert's. Hoyt's were as panicked as a cornered rabbit's. The expression in them begged for saving.

Albert couldn't take it anymore. The Balance Keepers were losing concentration, scattered like ants in the rain. He had to take control of the group and save Hoyt before it was too late.

"Come this way, hurry!" Albert shouted to all the others. He leaped from his final pillar onto the safe, solid ground of the cliff. The others followed, racing across the tops of their pillars toward the cliff.

All the while, the Lightning Rays attacked, and Hoyt got closer and closer to falling. He'd been hanging on for at least three minutes already.

When everyone was safely on the cliff (albeit with a few paralyzed hands and feet), Albert leaped back toward the pillars, back in the direction he'd already come.

"Albert, what are you doing?!" Birdie screamed.

"Someone has to help him!" Albert said.

"Whatever you're going to do, Flynn, you'd better do it fast!" Hoyt shouted. A Lightning Ray shot out of the waves. It managed to get Hoyt's foot, and the pain on his face was enough that Albert was afraid Hoyt was going to let go of the rope.

Still, Hoyt hung on.

Albert leaped from one pillar to the next one, dropping four feet before he landed. He took a deep breath
and leaped again, this time jumping the four feet up to
land onto the next pillar.

"HURRY UP!" Slink shouted from behind him. "He's
going to fall!"

Albert worked as quickly as he could, using the Jackalope symbol to leap over the gaps the Hammerfins had
caused. The wind was blowing as fiercely as a hurricane,
and once, Albert almost toppled over.

But one final shout from Hoyt, full of fear, was all
Albert needed to carry on.

He made it to the pillar closest to Hoyt. Hoyt hung
there, about seven feet away. "Help me!" Hoyt shouted.
"*Please.*"

The plan formed in Albert's mind almost instantly.
He'd never done this before. In fact, he hadn't even *practiced* this symbol, and he wasn't sure if he had the right
image in his mind.

But there it was, like a rubber band stretched tight.

The Stretch symbol. *I need longer arms, Tile. Please, help
me save Hoyt.*

Albert's arms tingled. He felt like he'd just dunked
them into icy cold water, and Albert watched, amazed,
as his arms grew. They stretched as if they were made of

rubber, slowly lengthening until they were twice as long as normal.

The whole world slowed down around Albert as he knelt on his pillar and reached his arm toward Hoyt.

He was still not close enough.

"You have to come closer," Albert said to Hoyt. "Inch your way, slowly, one hand at a time."

"I can't!" Hoyt's voice was high pitched.

Albert stared into Hoyt's eyes. "You have to, Hoyt. Just pretend we're in the Pit. If you fall, it's no big deal, right? There's a trampoline floor to send you right back up."

Hoyt closed his eyes tight. Slowly, he moved his hands a little to the right, toward Albert.

"Good," Albert chided. "You're doing good. Keep coming."

Albert noticed a strange popping sound, almost like the crackling of a fire.

He looked past Hoyt, to the boulder where he had originally tied the first end of the rope.

It was fraying, strands of it popping away one by one.

"Okay, Hoyt, you gotta move *now*," Albert said. He tried to keep his voice calm and collected. Hoyt picked up the pace, but only a little.

Another ray flew into the air, so close to Hoyt's head that he screamed. But the fear made Hoyt move a little faster, and he was a few inches closer to Albert.

"Just a little bit closer, and I can reach you," Albert said.

There was another *pop!* The fibers of the rope were fraying even faster. Hoyt started to sink lower as the rope sagged beneath his weight. It was going to snap.

"Hoyt, you've got to move faster than this!" Albert shouted. "Use your Speed Tile!"

Behind him, everyone screamed a warning.

"Grab my hand!!" Albert shouted.

The rope snapped, and Hoyt fell.

CHAPTER 25

The Silver Sea

Albert had never imagined he'd have to save Hoyt someday. They'd always been enemies, from the very beginning. Last term, Albert might not have risked his life for Hoyt's.

But now, as Albert lay on his stomach on a pillar hundreds of feet in the air, his extra-long arms screaming from pain as he gripped Hoyt and held him over the chasm, Albert knew that what he'd done was right.

"Pull me up!" Hoyt shouted from below.

Albert felt like his arm was about to rip out of the socket. He gritted his teeth and screamed, then pulled with all his might. Hoyt was just too heavy, and Albert's palms were slippery with sweat.

Strength. The word popped into Albert's mind, and he latched onto it. The Strength symbol appeared, and

Albert's Master Tile kicked into gear. Suddenly Albert felt strong enough to lift Hoyt over his head.

Albert hauled Hoyt up and onto the pillar. Hoyt collapsed against Albert, and the pillar was so small that they had to lean together, arms over each other's shoulders, to stay balanced.

"You," Hoyt said, gasping for air. "You *saved* me."

Albert felt ready to collapse, but he stood strong and steady, letting Hoyt lean on him. "It was the only thing to do."

"That's twice now," Hoyt said. "Why do you keep saving me, after I've been such a jerk all this time?"

The wind howled, and a Lightning Ray leaped. Albert and Hoyt ducked together, then stood back up again.

"Saving people is what Balance Keepers do," Albert said. He looked sideways at Hoyt. "We've got to move now. The others are waiting, and we're not out of danger."

Hoyt nodded, still trying to catch his breath.

Albert had turned to look ahead, to figure out a plan for getting the rest of the way across, when Hoyt spoke again.

"Thank you," Hoyt said. He stared at Albert with a strange softness in his eyes that had never been there before. "I didn't deserve it."

Albert shrugged, and what he said next came from his heart of hearts. "Everyone deserves saving, Hoyt. Even the bad guys."

Albert told Hoyt his plan, and together they leaped

across the remaining pillars, using Albert's Master Tile to cross the gaps from the Hammerfins, and Hoyt's Speed Tile to do it quickly.

Eventually, with the cheers of Birdie, Leroy, Slink, and Mo, both Albert and Hoyt made it to the safety of the other side.

The Counter on Albert's wrist said they only had ten hours left before the fate of the world ended in darkness and doom.

They walked until Albert's feet throbbed. His stomach ached from hunger, so they stopped and ate granola bars that Leroy had stuffed into his backpack. In the distance, the outline of the Silver Sea was the only thing the Balance Keepers had as their guide.

At the nine-hour mark, they crossed another rope bridge. This one was just as rickety as the first, like it was made of toothpicks and floss. Crossing it lasted almost an hour. Every step they took caused more wooden planks to snap or fall.

Just as the last of them stepped off, the rope bridge fell.

"How are we supposed to get back?" Birdie asked. "Everything we've crossed has basically been destroyed."

Leroy shrugged. "Don't ask me."

"We'll worry about that after we settle the Imbalance," Albert said.

Everyone was tired and windblown. Hoyt hadn't

spoken since the accident at the Path of Pillars, and Albert was starting to wonder if the guy was in shock.

At the eight-hour mark, they used another rope to hop across a shorter passage of pillars, and nearly lost Birdie to a Lightning Ray attack. The rays had doubled in number. They managed to paralyze both of Birdie's legs with their electric shock. Birdie only made it to safety because Slink stepped in and grabbed her just before she fell into the chasm.

After that, Albert noticed that something had changed between Birdie and Slink. Birdie looked right into his eyes to thank him, her previous shyness having melted away. Slink offered to carry Birdie piggyback style until she was able to walk again, and they chatted nonstop.

The farther they journeyed, the closer they got to the Silver Sea. At the seven-hour mark, they finally made it, stopping on a cliff that overlooked the center of the Realm.

Albert gasped. It was just as Professor Asante had promised.

The Silver Sea was like polished dimes, the water shimmering and bright, even as it churned. It was perfectly circular in shape, and it spanned at least two miles across.

"It's breathtaking," Birdie gasped. "And more than a little scary."

"You can say that again," Mo agreed.

Slink set Birdie down on the rocky cliff. "I can't believe we made it," he said.

The Silver Sea was a sight in itself, but the real masterpieces were the Ten Pillars.

They stood at least fifteen stories high, and each one was as wide around as a tour bus. They were arranged in a perfect circle, each Pillar about thirty feet away from the next one. They spun so fast that when Albert tried to pick out the individual Pillars, all he saw was a blur. Their color was a deep, dark chocolate. Using his Flight Vision to get in closer, Albert could also see the large holes in the Pillars' sides—though he didn't see any Jackalopes.

He let go of the Flight Vision and returned to gazing from the cliff. He confirmed what he suspected—there were no bridges from this cliff out to the Pillars—it was just hundreds of yards of Silver Sea between them and the Pillars.

"We made it this far," Albert said, sitting with his knees to his chest. "We should rest for a few minutes before we climb down."

"That's the best thing you've said all day," Leroy said as he flopped down onto his back and stared up at the sky.

Everyone sat in a circle, happy to get a few moments of rest after the long journey, but Hoyt crossed to the edge of the cliff and sat alone. His legs dangled over the edge.

"Wake me up when it's time," Leroy said. "I need a power nap." He rolled onto his side. Even with the howling wind, his snores could be heard within seconds.

"So what's the game plan?" Birdie asked. She was rubbing her legs, trying to get feeling back into them.

"We need to climb down this cliff first," Mo said. His face was covered in dirt and grime. Albert knew he probably looked just as filthy.

"The water is going to be freezing," Slink added. "We should start mentally preparing for that."

Albert wanted to stay and talk, but his mind was elsewhere. He stood up and crossed the cliff to where Hoyt was sitting.

"Mind if I join you?" Albert asked.

Hoyt shrugged.

Albert sat down beside Hoyt and took off his boots. It had never felt better to have his feet free. He let his legs hang over the edge of the cliff.

"Are you all right, man?" Albert asked.

Hoyt hadn't said a word since Albert saved him.

I've befriended Slink and Mo, Albert thought. *There has to be hope for Hoyt and me.*

Albert was afraid, with the way Hoyt was acting now, that Hoyt wouldn't be able to perform to the very best of his abilities once they were in the Silver Sea and climbing the Ten Pillars. Albert needed to get Hoyt talking. He needed to help him stay focused.

But Hoyt spoke first. "I've never liked you, Flynn. From the first day you set foot in the Core, I've considered you an enemy."

Albert readied himself for whatever rude thing Hoyt was about to say next.

But Hoyt turned to Albert and smiled. "It's because you're a great Balance Keeper. And I don't like to be shown up by anyone."

Albert laughed. "I'm just the same as everyone else in the Core."

In the harsh light of Ponderay, Hoyt's hair looked orange-black, positively Halloweenish. He shrugged. "You're different. You can't deny that, especially with that Master Tile around your neck."

Albert looked down at his black Tile. For so long, he'd hated it, and wished he'd plucked something else out of the Waterfall of Fate. But now that Albert had learned to use his Tile, it had become a lifesaver.

"We don't have to be friends," Hoyt said. "But we can be cool with each other. You saved me, which means I owe you one."

"Nah, you don't," Albert said, but Hoyt held out his hand.

"I'm saying thanks," Hoyt said, chuckling. "Accept it."

They shook hands, and just then, Albert was struck by an incredible amount of respect for the Realm of Ponderay. If they hadn't come here, Albert and Hoyt would still be enemies. Now, things were changing, and it was the Realm that had made it all happen.

"You ready for this?" Albert asked.

The wind blew, and Hoyt shivered. "Ready as I'll ever be, I guess."

"We should get everyone together," Albert suggested. "And start planning. It's time to move on."

Albert and Hoyt turned back to the group, only to find that Birdie, Slink, and Mo had fallen asleep, too.

Albert looked at Hoyt. "We could probably use the rest. I'll take the first watch and wake you up in an hour. Sound good?"

Hoyt nodded, and lay down near Mo.

Albert looked around. Even with his friends asleep, there was a determination that hadn't been there before. They were a real team now, and despite all the danger they'd faced, despite everything that had happened today, all the close calls and arguments and fear, Albert was happy.

Beneath the happiness was something else, something that made Albert wonder if he'd be able to nap at all.

Excitement.

CHAPTER 26

The Ten Pillars of Ponderay

T wo hours later, they had made their plan—or at least a plan for getting to and climbing the Pillars. They still didn't know what they'd do once they got to the top; they still didn't know how the Tiles and Pillars were marked.

"Nothing to do but climb down," Albert said, as he peered over the edge of the cliff, lying on his belly. The cliff simply dropped off, fading into a rocky beach that led to the shores of the Silver Sea.

Leroy was beside Albert, staring down into the abyss. "Hey, at least we haven't seen any Core creatures here at the sea . . . yet."

Albert laughed. "Way to be positive."

"I've been sort of a wimp this whole journey," Hoyt

said. "I'll lead the pack."

"Go ahead," Birdie suggested, waving a hand as Hoyt marched past her. She was hopping up and down, testing the strength of her legs. They'd finally become unparalyzed after their short rest.

Slink stood beside her, grinning like a madman. Albert was starting to think the guy had a crush on Birdie. And with the way Birdie smiled back at him, maybe she had one, too. Slink was cool, in Albert's eyes. He'd saved both Albert and Birdie in one day.

"We've got five hours left," Albert said. "And those Pillars are going to take at least a few hours to climb. Let's go."

They had to lie on their stomachs and scoot backward over the edge of the cliff to move down. It was scary work, and slow going with all the strong winds at their backs.

Hand after hand, foot after foot, the six of them made the descent. The closer they got to the bottom, the more Albert noticed just how big the Ten Pillars were. He could see sparks and flashes of color in the Silver Sea— Hammerfins and Lightning Rays upset by the Imbalance, getting ready for the attack.

He wondered briefly where the Jackalopes were. Maybe they'd get lucky, and not have to face them at all. *Probably not.*

Hoyt's feet touched the ground first. Everyone else

joined soon after, and they took a few minutes to rest on the rocky beach.

"We're really here," Birdie said, staring out at the Ten Pillars, her eyes wide. "Professor Asante wasn't kidding. The Pillars are, like, totally ginormous."

"That's not a real word," Leroy noted, and Birdie punched him in the arm. They started to bicker, and it comforted Albert to hear them acting the way they always did in the Core, where things were safe and fun and free.

The feeling only lasted a minute. The rest of the First Unit had gone to the water's edge, and Albert, Birdie, and Leroy joined them. Albert bent down and stuck his hand in. Cold was an understatement. Freezing didn't quite cut it, either. Bone-shattering, teeth-trembling, limb-snapping punishment was more like it.

"We're definitely going to need those gloves and booties and hoods," Albert called over his shoulder. Everyone unzipped their backpacks and put on the neoprene gloves and booties. Leroy took off his glasses and replaced them with the vision-correcting goggles Professor Asante had given him.

Albert stepped into the water up to his ankles. "Much better," he said. It was still cold, but not as horrible as before.

"Remember—we stick together!" Leroy shouted from the right.

"Definitely!" Albert answered.

To his left, Slink and Hoyt nodded, and to his right, Birdie just looked like she wanted to punch the water for daring to be so cold.

"On the count of three," Albert shouted. "One, two, three!"

They swam as best they could, heading toward the Pillars.

The Pillars stood as thick around as the Troll Tree in the woods outside of Herman, and they moved at such high speeds that great waves raged around them.

One of the waves slapped Albert in the face, and he swallowed salty seawater. He could feel the current tugging at his legs, like a great invisible hand, trying to suck him under. He and Birdie would be fine, with her Water Tile and his Master Tile, but everyone else would struggle the closer they got.

"We should link together!" Albert said. "Do what we did with Leroy in the Pit!"

It was awkward at first, for Albert to link arms with Hoyt, but they did it anyway.

"Can you use your Speed to swim with Birdie and me?" Albert yelled over the wind and the waves. Another one slapped him in the face, and he narrowly avoided bumping heads with Birdie.

"Is that even a question?" Hoyt yelled back. "Let's do this."

He kicked his legs like crazy, and Birdie and Albert followed suit. Soon, they were soaring across the waters like a pod of dolphins, all six of them linked together as strong as a chain. If they could swim fast enough to launch Slink, Mo, and Leroy to Pillars, then Birdie, Albert, and Hoyt could get to theirs on their own. But these Pillars weren't the pathetic Pit stand-ins. These were the real deal. They stood much too far apart for the Balance Keepers to jump between. Even Albert, with his Master Tile, probably wouldn't be able to make that leap.

It's almost as if the traitor knows the limits of my Tile, Albert thought. The idea chilled him more than the freezing water did.

And, just as they swam up to the first Pillar, a blue fin appeared in the waves.

"HAMMERFIN!" Slink and Hoyt shouted at once.

They all stopped swimming and watched as the giant blue shark leaped from the waters, soaring so high into the air that Albert was *sure* it was going to make it to the top and try to destroy the Pillar.

Instead, the Hammerfin turned in midair, doing a backflip that could rival the best Olympian diver. Then it rocketed down from the sky, its hammer-like head aimed right at Slink and Hoyt.

"SWIM!" Albert screamed.

Their human chain broke. They dove, fighting against the waves to escape the Hammerfin's destruction.

A wave exploded across from Albert as he watched the creature make impact. Water sprayed his face, getting salt into his eyes. When he blinked it away, he saw that the Hammerfin had missed Hoyt by just an inch. As the creature disappeared beneath the waves, Hoyt started screaming his head off.

"GET ME OUT OF HERE!"

Mo grabbed him, trying to calm him down, which Hoyt took as his cue to whizz off across the waters, with Mo clinging onto him for dear life. Hoyt kicked his legs so fast that he practically launched them out of the waves, landing them like flies on the side of the nearest Pillar. They clung to it, dripping wet and trembling. "We're good!" Mo called out. "Keep moving like we planned!"

"Let's go!" Albert shouted, waving his friends along.

Slink and Birdie went one way, with Birdie using her Water Tile to help Slink swim fast enough to grab onto a Pillar as it rocketed by. Leroy and Albert went the other way.

The Pillars soared past, like a merry-go-round on a sugar high, way too fast for anyone to grab onto. Albert helped rocket Leroy toward the closest one. Across from them, Hoyt and Mo began climbing their Pillar, and Albert could see Birdie and Slink in the distance doing the same.

"The handholds shouldn't disappear here," Leroy said, as he and Albert hoisted themselves onto the Pillar.

He was right, but now Albert understood the reason for the strange handholds in the Pit. As he grabbed ahold, his hand slipped on glowing blue-green algae. He barely had time to grab onto another divot in the rock before his left foot slipped, too.

Albert and Leroy managed to hang on. Every ten feet or so, there were giant holes in the Pillar. It was almost as if they were climbing a humongous termite mound.

"Aren't there supposed to be Jackalopes in here?" Leroy asked from below.

Albert stopped, peering into one. It was black as night, impossible to see more than a few inches inside. "Yep," he said. "But I don't really think I want to stick around to meet one."

"Good call," Leroy said. "Let's keep moving."

The climb was exhausting. For every few feet they moved upward, Albert felt like they'd move just as much back, and the Pillars were spinning so fast it made Albert's head wobble and his stomach roll.

Partway up, Leroy slipped and fell, knocking Albert down with him. They both tumbled into the Silver Sea. Albert splashed to the surface, coughing salt water, his eyes burning. "Leroy!" he screamed.

The Pillars whizzed past, shoving wind into Albert's face. He saw Birdie and Slink go by on their Pillar.

"Do you see Leroy?" Albert screamed.

"I . . . can't . . . hear yooooouuuuuuuu!" Birdie yelled,

as the Pillar whisked her away.

Albert dove under, using the Water symbol in his mind. Sure enough, Leroy was there beneath the surface, his foot tangled up in a chunk of seaweed, his black hair fanned out around him like a shadow.

Albert dove deep, stretching for his friend. He quickly untangled Leroy's boot, and they both zoomed to the surface.

Leroy coughed and sputtered for air. Then he lunged forward and gave Albert a floating water-hug. "Thanks, bro!"

"No time to thank me. We've got to get on a Pillar!" Albert shouted.

They started their journey again, grabbing ahold of a Pillar just as it flew past. The timing was perfect, for just as they left the water, a flock of Lightning Rays appeared, soaring from the waves like birds.

"Look out!" Albert shouted.

He hung from one hand, narrowly avoiding the electric beasts.

The Pillars swung round and round. Albert climbed, trying as best he could to make good time. Through the chaos he could see Hoyt climbing higher and higher by the second. It was hard to see, hard to breathe.

Albert passed by one of the hundreds of holes in the Pillar's side. It was so tempting. If only he could just duck inside for a second, get warm and catch his breath. He didn't *see* any Jackalopes. . . . He dove inside.

The cave was larger than he thought. There was plenty of room to stretch out, even stand if he wanted to.

"Look out!" Slink shouted, from somewhere outside.

Albert peered out of the hole.

Slink was on an opposite nearby Pillar, waving one arm like crazy, trying to get Birdie's attention. It was too little too late. Birdie was staring a giant Jackalope in the face. It had appeared in one of the dark holes, its antlers large as a deer's, its rabbit-like legs ready to pounce.

And pounce it did.

The creature reared from inside the hole. Its strong front legs punched Birdie, and she was catapulted away. She crashed into the waves, far below.

"NO!" Albert shouted.

Slink dove into the waves after Birdie, and they disappeared from view as Albert's Pillar carted him away.

Albert gasped, suddenly, as something occurred to him. If a Jackalope had been in the other hole, then that could only mean one thing.

Albert turned, slowly, to look into the darkness behind him.

There was a thumping sound, like a giant drum banging over and over.

A Jackalope raced forth toward the mouth of the hole. Albert screamed, but there was no time to react. The Jackalope turned in a flash and used its powerful back legs to kick Albert.

Albert felt like he'd just been shot out of a cannon. All the air left his lungs as he soared through the air, then crashed back into the sea below.

When he surfaced, there wasn't any time to waste.

"Albert, get out of there!" Leroy shouted as he swung past on a Pillar.

Albert turned. His whole body went rigid. The water was turning yellow with flashes of light.

Lightning Rays, by the hundreds, had appeared. They were swarming in the waves, like a fireworks show beneath the surface. They were heading toward Albert, and *fast*.

Albert thought of the Water symbol and swam as fast as his Master Tile would allow him, then reached out and grabbed a Pillar. A hand locked onto his, and Albert looked up into Hoyt's eyes.

"Climb, Flynn!" Hoyt shouted, as he helped Albert hoist himself onto the spinning Pillar.

"Thanks," Albert said. His feet were barely out of the water when the Lightning Rays reached the Pillar. "We'd better climb before they start leaping out of the waves."

"I couldn't agree more," Hoyt said. His suit had a big gash in it, and his arm was bleeding. It looked like he'd been scraped by a Jackalope's antlers.

Just as Albert thought it, there was a rumble, and from the holes in the Pillars, it was like an army of Jackalopes sprouted. Left and right, the antlered creatures poked their heads out.

Then they started leaping. Somehow, the Jackalopes leaped from Pillar to Pillar, using the handholds in the rock as little springboards. Every time their rabbit feet touched a Pillar, they'd ricochet off and leap for another, knocking down any Balance Keepers that got in the way.

It was like a game of tag, but it wasn't fun for Albert and his friends. Leroy was catapulted from a Pillar, landing in the water again. He climbed back up, and Albert cried out just as another Jackalope headed for Leroy, its antlers poised for the attack.

"Leroy, watch out!" Albert shouted.

He watched as, almost in slow motion, Birdie emerged from one of the dark holes and hauled Leroy inside in record time. The Jackalope decided to go after Slink then, but Slink was fast. He turned and shouted something at the Jackalope, using the power of his Creature Speak Tile. The Jackalope dove into a hole, but Albert guessed it wouldn't stay there long.

Slink turned to Albert and Hoyt. "There's too many! I can't talk to them all! You guys go on!"

Just then, a Hammerfin bashed sideways into Albert's Pillar, rocking it so hard that Albert almost lost his grip. Hoyt grabbed his wrist, helping him hang on.

"You all right, Flynn?" Hoyt shouted from above.

"I'm good!" Albert yelled back. "We have to end this, before it gets worse!"

And he was right. The Counter said it had been two

hours since they climbed down the cliff. Two solid hours
of swimming and climbing, swimming and climbing. If
they continued this way, they would exhaust themselves
before time was up. They had to finish the job.

Albert was about to call Leroy over so he could logic
out a new plan, when Hoyt turned and shouted, "Slink!
Come here!"

Slink climbed over to Albert and Hoyt. He was dripping wet, and he looked like he was about to drop.

"Ask a Jackalope to take me and Albert to the top of
this Pillar," Hoyt said.

Slink looked like Hoyt had just told him to put on a
dress. "I can't do that! I'm not good enough yet. I only
know how to say a few words to them, and besides,
they're angry from the Imbalance."

Hoyt looked Slink right in the eyes. "You *are* good
enough, Slink. I know you can do it. Just try."

Albert was grateful to Hoyt right then, for his pep
talk seemed to have worked. Slink climbed back up and
approached the hole where the Jackalope was hiding.
With a deep breath, Slink climbed inside.

Albert gripped the Pillar so hard his fingers ached.
What if Slink can't do it?

"He's got this," Hoyt said.

A full minute passed.

Slink poked his head out and called down. "Get in
here, boys!"

Albert and Hoyt climbed up the Pillar as quickly as they could. Had Slink done it? Had he tamed a Jack-alope?

They reached the hole, and both Albert and Hoyt climbed inside.

There sat a Jackalope, with horns as long as Albert was tall. It hardly fit inside the cave, and with three boys inside as well, the Jackalope looked like it wanted to bolt. Or attack.

"He'll do it," Slink said. He reached out and patted the wild Jackalope on the neck. It flinched, and its eyes widened, but when Slink spoke something to it in Creature Speak, the Jackalope relaxed. "Better go now, while you can. I'll go find Birdie and Leroy and see if we can tame some more."

"You're a lifesaver," Albert said to Slink.

"I knew you could do it." Hoyt grinned.

Slink said one more thing to the Jackalope, and dove out of the hole.

The Jackalope pawed the ground, as if to say, *Let's get this over with.*

Albert approached it first, his hands outstretched. The Jackalope's fur was soft as silk. Albert climbed on the creature's back and grabbed onto its horns for support.

"No one in the Core needs to hear about this," Hoyt said. He climbed on behind Albert and wrapped his arms around Albert's stomach. "Got it?"

"Got it," Albert said.

He wasn't sure how to control the Jackalope. He clicked his teeth and kicked his heels, almost like he was riding a horse. The Jackalope huffed and bent its back legs. Then, before Albert or Hoyt could change their minds, the creature leaped.

Really leaped.

It was like Albert had been in a car that suddenly went from zero to one hundred in an instant. His stomach went out from under him, and he and Hoyt both screamed.

The Jackalope carried them through the air, across to the next Pillar. There, its back feet kicked off a handhold. It leaped again.

Jump after jump, the Jackalope carried Albert and Hoyt into the sky.

Finally, they landed on top of a Pillar.

Albert and Hoyt slid off the Jackalope's back. It shook like a dog after a bath, but it stayed put.

"Wow," Hoyt gasped. "Look at this, Flynn."

They peered over the edge of the Pillar as it spun them round and round and round. From here, they could see the rest of the Realm, all the cliffs and chasms they'd journeyed across to get here. Down below, Albert could see Slink and Mo on one Pillar, Birdie and Leroy on another. He hoped they'd get up here soon. Albert and Hoyt needed all the help they could get. The Counter said they had only two and a half hours to finish this thing.

Probably shouldn't have slept so long on the cliff, Albert thought. *But too late now.*

"On to the Tiles," Albert said.

He sat up and looked around. Sure enough, right there on the top of the Pillar was a narrow opening. There was something sticking out of it.

"The first Tile!" Albert said. It was just like the Tiles they wore on their necks, but bigger, about the size of a piece of toast.

Hoyt reached for it and yanked it out, holding it in front of him.

There was an ancient-looking symbol on it, like a knife had scratched it. The symbol was a diamond—or a rhombus, as his math teacher had called it during their geometry lesson earlier this year. Albert did pay attention in school *sometimes.*

"What should I do with it?" Hoyt asked.

Albert shrugged. "Keep it, I guess. Not much we can do with it until we know how the Pillars are marked."

Hoyt stuck the Tile in his backpack and zipped it tight. "Now what?"

Albert looked around. The rest of his teammates were still climbing Pillars; Slink apparently hadn't tamed any more Jackalopes yet.

"Ready for another ride?" Albert asked. "We should go and grab another Tile and see what the symbol is. Maybe it will spark something for us. If the goal is to rearrange the Tiles, and get them back to their original Pillars, then we've got to see if we can decipher the pattern."

They climbed back onto the Jackalope. It bristled, but allowed them to stay on.

"Take us to the next Pillar," Albert said, picturing the Creature Speak Tile. His words came out in a mixture of strange huffing and clicking noises.

The Jackalope bent its back legs, wiggled its butt, and leaped.

This time Albert resisted the urge to scream. The wind was ice-cold on his face, but it made him feel alive.

The Jackalope landed hard, on the next Pillar. Hoyt fell off, and Albert almost landed on top of him.

"Sorry," Albert said, as he brushed himself off.

"It's fine. Look!" Hoyt yanked out the next Tile. This one had a carving of a triangle. "Should I put this in my backpack, too?"

Albert just shrugged. He hated that they didn't really know what to do next. *Had* they checked the Pillars for markings on the way up? Albert certainly hadn't and it wasn't like he wanted to interrupt Leroy to ask him now—he was dangling precariously near a Jackalope hole. Maybe Albert could do a quick check himself.

He pictured the Flight Vision symbol once again and looked over the edge of his Pillar, searching for a symbol.

But it was just rock! Just stupid, algae-covered rock.

He moved his vision to another Pillar where his friends were climbing around the sides. He watched Birdie try to climb around a corner on one Pillar, and Leroy nearly slip over a rounded edge on another, but he didn't see any symbols.

He saw Slink talking to the Jackalopes, trying to reason with them, and Mo was in the waves below.

Still, no markings caught Albert's eye. "I've got nothing," Albert growled in frustration, shaking off the Flight Vision.

Just then, a splash sounded from below. A Hammerfin flew through the air.

"Duck!" Albert shouted. He tackled Hoyt just in time, and then caught the Triangle Tile, which had flown from Hoyt's hands. The Hammerfin did a flip, and its giant tail swooshed less than a foot from Albert's head.

Albert scrambled to the edge of the Pillar and peered over. The Hammerfin had disappeared back beneath the waves. But more would be back.

"We have to keep going," Hoyt said, as he and Albert brushed themselves off. Albert tucked the Triangle Tile into his backpack and climbed onto the Jackalope. "Take us to another Pillar," he said to the Jackalope, using Creature Speak.

"I'm glad you've got that Master Tile," Hoyt said, climbing up beside Albert onto the Jackalope's back. The beast reared and leaped, and soon they'd landed on another Pillar.

Hoyt quickly bent down and plucked out a third Tile. He held it up and Albert noted the rectangle shape.

Just then, everything changed.

There was a great, resounding *CRACK-BOOM-CRACK*, an angrier noise than Albert had ever heard. The ground shook, and the Silver Sea roared from far below. The Pillars jerked violently. Albert and Hoyt fell to their knees to avoid going overboard, Hoyt barely keeping ahold of the Rectangle Tile.

This is the end, Albert thought. *The Counter must have been wrong. We're too late.*

The Pillars' insides buzzed like a car's engine revving up. Albert braced himself for the Pillars to pick up even more speed, but instead, the Pillars jolted to a hard stop, like when his mom slammed on the brakes at a red light. Albert and Hoyt instinctively each grabbed the Tile slot in the middle of the Pillar to keep from flying off.

Albert had turned to make sure his friends were okay when the Pillars jerked into motion again, this time rotating in the opposite direction.

Well, that could be worse. A direction change isn't so—

The Pillars halted again, and rotated back the *other* way.

Then the other way.

Then back the other way again.

Every few seconds, the Pillars halted and switched direction, churning back and forth, back and forth. It was like Albert was in a giant washing machine set to the "heavy duty" cycle. Below them, the waters of the Silver Sea churned with waves higher than Albert had ever seen. Albert and Hoyt held on to the Tile slot as best they could, but after a particularly heavy jolt, Hoyt started sliding away from Albert, the unexpected momentum tugging at him like an invisible hand. Albert tried to hang on to him, but the churning was just too strong.

Hoyt's legs dangled over the edge.

"Don't let go!" Hoyt screamed.

Albert didn't let go.

Not even when the Pillars churned harder. Not even when Hoyt's weight became too much. Together, they went overboard and plummeted toward the Silver Sea.

CHAPTER 27

The CoreBow

There was nothing they could do. It all happened so fast.

Albert saw the Lightning Rays below in the water, ready to shock him and paralyze him. He was going to die down there, even if he survived the fall.

Down and down they fell, tumbling head over heels.

I should have been nicer to my siblings, Albert thought, as he came closer and closer to death. *I should have called my mom one more time before I entered the Realm, to say good-bye.*

He thought of Farnsworth's bright blue eyes, and Professor Flynn's glittering smile, and the very first time Albert had seen the Core. He imagined he was just about to dive into the Waterfall of Fate, not the Silver

Sea, and . . . suddenly something floated into his line of vision.

It was the Tile Lucinda had given him, back in the Main Chamber.

The Chance Tile.

Albert wrapped his fingers around the Tile, clutching it with all the hope he could muster. *Please*, he thought, as he came closer and closer to his end. *Please don't let me die like this.*

The Tile burned beneath his fingertips. The wind rushed and roared into Albert's face as he fell. For one fleeting moment, he thought he heard music, the voice of someone or something sweet, telling him to hold on.

BAM!

The breath left Albert's lungs in a whoosh as he landed, hard.

But it wasn't into the Silver Sea. He'd landed . . . *on the back of a Jackalope? And Leroy was controlling the creature?!*

Leroy had come out of nowhere, riding on a Jackalope like it was a quarter horse. It had bounced from one Pillar to another, angling itself perfectly so that Albert fell across its back.

Albert gasped and held so tightly to Leroy's waist that Leroy yelped. But Albert didn't care. He was *alive*.

"What the heck?" Albert yelled.

Leroy's laugh was triumphant. "It was me! I saw you and Hoyt struggling up there, and there was nothing I could do, but suddenly it was like I heard this voice, talking about horses. Can you believe that? So I put two and two together, and figured out that Jackalopes are just like horses, really. And once I knew that, it was much easier for Slink to use his Creature Speak to communicate with them. We all hopped on Jackalopes the second you fell."

Albert looked to the left, to see Mo and Slink each on their own Jackalopes. The real shock was Birdie, who'd gotten stuck with saving Hoyt (who was hugging Birdie's waist so tightly she looked like she couldn't breathe).

"You're a genius!" Albert shouted.

"Take us sky-high, noble steed," Leroy said, and though the Jackalope couldn't understand his words, when he lightly kicked the Jackalope's sides, it responded. It bounced higher and higher, using divots in the rock to reach the top, navigating the Pillars easily, even with their crazy churning.

Albert and Leroy landed safely on a Pillar, Slink and Mo beside them.

Hoyt and Birdie landed on the Pillar Albert had just fallen from, directly to their left.

They all dismounted—Hoyt in record time.

He must really hate these Jackalopes, Albert thought, but then Albert saw why Hoyt had jumped off so fast—he was now plugging the Rectangle Tile back into the Pillar.

The churning motion died down instantly. The Pillars

went back to what Albert had come to think of as their normal spinning.

Albert looked to Slink, Mo, and Leroy for an explanation, but they all just shrugged.

Hoyt, on the other hand, nodded to himself, then stooped down and plucked the Tile *back* out.

CRACK-BOOM-CRACK!

Albert's stomach lurched as the Pillars jerked violently. The churning began again, but it didn't reach its full extremes before Hoyt had plugged the Tile back in.

"What's he doing?" Albert asked.

It was Leroy who answered. "I think he's just discovered another challenge to the Means to Restore Balance. How many Tiles are in your backpack, Albert?"

Albert swung his backpack forward. "I've got one, and Hoyt has one, plus the one he just put back in."

Leroy nodded. "I think that when more than two Tiles are removed at the same time, the Realm reacts very, very badly."

Albert thought back. The churning *had* happened right after Hoyt had removed their third Tile.

"So we can only remove *two* Tiles at once," Albert said. "My dad and Tussy didn't figure that out, because they'd only managed to climb two Pillars when they came."

"Great," Mo said. "As if this wasn't hard enough."

"Statistically speaking, if we were to remove *four* Tiles at one time, things could get a whole heck of a lot harder," Leroy said.

Birdie glared at him, and Leroy's mouth snapped shut.

"Well, we've got to move forward," Albert said. The Counter on his wrist now blinked with a red number two. "We're running out of time."

Mo whistled and waved his arms to get Birdie's and Hoyt's attention. They quickly hopped onto their Jackalope, and when Albert called out *come here* in Creature Speak, their Jackalope leaped over the gap.

Now all six of them were together again.

"We've figured out the whole only-remove-two-Tiles-at-once rule," Albert said. "At least, Hoyt did." He gave Hoyt a congratulatory slap on the back.

"So now what?" Birdie asked. "We've got Ten Pillars, and we can only remove two Tiles at a time."

"And," Mo added, scratching his head like a Hexabon, "we still haven't figured out the markings on the Pillars."

Time was running out. It was Slink's idea to call up more Jackalopes.

In pairs of two, the Balance Keepers rode around, searching for markings. There was nothing. Once, Albert and Leroy dismounted, and spent twenty precious minutes trying to find *any* type of sign.

"I can't see anything that stands out!" Albert called to Leroy. He was trying to climb sideways around the Pillar to reach Leroy, but there was a jagged point in the Pillar's side making things difficult. He looked across, to where Birdie and Slink were carefully scaling a particularly sharp-edged portion of a Pillar. Albert was glad he wasn't on that one. Hoyt and Mo were on a third Pillar, looking like koala bears stuck on the trunk of an extra-large eucalyptus tree. *They* didn't have any weird lumps to climb around. *They* didn't have any sharp edges to navigate. . . .

"Holy crap," Albert gasped, as it hit him. The Ten Pillars were shaped differently. He had assumed the Pillars were all basically the same, but looking again . . .

Excitement buzzed in his chest. If he was right, and he'd figured out the solution to the problem. . . .

They were going to save Ponderay.

Albert called the Jackalope forth, and he and Leroy climbed back on. When they got back to the top of a Pillar, Albert confirmed his suspicions.

The top of the Pillar he was on was a rough star shape. The top of the one Birdie and Slink were on was a little more like a triangle. How had he not noticed that before? He used the Flight Vision symbol to take his vision skyward, until he had a bird's-eye view of the Ten Pillars. Albert saw that the Pillar directly across from him—the one Hoyt and Mo were on—was a perfect circle. The next one was a rectangle, and the next one was a rhombus, like the shape that was on the Tile Hoyt had in his backpack!

The Pillars were different shapes, so that meant that each Pillar had a Tile with a symbol shape to match it. That had to be it!

Albert returned to normal vision and called his teammates in.

Once all the Balance Keepers were back together, Albert explained what he'd figured out.

"Awesome, Albert!" Mo said.

"Yeah, Albert, way to use that Master Tile," Birdie chimed in.

"So now all we have to do is match the Triangle Tile with the Triangle Pillar and so on. Easy peasy!"

"Not so easy," Albert said. "The Tiles are scrambled, remember?"

"And we can only take out two at a time," Hoyt said.

Mo stepped forward. "We need to create a map first. Figure out the shapes of all the Pillars."

Hoyt nodded and pulled his pocketknife out. "We'll carve it into the top of this Pillar, and use it as a guide map for when we start unscrambling the Tiles."

"I never thought I'd say this, boys," Birdie said, as she tightened her ponytail like she was gearing up for battle, "but you're brilliant."

Albert called forth the power of his Master Tile, and as he used Flight Vision to get an aerial view of the Pillars, he called out the pattern.

"The one we're on is a star," he said.

He could just hear the scratching of Hoyt's pocketknife over the wind as Hoyt carved a little star on the Pillar.

"The one directly to our left is a square," Albert said. "To the left of the square is eight-sided."

"An octagon," said Leroy.

Albert nodded. "Yeah, that's the one. Next is a trapezoid. Then a pentagon."

He called out shape after shape (thankfully he'd actually paid attention for that portion of his math class this year) until all Ten Pillars had been accounted for.

Albert called his vision back to his head. He looked down and saw the crude, caveman-like map Hoyt had carved. The shapes were a little off, but it did the job. Now they had a solid plan for which Tiles were supposed to go where.

Albert's Counter beeped.

Then it started blinking, a fat red *60* that made everyone stop and stare.

"An hour left," Leroy said.

"Can we make it?" Slink asked.

"We have to try," Mo answered.

Albert was expecting nerves to flow like a raging river into his system. But instead, a wave of calm rushed over him. He knew what he needed to do next.

He reached into his backpack and pulled out the Core-Bow, unfolding it to its regular size. "We should all take a Jackalope to our own Pillars. That will cover six Pillars, and six Tiles."

Slink nodded, then leaned over the side of the Pillar

and shouted something in Creature Speak. Three more Jackalopes started toward them.

"Everyone head for a Pillar," Albert said. "Then wait for instructions."

They all nodded, climbed onto Jackalopes as they arrived, and bounded off to five separate Pillars. Albert stayed on the star.

Albert unzipped his backpack and pulled out the Triangle Tile. He looked around the ring of Pillars. Hoyt was sitting atop his Jackalope on the Triangle Pillar. Albert waved his arms to get Hoyt's attention. Then he plugged the Triangle Tile into the CoreBow.

It wasn't like last night in Cedarfell, where aiming the bow had been a breeze. From here, with the Pillars spinning like wild, and the wind raging at top speeds, aiming seemed impossible.

Even if Albert shot it straight toward Hoyt, the wind would carry the Tile away.

Aim a little to the left of him.

It was Professor Flynn's voice that popped into Albert's head, a memory from the time his dad had taught Albert how to shoot a BB gun in the woods outside of Herman. It was windy that day, and aiming to the left would compensate for that.

"Thanks, Dad," Albert whispered to himself.

He leveled the CoreBow toward Hoyt, then swung a tiny bit to the left, and squeezed the trigger.

The Tile shot out of the bow like a bullet, spiraling toward Hoyt so fast that Albert was afraid Hoyt wouldn't be able to catch it.

But Hoyt did.

Everyone cheered from their spots on separate Pillars.

Albert tried to yell a command to Hoyt, but his voice was lost in the wind. He closed his eyes and pictured the Black Book, all the countless symbols. With a little help from the MegaSpeak symbol (which resembled a megaphone), it was like Albert was speaking into a microphone. "Unplug the Tile on your Pillar, and plug the Triangle Tile in *immediately* after. That will mean, for just a second or two, that we'll have three Tiles out. Everyone brace yourselves for that to happen!"

Hoyt did as Albert asked.

The *CRACK-BOOM-CRACK* sounded, and for one horrifying moment, the Pillars responded, trying to throw everyone overboard. But in seconds, Hoyt had plugged the correct Tile into the Triangle Pillar.

The Pillars slowed just slightly, and Albert continued with his orders.

It took a while to get a steady pace going at first, but with the help of the CoreBow, and with Slink also offering to bound back and forth on his Jackalope and help trade Tiles, they got their system down.

Tile after Tile, Pillar after Pillar, the Imbalance in Ponderay was one step closer to being solved. They got really good at switching Tiles out to avoid any chance of activating the churning, and the Pillars slowed their spinning with each Tile they plugged in.

A couple of times, Albert was tempted to check the Counter on his wrist, but he didn't want to get distracted stressing out about time.

Just keep going, Albert, he thought. *The world is counting on you.*

Still, by the time all the Balance Keepers were back on the Star Pillar, Albert had a feeling it was getting down to the wire—and they all looked exhausted. Everyone was breathless and ready to drop. Their faces were red, their skin chapped from the wind. Albert longed to finish the Means to Restore Balance if not to save the world, then just so he could get some sleep.

Leroy had just plugged in the Star Tile and pulled out a Parallelogram when Albert's Counter flashed an angry blood red like a flashing police car light on the streets of New York City. Albert had been right about it being close.

"We have five minutes left," he said, a rush of adrenaline suddenly giving him a jolt of energy. It was tight, but the Parallelogram was the last Tile—they might actually make it.

Albert looked at the map. The Parallelogram Pillar was directly to their right. He called a Jackalope over and readied himself to mount it.

"Ready?" Albert said to the others. "I'm going to end this!"

"Do it, dude," Leroy said.

"Then we can go home." Birdie nodded. She looked barely able to stand.

Hoyt had a strange glint in his eyes, but Albert figured it was because Hoyt was proud of himself for helping save the day.

"Thanks, man," Albert said. "You've been an awesome teammate today."

"Same to you," Hoyt replied.

They shook hands, and Albert mounted his Jackalope. He rocketed off the Star Pillar, and stopped on the only Pillar that was left. The Parallelogram.

With his back to his teammates, Albert bent down, ready to plug the last Tile in, but then he heard Leroy shouting something.

Albert whirled, and what he saw made his stomach drop to his toes.

Hoyt had taken the Star Tile out of the Pillar and had leaped to the Square Pillar.

Albert watched from afar, horrified, as Hoyt dismounted and stooped to one knee on the Square Pillar.

"No," Albert gasped, as Hoyt reached down, his fingers an inch away from plucking out the Square Tile. "NO!"

Hoyt removed the Square.

That made three Tiles loose. Three at once.

It was the only rule, and Hoyt had deliberately broken it.

All of Ponderay began to quake.

CHAPTER 28

The Traitor

Albert didn't know if the Pillars had feelings. But if they did, then right now, they were *angry*. Really angry. Did the Realm know the difference between *by accident* and on *purpose*? It seemed as furious at Hoyt as Albert felt.

The churning from before was nothing. The Pillars went from their lazy spin to full-speed again, churning faster and more violently than Albert thought possible. Back and forth, back and forth. The ocean below responded with tidal waves, and the creatures reacted in turn.

The Lightning Rays leaped from the water, their electric hides flashing as they tried to strike out at anything they could touch. The Jackalopes went nuts, rearing and trying to leap away. It took everything Slink had to keep them under control.

Suddenly, the Pillars began to rocket up and down, too, like pistons. Now Albert felt like he was flying and falling at the same time, all while trying to combat the churning, too. He clung to his Jackalope, the only thing that kept him from tumbling into the Silver Sea as the Pillars rose and fell.

"Put it back, traitor!" Albert could hear Leroy shouting to Hoyt.

"NO!" Hoyt shouted back. "Albert has to put his in first! He doesn't get to be the hero today!"

"I'm gonna come over there and push you overboard if you don't put. It. BACK!" Birdie screeched.

That's what this was about? Being the person to plug in the last Tile?

Of course. Hoyt wanted all the glory.

Albert was in shock. It took all his concentration to magnify his voice with his Master Tile. "Put the Tile back before you kill us all!" The wind seemed to find more energy. Albert nearly fell off his Pillar.

But Hoyt shook his head.

Everyone else just stood there with their mouths hanging open.

"You put yours in first, Flynn!" Hoyt shouted across to Albert.

Behind Hoyt, a Jackalope that wasn't under Slink's

control appeared, bouncing onto the Pillar. Hoyt didn't notice the creature. Albert waved his arms and pointed, trying to get Hoyt's attention. But he wasn't listening.

The Jackalope bounced once, twice, and on the third time, he tackled Hoyt like a linebacker.

The Tile shot out of Hoyt's hands. It ricocheted off the stone floor of the Square Pillar and headed toward the edge. Then, with the next violent drop of the Pillar, the Tile fell toward the Silver Sea.

"NO!" Albert screamed.

Albert's body reacted, and fast.

He plugged the Parallelogram Tile into the Pillar where he stood, then leaped onto his Jackalope. The Jackalope soared across the chasm between the Pillars, a flash and a blur.

Albert could see the Square Tile, falling as if in slow motion, just as Albert and Hoyt had fallen earlier.

His body burned with the desire to save the day, to save everyone in the Core and on the surface.

It was like magic, what happened next. Albert didn't picture the Stretch Tile in his mind. His body took over. The Master Tile buzzed against his collarbone, and Albert watched as his arms doubled, tripled in length, just like they'd done earlier when he saved Hoyt.

His fingertips grazed the Square Tile. He grabbed ahold, just before it was out of reach. His arms snapped back toward his body like a rubber band, and he clutched the Square Tile to his chest like it was a new-born infant.

Albert's Jackalope landed on the Square Pillar. Albert leaped off and rolled to his feet.

Around him, Ponderay settled, as it realized that only two Tiles were out now. Albert quickly plugged the Square Tile back in, then stooped to one knee beside Hoyt, who sat there, still holding the Star Tile and staring at his hands.

"You betrayed us," Albert said, so that only Hoyt could hear. The next words he said came forth with such a vengeance that Hoyt trembled as he met Albert's eyes. "You're a traitor, Hoyt. You don't deserve to be a Balance Keeper."

Hoyt said nothing, but the silence was interrupted by the Counter beeping and blinking like crazy.

One minute left.

Albert grabbed the Star Tile from Hoyt's hands and mounted the Jackalope.

Forty seconds . . . thirty seconds . . .

He leaped back to the Star Pillar.

Fifteen seconds . . . ten . . . nine . . .

Albert dismounted the Jackalope.

Seven . . . six . . .

Without hesitation, Albert plugged the Star Tile in.

Three . . . two . . .

CRRRRACK! The entire Realm trembled. The sky

roared, and all around, the wind whistled like an angry beast.

Then, suddenly, the Realm of Ponderay fell silent. The Pillars moved inward and slowed to a stop.

Albert looked down at the Counter on his wrist. They'd finished just in time, with not a second to spare. But that no longer mattered.

Balance had been restored.

The ride down was peaceful and quiet.

Hoyt and Mo took a Jackalope down together. Slink and Birdie took another, and Albert and Leroy rode together in the back of the pack. The Hammerfins stayed out of the way and the Lightning Rays took their leave.

At the bottom of the Pillars, they discovered something surprising—Jackalopes could swim. Last time, in Calderon, Hydra had celebrated and laughed, enjoying their time as they left the fixed Realm. But today, as they rode back toward the shores of the Silver Sea, all Albert could think about was how Hoyt had put everyone's life in danger, not just in the Core, but on the surface above. All so that he could look like the hero by placing the last Tile in the Pillar.

They'd worked together like friends, and Albert had enjoyed it. But now he could never imagine being friends with someone who would do something so selfish. He could never trust Hoyt again. It was too risky.

The Jackalopes carted the Balance Keepers to the top of the cliff that overlooked the Silver Sea, and they rode onward.

"How will we make it back?" Birdie asked as they headed for home. "We ruined all of the bridges." She slowed her Jackalope down so she could ride beside Albert and Leroy.

Leroy patted his Jackalope's neck. "These guys can jump higher and farther than any creature I've ever known. I'm sure they can handle a few chasms."

When the first chasm appeared, the Jackalopes bent their back legs and took a *huge*, bounding leap over the edge. The Balance Keepers all held on tight, and they landed safely on the other side.

"They're like real Energizer Bunnies!" Birdie shouted. "It seems like they aren't even tired!"

"Probably all that practice, leaping between Pillars in the Silver Sea," Slink suggested.

Albert looked down at his Counter, which he had figured out how to set to count upward, instead of down. They'd spent two hours riding so far, and were already halfway back to the edge of the Realm. They were making great time, and at this rate, they'd be back to the Core in just a few more hours. Albert closed his eyes and tried to imagine what was going on inside the Core right now. Even though it was early morning, they were probably celebrating, while everyone on the surface was probably scratching their heads, wondering why the worst storm ever to hit the western United States had suddenly disappeared.

Albert forced himself to relax, to take the time to look around and remember Ponderay as a beautiful place. It really was gorgeous—the orange of the cliffs against the silver water, the dust of the rocks in contrast with the sparkle of the streams below.

At least I bonded with Slink and Mo, Albert thought, *made real friends out of them*. And Leroy was having a blast. He was laughing like a maniac, making *yeehaw* noises as he and Albert rode together. Sometimes, Albert had to hold on at the last second as Leroy made their Jackalope do tricks like rear up onto its back legs and spin in circles.

They leaped across more chasms, soared right over the Path of Pillars, and made it across the final chasm within the next hour and a half.

The tunnel to the Core came into view not long after. It was like a dark, yawning mouth, which was oddly comforting to Albert. It also made him realize how exhausted he was. They had battled the Imbalance all through the night.

The Jackalopes slowed as they got closer. Birdie clapped her hands with excitement. "I can't wait to see Jadar!"

"I can't wait to sleep," Slink said.

"I can't wait to take a warm bath," Mo added.

"I can't wait to see my dad and call my mom," Albert said, stifling a yawn.

Hoyt said nothing, just stared ahead like he had the entire time since Balance was restored.

Finally the Jackalopes stopped at the entrance to the tunnel. Everyone slid off their mounts except Leroy. The other Jackalopes raced away, back toward their homes inside the Ten Pillars. But Leroy wouldn't come down.

"I don't want to leave Geoff," Leroy said, patting his Jackalope on its head, right between its antlers. The creature leaned into his hand, looking very pleased with itself. Albert wondered if this was another Jadar–Birdie moment, like last term.

"Geoff?!" Birdie squeaked. Her ponytail was all puffed up from the wind. "What kind of a name is that for a Jackalope?"

"The best name." Leroy frowned. "What kind of name is Jadar for a Guildacker?"

Birdie sighed. "Fair enough."

The Jackalope wiggled its nose, then leaned forward and sniffed at Leroy's pocket like it was hoping to find a snack.

"Well, I got to keep Jadar," Birdie said, petting the Jackalope's nose.

"And I have Farnsworth," Albert added. "So I don't

think anyone in the Core would mind if you kept Geoff."

"I knew you guys were good friends," Leroy grinned. He patted Geoff's neck and shouted, "Onward, Geoff! Go forth to the Core!" Then he hopped away like he was a great knight atop a noble steed.

CHAPTER 29

The Return to the Core

H undreds of voices exploded into shouts and cheers as soon as Albert and his team arrived in the Core.

"You did it!"

"Ponderay is saved!"

"Gooooo Hydra and Argon!"

As the six Balance Keepers made their way inside, they were pulled into hugs and patted on the back. The boys were even given kisses on the cheek by a few of the girls (which Albert promptly wiped away). Leroy rode in on Geoff, and the claps and cheers grew even louder, a roar that could threaten even Jadar's greatest volume. Everyone crowded around Leroy and Geoff, and Leroy looked like he was so happy and proud he was about to burst.

Hoyt didn't say a word. He smiled and nodded his head, then mumbled something about needing sleep.

There was a roar, and Jadar came to greet Birdie, soaring on outstretched leathery wings.

"Jadar!" Birdie ran to him and flung her arms around his thick neck. "It's good to see you! You wouldn't have liked Ponderay, it was cold and wet." Jadar hissed and snapped his beak, and Birdie laughed, pulling him into another hug. "Don't worry, you're safe and warm here!"

Where's my dad? Albert wondered. Professor Bigglesby was handing out fizzy blue sodas, and some of the Core workers had wheeled out a giant cotton candy machine, passing giant cones of pink sugary fluff around.

In the middle of the crowd, Albert caught Petra waving. Albert was relieved to see the Homing Tile, still safely around Petra's neck.

"Hey, Albert!" Petra shouted.

"Hey!" Albert waved back. He was about to cross to see his friend when he heard a dog bark twice.

Albert turned and saw his dad's familiar mouse-brown hair peppered with gray, his shimmering emerald jacket. Professor Flynn stood on the arched bridge, looking like he belonged in the Core. Farnsworth struggled in his arms, trying to wiggle away and run to Albert.

"I'm coming, buddy!" Albert laughed, and Farnsworth barked again as Albert ran to them, a smile lighting up his face.

"You did it again, kiddo. My son, the twice hero! Everything in the Core is back to normal. Even the Heart of the Core has regained its color." Professor Flynn handed Farnsworth over, then pulled Albert into a bear hug. "I knew you could do it. I knew you'd be all right. How was it? I want to know everything."

He hugged Albert tighter than he ever had before.

When Albert pulled away, he saw relief in his dad's eyes.

"You really were worried, huh?" Albert asked. "It was crazy, Dad. You should've seen the Hammerfins, and the Lightning Rays, and *man* it was cold! And Leroy brought back a Jackalope, if you haven't seen. They helped us get home, because the bridges weren't going to work the second time around and, what?"

Professor Flynn was laughing, shaking his head. "It's nothing," he said. "I'm just looking at your excitement, and it reminds me of the first time I went into Ponderay. It's a dangerous Realm. I'll never forget my first visit there. I had faith you would be able to handle yourself. You're a Flynn! But of course, with a traitor in our midst, it was natural for a father to be concerned."

"Yeah, Dad, about that . . ." Albert pulled his dad aside, away from the cheering crowd. They stood with their backs against the cool stone of the curved Main Chamber wall. "Is it Trey? Is he the traitor?"

Professor Flynn pulled back and almost lit his hair on

fire from one of the blue torches. "What? Trey?!"

"I can explain," Albert said. "I've noticed him follow-ing me. He was hunting around by Professor Asante's office, and I think maybe he was in the Library the other night and . . ."

Professor Flynn held up a hand. "It's not Trey. Trust me on that, Albert. I'll explain his behavior later. For now, let's go and enjoy the celebration. You deserve it! The Float Parade is this afternoon. The festivities have only just begun!"

Albert could still see a hint of something strange in his dad's eyes, something he couldn't quite place. It didn't sit right with him, and for some reason, it made his stomach turn. He could tell his dad was holding on to a secret.

But what was it?

Albert wanted to talk more, but he had to admit, he was exhausted, both mentally and physically. And he wanted to find his friends.

"I'll see you later, Dad!"

He gave his dad another hug, then found Leroy and Birdie in the crowd. Birdie was trying to coax Jadar into letting Slink pet him, and a crowd of girls stood around Leroy and Geoff, giggling away.

Tussy approached from the crowd. For once, her face wasn't freshly cut or scabbed, and her hair was smoothed into a bun. She looked, for the most part, harmless.

"You did your job, and you did it well," Tussy said.

Albert shrugged. "I didn't do it alone." He looked over his shoulder again, at his friends. He thought of what Hoyt had done in the Realm. Albert could turn Hoyt in right now. After all, Hoyt's mistake had almost cost everyone their lives.

"There's something you should know," Albert started to say, but then his voice trailed off.

What would that really do, turning Hoyt over to Tussy? He'd create even more of an enemy out of Hoyt. No, Hoyt had made his choice, and now his own teammates knew his true colors. In time, Hoyt would probably end up losing all the power he held in the Core. It wasn't much to begin with.

"What were you saying?" Tussy asked.

Albert shook his head. "I forget," he said. "Sorry, I guess I'm just really exhausted. Thanks for coming to say hi. I'm gonna go find my teammates."

"Rest up," Tussy said. She clapped a hand over Albert's shoulder and smiled. "You deserve it."

Albert smiled and backed into the crowd. When he found Leroy and Birdie, he pulled them off to the side. "How about we go grab some food, then find some peace and quiet?"

Leroy slid down from Geoff's back. "You don't have to ask me twice."

"You never change," Birdie laughed. She linked her

arms through Albert's and Leroy's, and together, the three of them headed away from the crowd with their heads held high, and Farnsworth's bright blue eyes to keep the darkness away.

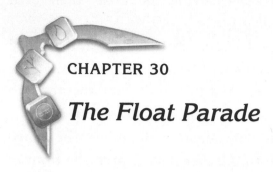

CHAPTER 30

The Float Parade

That afternoon, Albert, Birdie, and Leroy sat atop Petra's float, hidden in the shadows of a tunnel. In front of them, five more student floats were waiting.

"I think we might win," Albert said to Birdie and Leroy. All three of them had squeezed in quick naps after the morning's excitement. Now they were ready to kick some butt at the Float Parade.

Petra was inside of the Guildacker's belly, running the gears. He opened up the hatch on its back and peered up at his friends.

"You guys ready? Big smiles. Lots of waves."

"We'll steal the show," Albert promised.

Somewhere out in the Main Chamber, Trey addressed the crowd with the MegaHorn. He sounded like a real sports announcer, even giving the floats their own names.

From the back of the line, Albert could hear the crowd erupt into cheers as the first float rolled into view.

"Created by the Girls of Belltroll!" Trey shouted into the horn, his voice carrying back into the tunnel.

The floats rolled out, one after the other. The crowd went wild. As the Guildacker float neared the front of the tunnel, Petra, somewhere inside the belly, revved the engine. The Guildacker rolled out into the Main Chamber.

People ooh and aahed, and some even backed away. Petra revved it again, and this time, blue flames shot out!

"Amazing!" Trey shouted, and the crowd went nuts.

The Professors came with their floats next. First came Calderon. Professor Flynn stood atop an incredible replica of the Realm. It had all the rings, Calderon Peak in the center, and a metal King Firefly that spit real orange flames.

"A tough competitor, as always!" Trey announced.

From his spot atop the float, Albert saw Hoyt's face in the crowd. Hoyt didn't look smug. He just looked sad. Albert wanted to feel sorry for the guy. But he couldn't. Not after what Hoyt did in the Realm.

After all the Professors rode their floats out, the judging began. Petra came out of the belly of the float, his face white from nerves as he sat beside his friends, waiting for an answer.

"We've got this," Birdie assured him. "The people were terrified when he roared! It was *awesome*."

Petra nodded, looking like he was about to pass out. Trey, Tussy, and Fox moved up and down the line of floats, tallying points on clipboards. When they stopped to look at the Guildacker, Albert tried to read the expressions on their faces, but they were solid as stone.

Albert leaned over to Petra and said, "Even if we don't win, you know ours is definitely the coolest-looking float out here, right?"

Petra chuckled under his breath. "I can't argue with that."

Albert crossed his fingers and waited. Petra deserved to win something. He'd wanted, all his life, to be a hero. *Please*, Albert thought, *just let him win*.

He didn't need to be worried at all. The Apprentices lined up side by side. Trey took the MegaHorn from Tussy.

"First runner up—the Belltroll Professor's float!"

Professor Bigglesby looked three feet taller than he was. *It* was *an impressive float*, Albert thought. He'd never seen so much weaponry in one place before.

"And the grand champion of this year's Float Parade is . . . the Guildacker float!"

Petra nearly tumbled from the Guildacker's back. A cannon of confetti went off, and as the crowd went wild, celebrating and rushing toward the Guildacker, Albert realized something.

He looked sideways, at Birdie and Leroy, and at Petra.

He looked around, at all the people in the Core, the smiles on their faces, the way they were so alight with life.

The Core was dangerous, and scary at times, sure.

But it was also amazing. And Albert knew, in that moment, that he was the luckiest guy in the world.

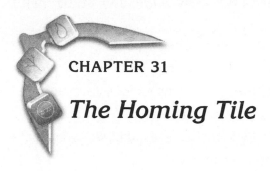

CHAPTER 31

The Homing Tile

The dancing went on all night. It was nearly time for breakfast when Albert, Birdie, and Leroy decided to call it quits.

They needed a day of sleep (and food, according to Leroy), so they left the party behind with Farnsworth in the lead, making their way into the silence of the tunnels that led to their dorms.

Birdie was about to say good-bye to the boys and head her own direction when Leroy let out a gasp.

"What?" Albert turned to look at him. "What is it?"

"The Homing Tile!" Leroy pointed at his chest.

Farnsworth growled.

Albert's jaw dropped. Birdie swallowed hard. Sure enough, the Homing Tile was reacting. It had just barely begun to float off of Leroy's chest, like a butterfly trying to head for home.

"What do we do?" Albert asked.

Leroy's exhaustion disappeared in a snap. "We see where it leads us. It's set to take us exactly to its match."

"Let's hope it doesn't lead us into too much trouble." Birdie nodded. The look in her eyes said she was ready for what was to come, either way.

"And to think I was *this* close to finally getting some sleep," Albert groaned, but inside he felt a flame of excitement.

They followed Leroy's orders as the Tile tugged and tugged at his neck, trying to get back to its partner.

The door to the Library opened with a terrible, horrible creak, and if they had any hope of sneaking inside, it was gone now.

It was dark, and empty as a tomb.

"Which way, Leroy?" Albert whispered.

"Left." Leroy pointed.

The Tile kept on tugging, looking very much like it was ready to snap itself off its cord and rocket toward its match.

Carefully, silently, they tiptoed across the floor. Farnsworth headed up the pack with his eyes turned off until Albert was ready to give the command.

The Tile led them farther and farther in, and then it

fell slack against Leroy's chest.

Albert's heart sank. *Not here*, he thought. *Please not here.* They were huddled in the entryway to Lucinda's Core Canteen.

"Lucinda," Birdie whispered. "It can't be her. She wouldn't deal in bad Tiles, would she?"

"There's only one way to find out," Albert said. His heart was in his throat.

The three of them tiptoed farther into the Canteen. They turned the corner and peeked inside.

Lucinda was there in the darkness. She sat on a stool with Kimber slithering across her shoulders.

Albert saw something that made his heart sink all the way to his toes.

The black box, and beside it, the Book of Bad Tiles.

CHAPTER 32

The Truth Comes Out

They ran all the way to Professor Flynn's office.

The party was still going when they passed, and Albert felt sick to his stomach.

"We trusted her!" Leroy said, as they reached Professor Flynn's door.

"I thought she was our friend," Albert said.

Farnsworth whimpered, his ears drooping. His headlights faded to a solemn blue. Albert nearly kicked open the door to his dad's office, and they raced inside. Farnsworth yipped, announcing their arrival. When they rounded the Waterfall of Fate, Professor Flynn and Trey were already there, having what looked like an important discussion.

"What's going on? Why aren't you at the party?"

Professor Flynn asked as the three of them burst into the room.

Albert stooped over to catch his breath. "Book of Bad Tiles," he gasped.

"Homing Tile," Birdie added.

"It's . . . soooo . . . bad. . . ," Leroy groaned.

"Everyone calm down," Professor Flynn said. "What's this all about?"

They told Professor Flynn everything, from seeing Trey spying on them, to the Book of Bad Tiles, to thinking Trey was behind it. They told him about the Homing Tile and how Petra had gotten it for them, and how they used it. And finally, they explained their discovery this morning. Lucinda, leaning over the box in her Core Canteen, when she thought no one was looking.

When Albert was finally done talking, he felt like a million pounds had been lifted off of his shoulders.

"It's true," Trey said, finally breaking the silence. "I followed Lucinda back to her shop tonight a little while ago. I saw her with the box."

Professor Flynn frowned. "This is unfortunate news, indeed."

"Why is she doing this?" Albert asked.

"I thought she was our friend," Birdie said, putting her chin in her hands.

"She's always been so nice," Leroy sighed. "Strange, but nice."

Albert sat back in his chair. His back ached, and all he wanted to do was sleep.

"You should have come to me sooner," Professor Flynn said.

"We're sorry," Birdie squeaked. "We just didn't know what to do."

Professor Flynn held up a hand. "I understand. I would've been afraid to come forth with such accusations as well. Keep in mind that Lucinda's retrieval of the Book of Bad Tiles doesn't prove that she's the one behind the Imbalance."

"But she must be," Albert said. He looked at Leroy for help.

"The odds are pretty high," Leroy admitted. "Why else would she take it?"

Professor Flynn nodded, deep in thought. "We'll keep this under wraps for now. I'll alert the other Professors, and we'll investigate."

Trey leaned forward and whispered something into Professor Flynn's ear.

"Yes, I know. It's time to come clean, I agree." Professor Flynn nodded.

Just then, Albert saw it: his dad looked *sad*. Like he had terrible news to share. Albert wasn't sure if he really wanted to hear it.

"I should have told you this the moment you received your Master Tile, Albert," Professor Flynn said. He sighed.

"It isn't the only one of its kind."

"WHAT?" Albert, Birdie, and Leroy all said at once.

Professor Flynn nodded. "There are three Master Tiles. One of them once belonged to your Pap. Another is around your neck, right now. And the third one, the final Master Tile, once belonged to me."

Albert felt like he'd just been slapped. He didn't know what to say. In fact, he didn't have words. They just wouldn't come.

So Professor Flynn went on. "Your Pap and I assumed there were only two. But then you came along, and a new Master Tile chose you. For whatever reason, our family line has been chosen, Albert."

"But you have a Creature Speak Tile," Leroy said unexpectedly. He seemed to be mulling something over in his head, but he wouldn't say what it was.

"Indeed, Leroy. I had a Creature Speak Tile last term," Professor Flynn admitted. "You see, I lost my Master Tile."

This time, the words flew out of Albert's mouth. "You did *what*?"

"I know, I know." Professor Flynn nodded. "But I think it would be more accurate to say that my Master Tile was stolen, not lost. I traded my Creature Speak Tile for Pap's Master Tile a few months ago and have had that since, but I'm afraid there's bad news about that Master Tile as well. "

"That one has been lost—or stolen—too?" Leroy asked. The wheels were turning in his mind.

"You had a Master Tile," Albert said, still trying to process everything. "And Pap, too? Why didn't you guys ever tell me?"

Professor Flynn looked disturbed. "You and your Tile learn from each other. You become one. And Master Tiles are tricky; each of them is different in its own way. I didn't want you to feel any less special because Pap and I had them before you. But there's more than that."

"Professor," Trey interjected.

But Professor Flynn waved him off. "They need to know. It's time." He looked Albert right in the eye. "Someone is—"

"Someone is collecting Master Tiles," Leroy said. By the look on Professor Flynn's face, Leroy was right. "But I thought a Tile had to stay in its family line?"

Professor Flynn nodded. "Normally I would say yes, that's true. But Master Tiles are mysterious. We know so little about them."

"It would explain a lot," Albert said. "These huge Imbalances couldn't have been created by just anybody— a normal Balance Keeper wouldn't have enough power to even make it through the Realm alive on their own, let alone wreak havoc on it. But if they had a Master Tile . . ."

"Or two or three Master Tiles . . . ," Birdie said.

Professor Flynn glanced at Trey, then back at Leroy, Birdie, and Albert.

"Pap's Tile was taken from me while I slept only just last night," Professor Flynn said gravely. "I sleep lightly, so someone must have slipped something into what I drank or ate during the festivities last night. I do remember feeling unwell, very tired."

"It would have been the perfect time," Leroy said. "Everyone in the Core was celebrating, distracted. And you were here all alone."

"Precisely," Trey said.

"We know the Imbalance someone with one Master Tile can create," Birdie said. "Ponderay was pretty messed up."

Albert gasped. "Did the traitor create the Imbalance in Calderon, too?"

Professor Flynn shrugged. "It's very, very possible, Albert. And if that's the case, and Calderon and Ponderay have been hit, it's quite possible that we could be dealing with another Imbalance soon, unless we discover who this traitor is."

"Two Master Tiles might mean double the trouble," Albert said. He touched the Tile hanging around his neck, and looked up. Everyone was thinking the same thing.

"Albert, you may be the only thing standing between total destruction of the Core and the Realms," Professor

Flynn said. "For now, we must get you to the surface as quickly as possible. We must protect you from whomever we're dealing with."

"No way," Albert said. "I'm not leaving you all here. I can help."

There was silence in the room, and then Trey spoke. "They might be willing to harm you for it, Albert."

"Forget about harming," Leroy said. "I'm thinking they would kill you to get their hands on the last Master Tile."

Albert sat silently, thinking about how serious the situation had become. Getting beaten up because of his special Tile was one thing. But getting killed because of it? That was something Albert had never thought of.

"This is why I've had Trey following you, in case someone tried to steal your Tile," Professor Flynn said.

"So that's why we saw you snooping around all the time," Leroy said.

"I'm sorry I've been cold," Trey said to the trio. "Professor Flynn didn't want to worry you."

Professor Flynn leaned forward and placed his hands onto his old oak desk. "I'm going to have to come clean to the other Professors. I need to turn myself in, tell them about the two missing Master Tiles. One missing Master Tile was serious, but two is far too dangerous to cover up."

"Won't you get in trouble? Like, major trouble?" Albert asked.

His dad nodded, and there was sadness in his eyes. "I'm afraid so, kiddo."

"What will they do?"

Professor Flynn smiled weakly. "Right now the only thing that matters is getting you three out of here as quickly as we can."

"No one can be trusted," Leroy said as he cleaned his glasses. "Not anyone except for us, the five of us in this room."

Leroy put his glasses back on and looked directly at Professor Flynn. "You can tell the other Professors about the missing Master Tiles if you want to, Professor Flynn, but I think you should wait. Out there, anyone could be guilty. If they punish you for bringing this up, we'd lose you, and we can't afford that. You have to stay quiet, for now. For us."

Trey and Professor Flynn looked at each other for a long moment, and then Trey nodded. Professor Flynn turned to the rest of them and nodded as well.

"I hate to say this, but I do have my suspicions about at least one of the other Professors. For now, we keep it quiet."

"You'll leave for the surface immediately," Trey said to the trio. "Keep everything we've spoken a secret. We'll contact you with news as we hear it, and we'll continue to track Lucinda and our other leads."

"The Path Hider does repairs in other parts of his

domain when no one is coming or going," Professor
Flynn said, glancing at his watch. "He's rarely at the
relay station at this early hour."

"And I'm guessing you know how to work the controls?" Trey asked Leroy.

"I do," Leroy admitted. "I can't help myself. I memo-
rize everything I see."

"Synapse Tiles are awesome," Birdie said, slapping
Leroy on the back.

"You have the only remaining Master Tile, Albert,"
Professor Flynn concluded. "Keep it close. Keep it around
your neck at all times, and don't let anyone touch it. And
use your powers wisely, especially on the outside. If the
thief gets his or her hands on the last Master Tile before
we can discover who this person is, it could mean the
destruction of the entire world."

Albert's Tile felt a whole lot heavier around his neck.
He reached up and closed his fingers around it. He'd
guard it with his life.

He'd go back to his mom's apartment and he'd study
the Black Book every day.

He'd learn how to become the best Balance Keeper
of all time. And when he returned to the Core and his
enemy was revealed, Albert Flynn would be ready for
whoever it was.

CHAPTER 33

Leaving for Home

When the last of the partygoers had finally cleared out of the Main Chamber, Albert, Leroy, and Birdie stood on the edge of the cavernous space, ready to head for home.

"Even though there's lots of scary stuff going on," Birdie said as she hugged Jadar good-bye, "I still don't want to leave. Probably even more so than last term."

"But it'll look suspicious if Albert leaves suddenly, and we don't go with him, too," Leroy said. He pretended to be tough and wiped away tears as Geoff hopped across the bridge and out of sight, heading back to Cedarfell. "But I wish we could stay, too."

Farnsworth whimpered as he watched his new companion friends fade away.

"I feel like the Core needs us now even more than ever," Albert said. He scooped up Farnsworth and looked back at the Main Chamber, committing every detail to memory. What if the traitor struck again, while Albert was gone? What if something horrible happened, and he couldn't make it back here fast enough?

But he trusted his dad. He trusted Trey. And he knew that the only safe thing to do right then was to get himself and the last Master Tile out of the Core, away from danger.

"We should go," Birdie said, putting her hand on Albert's arm. "I know it's hard. But we have to get that Master Tile out of here. Far, far away."

"It's for the best." Leroy nodded.

"I know," Albert said with a sigh. It was hard, like ripping off a Band-Aid, but he turned his back on the Main Chamber, then pushed through the doors, leaving his dad and his friends, his second home, behind.

The gondola ride was as thrilling as always. The rush of wind hit Albert in the face, giving him some needed energy, soothing his thoughts. He was worried. More worried than he'd ever been, and leaving the Core didn't feel quite right.

When the gondola stopped at its station, the Path Hider was nowhere to be found. Farnsworth raced back and forth through the maze of pipes, sniffing away in search of him. But just as Professor Flynn had expected, the Path Hider was down some dark tunnel where smoke and steam poured out like witch's brew. Albert, Birdie, and Leroy were glad of this, because the Path Hider might ask questions or call one of the Professors for clearance to let them go.

Farnsworth turned on his high beams, and Leroy walked right up to the knobs and levers that controlled the entry and exit to the Path Hider's domain. "I've watched him. I know what to do."

"Gotta love that Synapse Tile," Birdie said.

Leroy turned knobs and cranked levers like he'd been doing it for years. When he was done, Albert, Leroy, and Birdie made a race of things, running as fast as they could back to the orange platform, then scurrying through the tangle of vines once they made it to the Troll Tree.

Albert burst through the door first, breathless.

His IceBlitzer sat waiting for him, covered in a fresh sheet of snow.

"I'm going to check in on you guys, like, every day," Birdie said, as they stood outside, saying their final good-byes.

"Yeah, if you need us, man, just call," Leroy added.

Albert pulled both of them into a hug. "Stay safe out there."

"We'll see each other soon enough," Birdie promised. "I'll miss you like crazy."

"Me too," Albert said to both of them.

They went their separate ways, and Albert could tell the Path Hider's tools were set perfectly in motion by Leroy. Soon, Leroy and Birdie were gone, down a path he could not see.

"You ready, buddy?" Albert asked Farnsworth.

Farnsworth barked happily and Albert revved the Ice-Blitzer. Together, they raced across the snow toward the town of Herman, Wyoming.

Epilogue

It was late Christmas evening when Albert's mom finally picked him up at the airport in New York City. His dad had scheduled the first flight out, Pap had dropped him off at the closest airport to Herman, and now, hours later, here Albert was, wrapped in a giant mother-bear hug back in New York City.

"I missed you," Albert's mom said as they drove home. Her makeup was runny from crying. "Did you have fun?"

"I missed you too, Mom," Albert said, laughing. "I'm glad I could surprise you and make it back for Christmas. I had a blast in Herman, as always. But it's so good to be home. I'm glad you're okay."

"We're glad, too," she said. "It got scary for a moment,

Albert. I'm so relieved you weren't there. It's just nice to know you were off having fun. It was a mess."

Farnsworth sat in the front seat. He growled playfully and licked Albert's chin. "Farnsworth had fun, too."

Albert's mom reached over and patted the little dog on the head. "New York just isn't the same without you boys."

The blizzard had let up, and as the city came into view, Albert grinned.

He loved the Core with all his heart, but New York was home, too. They piled out into the snowy streets.

Farnsworth raced ahead of them, yipping and snapping at snowflakes.

Albert smiled, remembering the Realm of Calderon and the Realm of Ponderay. He'd faced two of them already, and he'd come out alive.

Next term, he'd be ready for the traitor.

Deep in the Core, the Master sat waiting. He wore a dark cloak, and the hood concealed his face from the shimmering lights all around him.

He hated the Cave of Whispers. It was too happy, too bright, and it didn't help the impatience that flared as hot as dragon's fire in his heart.

His Apprentice was late, and if he didn't arrive soon, the Master would not be pleased. There was a creak of door hinges, followed by footsteps that echoed down the tunnel.

The Apprentice stepped into the light at the mouth of the cave.

"You're late," the Master said. "There isn't time to spare."

"My deepest condolences," the Apprentice said. He rushed to the Master's side and stooped to one knee, then bowed with his hands outspread and offered up a small bundle of black silk. "I brought it, just like you asked."

The Master plucked the silk bundle from the Apprentice's hands and unraveled it. An empty glass vial fell into the Master's lap. "I had plans to use this same poison to kill you for your failure in Ponderay," he said.

The Apprentice stiffened, but did not run.

"But you have redeemed yourself with this," the Master said. "You've done well, and you will be rewarded greatly for your allegiance."

The Apprentice nodded. "I am yours, whatever you should ask of me."

The Master nodded. The plan was in place. Soon, the Core would face dangers greater than anything it had ever known. Albert Flynn would return, and he would die in vain, trying to save a world that was already lost to the Master's control.

The Master threw his head back and laughed. Around his neck, two black Master Tiles hung side by side, as dark and menacing as the poison that had been used to help acquire both Tiles.

His laughter intensified throughout the Cave of

Whispers. The colors brightened and flashed, and the ground trembled in protest. Gems and diamonds crashed from the ceiling.

By the time the Master left, the Cave of Whispers was shattered and broken. Soon the Core would be forever under the Master's control.

Acknowledgments

It's so exciting to write a second set of "thanks" for Balance Keepers. I can't believe how much support and love I've gotten so far. Here's to all of you:

As always, to God, for having a plan for my life and easing me into it. You're the one who gave me the gift of writing, and for that, and everything else you've done to save me, I'm so thankful.

To my family: Lauren Cummings, Karen Cummings, Don Cummings, for helping me stay sane when I start to panic about due dates and reviews and everything that comes with being a writer. My husband, Josh, who listens to me whine and tells me that everything will work out. You're always right, but I'll never admit that (oops, I just did. I love you). To my extended family, the Ryans, the Burlesons, and all of my friends, for supporting me!

My cousins Abby Haxel and Landon Davies, because you're the only members of my family who love books about as much as I do. You guys = awesome.

Everyone at HarperCollins, for *again* giving me a chance to tell my stories. My editor, Katie Bignell, for making this book shine and understanding my love of flowers that match book covers. Katherine Tegen, for having a rockin' imprint. Patrick Carman, for being a constant support and guiding voice in this process. Peter Rubie, for helping get this series a home. The cover artist and designers, because you guys have given this series AMAZING covers so far, and I just can't stop staring at them.

My agent, Louise Fury, who just seriously rocks in a million, bazillion different ways.

My army of animals, for inspiring me constantly, and here's to hoping my husband will let me get a black beagle that I can name Farnsworth. Wink wink.

Nicole Caliro at Barnes and Noble, who has been endlessly supportive toward all of my books—you have helped Balance Keepers make it in this crowded book world. HUGS.

To my teeny-tiny little town of Celina, Texas. Because I didn't think I'd like you, and it turns out moving here was the best thing I could have done for my writing career and life in general. Lifeway Church, for the prayers. Linda Long at CHS, for welcoming me.

To my readers, who have loved this series from book one. To all the amazing school students I've visited, who have supported me and followed me on Instagram and kept up with all of my shenanigans.

To my army of #booknerdigans, for being rock stars, and always jumping to help promote at the drop of a hat (or a sudden email). Sasha Alsberg, for being my social media marketing maven. Abi Ketner and Missy Kalicicki, whose prayers and love and support are wonderful. Erin Gross, for all the hard work and support! Rebekah Faubion, for being another piece of my sanity.

The YA Valentines, who have shown constant love for me and been my voices of reason for several years now. Y'all. Are. Awesome.

To everyone I left out by accident, because I'm sure, inevitably, I will.

Lastly, to all the other writers and dreamers out there struggling to make it in this crazy business. You can do it. And you will.

Thank you.

Follow Albert Flynn in all his
fantastical adventures to restore
Balance to the Core and save
the world from chaos in the

SERIES

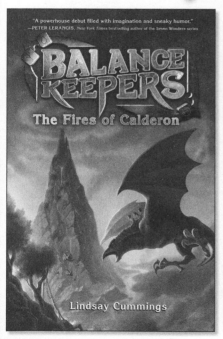

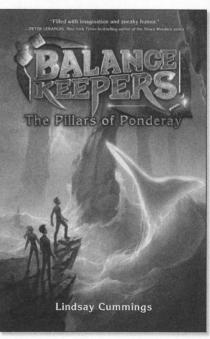

KATHERINE TEGEN BOOKS
An Imprint of HarperCollins*Publishers*

www.harpercollinschildrens.com